The Body in Seven Dials

Dear Rae,

I hope you enjoy this story of the first female superintendent!

The Body in Seven Dials

A Lady in Blue Mystery Novel

H L Marsay

With best wishes

Helen

The Body in Seven Dials
Copyright© 2023 H L Marsay
Tule Publishing First Printing, October 2023

The Tule Publishing, Inc.

ALL RIGHTS RESERVED

First Publication by Tule Publishing 2023

Cover design by Patrick Knowles

No part of this book may be used or reproduced in any manner whatsoever without written permission except in the case of brief quotations embodied in critical articles and reviews.

This is a work of fiction. Names, characters, places, and incidents are products of the author's imagination or are used fictitiously. Any resemblance to actual events, locales, organizations, or persons, living or dead, is entirely coincidental.

ISBN: 978-1-961544-12-3

Dedication

In memory of Nina Boyle, Margaret Damer Dawson, Mary Allen and Dorothy Peto.

Chapter One

STANDING IN THE impressive foyer of Marlborough Street Police Court, Dorothy Peto clutched her notebook and pencil tightly to her chest and tried to steady her breathing. Waiting alongside her in their bowler hats and puffing on their cigarettes were the gentlemen of the press. Despite their noisy chatter about the recent assassination in Sarajevo, she was sure they must be able to hear her heart pounding beneath the heavily starched shirt she was wearing. She had 'borrowed' the shirt from Raymond, her brother, along with his necktie and tightly belted riding breeches. To complete her disguise, she had piled up and pinned her long dark hair under one of his trilbies and the collar of his huge overcoat was turned up high enough to hide half her face. Although Raymond was sympathetic to their cause, she wasn't at all sure he would approve of what she was doing. Fortunately, he'd left early that morning for his job in the Foreign Office. The archduke's murder was keeping him occupied too.

Standing in front of the looking glass in her bedroom over in Bloomsbury, she had felt confident and almost giddy with excitement, laughing at her reflection with Nina and rebuffing her friend's more outlandish suggestions of adding a moustache or pipe to complete her new look. But now, standing here alone, all her bravery seemed to have deserted her.

It had been Dorothy's idea to try to enter the court in disguise. All members of the Women's Freedom League had been banned from the place since staging an obstruction protest there the previous week. Nina and half a dozen others had stood in the lobby with chains looped around their waists and fastened them across the door into the courtroom, preventing any witnesses from entering. Then, when they were arrested and brought before the magistrate, they had given false names, argued with the lawyers and generally delayed the proceedings for several days.

Writing afterwards in their magazine *The Vote*, Nina had declared the protest to have been a success 'beyond her wildest dreams'. Unfortunately, it had also meant they were unable to continue their work cataloguing the many cases of injustice women suffered under the legal system.

Dorothy had not taken part in the obstruction protest and with her tall, angular frame, she was the only one of their number who could possibly pass for a man. Eagerly she had volunteered to act as a court reporter. She was desperate to feel like she was making a contribution. It had been almost a year since she had joined the League and although she regularly typed up the court reports for *The Vote*, she was still a little in awe of the other, older members who all seemed so brave. They thought nothing of giving rousing speeches, chaining themselves to buildings, enduring prison and even going on hunger strikes, all to try to convince the powers that be to give women the vote. Today it was Dorothy's turn to play her part.

Suddenly, to her left, a heavy oak door swung open and Sergeant Munro, a large Scotsman with an impressive set of ginger whiskers, strode out. Dorothy held her breath. If he looked closely, he was sure to recognise her. Then, to her relief, a distraction arrived. Out of the corner of her eye, Dorothy could see Nina and the others appear at the main entrance and begin to argue loudly with the two policemen on duty there. They soon attracted quite a crowd as they started to sing, and Nina began waving a huge flag bearing the initials of the WFL. Sergeant Munro stood surveying the scene for a moment with his hands on his hips and his large feet planted firmly on the ground. As it became clear the two constables were having little effect subduing the women, he strode over to deal with the disturbance himself.

At the same time the door to Court No.1 opened and the gentlemen of the press began to file in. Dorothy followed them, walking in what she hoped was a manly fashion. Glancing back nervously, she caught Nina's eye, who gave her a quick reassuring smile. She felt a little better until she heard the journalist next to her mutter, "Bunch of bloody harridans! Give them the vote? They should lock them all up and throw away the key!"

Inside the courtroom, Dorothy carefully kept her eyes lowered and silently prayed she would go unnoticed. Feeling very self-conscious, she slipped into a seat at the back, as far away from everyone else as possible. She breathed in the scent of the place. It was a mixture of leather, tobacco and furniture polish. Up in the gallery, several anxious-looking young women were huddled together, and two older ladies sat on the front row, knitting. Everyone else present was male. The journalists, police officers, clerks, ushers and of course the lawyers. With their black gowns and sharp beady eyes, they reminded Dorothy of the ravens at the Tower.

Presiding over them all was the magistrate, Frederick Mead. At first glance, he had the appearance of a kindly country parson, but Dorothy knew he was nothing of the kind. Of all the magistrates the WFL had catalogued, Mr Mead was by far the worst. Often in his presence, female witnesses and victims were treated more harshly than the males who stood accused. During cases against suffragettes, when he felt the prosecution was not being robust enough, he would sometimes take over the cross-examination himself.

As the clerk of the court announced that proceedings were about to begin, Dorothy quickly opened her notebook and held her pencil at the ready. The first accused, a large man with black hair and a thin mouth, was brought up to the dock. Dorothy began scribbling as the charges against him were read out. Assault where the victim sustained a broken nose, blackened eye and extensive bruising to the torso. The plea was guilty as charged.

"Three months in the second division," proclaimed Mead briskly. The man in the dock gave a small shrug and waved up at the public gallery as he was led away. A few moments later, his place was taken by a woman of about thirty years old, with a bruised and swollen face. Her head was bare, her hair tangled, and Dorothy could see her lip was still bleeding and dried blood stained the collar of her white blouse. The magistrate glared across at her.

"I see the next is a filthy and disgusting case. All females out of court," he ordered. Dorothy sank lower into her chair and buried her chin further into Raymond's coat as Sergeant Munro ushered the other women from the court, as always happened when Mead was handling indecency cases.

Mead waited until all the women had been removed from the gallery and the heavy wooden doors were closed with a thud, before continuing.

"So," he began, "the victim of the previous case now stands before me as the accused, charged with soliciting. What is the plea?"

"Guilty as charged," replied the defence lawyer, without bothering to look at his client.

"Nine months' hard labour," declared Mead. Dorothy drew a sharp intake of breath. Such a sentence was harsh even for Mead. Her eyes darted to the defence lawyer, but he made no move to appeal.

"What?" screeched the woman in the dock. "That bastard got three months and look what he did to me." Her swollen eyes flashed with anger as she pointed at her face and a trickle of blood began to weep from the cut to her mouth. Mead's face was expressionless as he fixed his cold eyes on her.

"Madam, this is your third time before me. If you are unhappy with your sentence, I suggest you find another occupation. Take her away. Next case."

Two policemen dragged the woman out, her shouts of protest still echoing round the court after she had disappeared from sight. Dorothy wanted to shout out herself. It was so blatantly unfair. That the man should only serve a third of his victim's sentence, and in second division. That was barely prison at all. He would have frequent visits, be allowed to wear his own clothes and buy in his own food, while that poor woman would spend the months sleeping on a plank bed, with basic rations and picking oakum until her fingers bled.

The shouting woman's place in the dock was taken by a short, smartly dressed man, named Archibald Abbey. He had a thin moustache and wore steel-rimmed spectacles. The charges were several sexual offences against a minor. He was pleading not guilty. The first witness to be called was the alleged victim in the case. A side door opened and Sergeant Munro guided a young girl into the witness box. She looked terrified and was so small, Munro had to find her a stool to stand on. Following closely behind them was a woman with a pale, pinched face. She was clutching a shawl tightly around her shoulders. Mead watched her approach the witness box and scowled.

"Was I unclear in my instructions, Sergeant Munro?" enquired the magistrate, sarcastically. "I will have no females in court during hearings of indecency cases."

The policeman's face flushed red with embarrassment as he turned apologetically to the woman.

"But I'm her mother—she's only twelve," she cried as Munro placed a hand on her shoulder. Dorothy winced at the anguish and confusion in her voice.

"Remove this woman," ordered Mead again.

"What he did to my little girl was more than indecent. He's a monster! Be brave, sweetheart. I'll be right outside here waiting for you. Be brave!" the mother called, shaking her head in anger and disbelief as Munro led her out of the court. Dorothy stopped her furious scribbling and looked around the court in horror. Surely someone, a lawyer or a journalist, would speak up. The little girl began to quietly weep.

Mead raised an eyebrow. "Come now, young lady. I see here that you reside with your mother in a public house on the Horseferry Road. I therefore doubt you are quite as innocent, as you would have us all believe."

A small, satisfied smile crossed the lips of the man standing in the dock as the girl's sobs grew louder. This was too much for Dorothy. Indignation and frustration bubbled up inside her. To hell with the reporting. She leapt to her feet. Her hat fell to the floor and her hair tumbled down.

"This is wrong!" she shouted. "This girl should have her mother with her. By law, she is allowed her mother." Every head in the room turned to stare. A sea of shocked and frowning faces.

"Remove that female immediately!" bellowed Mead, his face turning puce. Dorothy continued to protest as Munro and one of the ushers rushed towards her.

"Not again, Miss Peto! Will you women never learn?" he muttered as they took her firmly by each arm. Dorothy tried struggling as they dragged her along, but they were too strong and her feet barely touched the ground. In desperation she attempted to appeal to the rest of the court.

"Gentlemen, please, I beseech you. What's happening here today is not fair and it is not legal. Will nobody help?" But her pleas were ignored. Not one of the men would even look her in the eye. Did none of them have daughters or granddaughters?

"Shame on you all!" she cried as she was hauled out of

the court. The last thing Dorothy saw before the door slammed behind her was the little girl's pale, frightened face staring back at her.

The two men roughly deposited her outside the main door. Dorothy tried to keep her balance when she was released from their grip, but missed her footing and fell down the two steps leading up to the court, landing in an ungainly heap on the pavement. People hurried past her tutting and shaking their heads until a hand reached out and took hold of hers.

"Well, you lasted longer than I thought," said Nina with a grin as she hauled Dorothy to her feet. "You're not hurt, are you?"

"Not really, just a twisted ankle," replied Dorothy, brushing down her clothes, "but I swear Mead gets worse each day."

Nina wrinkled up her face in disgust. "That man! It's a miracle he didn't have you arrested. Now let's get you back to the office. You can have a nice cup of tea, then write up what you witnessed."

Nina took Dorothy's arm and let her lean against her as she limped along. Constance Antonina Boyle, or Nina as everyone called her, was the leader of the Women's Freedom League. Her petite frame and delicate features were deceptive. She was a passionate journalist and speaker, and an expert at coming up with ingenious ways to promote their campaign. She was almost twenty years older than Dorothy, but the two women had become firm friends after Dorothy had joined Nina on one of her more daring escapades.

Nina had been banned from attending the House of

Commons since chaining herself to the railings outside, so had instead decided to take a boat down the Thames and make her demands while the honourable members were enjoying their tea out on the terrace. When she'd heard Dorothy had been boating on the Isle of Wight, she immediately roped her younger colleague in to steer the motor launch. They had arrived unnoticed, and Nina managed to deliver most of her speech from the roof of the boat. Unfortunately, some politicians had become so irate at the disturbance that they had started pelting them with bread rolls and the two women had only narrowly escaped being captured by a police boat. It had been Dorothy's first taste of campaigning. She had found it terrifying and exhilarating in equal measure.

"Here she is the heroine of the hour and armed with plenty more ammunition to fire at our so-called justice system," declared Nina dramatically as the two of them returned to the offices of the Women's Freedom League on Robert Street. Dorothy felt herself blush. Unlike Nina, she hated being the centre of attention. Before arriving in London, she had been educated at home along with her sisters and still found being part of a large group a little daunting.

"Tell us all about it, Dorothy dear," said Jean Bagster with a gentle smile. She was one of oldest and kindest members of the League.

"If you don't mind, I'll leave that to Nina," replied Dorothy a little apologetically. "I want to start writing my report straight away, while everything is still fresh in my mind."

She took a seat behind one of the typewriters and began bashing away at the keys as she listened to Nina begin regaling the others with what Dorothy had told her. Naturally, Nina's version was even more dramatic, culminating with Dorothy being flung down the courtroom steps rather merely suffering a stumble.

"Well, I only hope those men in court today reflect on the way you were treated and see the error of their ways," said Lucy Summerton blinking back tears. She was one of the League's newest recruits. A pretty, young blonde woman, she was very enthusiastic if a little over-emotional at times. Dorothy looked up from her work and shook her head at Lucy's optimism.

"I doubt seeing me hauled out will make much of an impact on their consciences if they were happy to sit back and watch that poor young girl weeping in the dock. I don't think I shall ever forget her face."

Jean came over and patted her on the shoulder.

"Let us hope the little mite remained strong enough to give her evidence and convict that dreadful man."

"Yes, let's hope," agreed Dorothy, but she didn't feel very confident.

Chapter Two

BY FIVE O'CLOCK that evening, the others had all left and Dorothy was finally happy with the piece she had written about the morning's events. She stood up, stretched and pulled on her coat. Before leaving, she spent a few moments tidying the place up. The other members of the League might be fearless campaigners, but they were definitely less keen on housekeeping. She emptied the wastepaper basket containing her crumpled-up drafts and also Nina's overflowing ashtray. Then she cleared away the dirty teacups and began folding the newspapers that were scattered across the table in the middle of the room. A photograph in *The Times* caught her eye. She stopped tidying and began to read.

For once the pages weren't full of the situation in Europe. Instead, the headlines were about an actress who had been found dead in her theatre dressing room. Dorothy recognised the woman in the photograph immediately. It was Edith Devine, a beautiful young woman and one of the most popular actresses in the West End. She was currently appearing in a revival of Oscar Wilde's *The Importance of Being Ernest*.

In fact, Dorothy had watched the play the previous evening. Her brother Raymond was a huge fan of Miss Devine.

His good friend, George Sledmere, had given him a front-row ticket for last night's performance, but he was so busy at the Foreign Office, he'd given his ticket to Dorothy instead. To repay his kindness, Dorothy had managed to get backstage and asked Edith Devine to sign her programme. She had then presented it to her delighted brother. As Dorothy continued to read, she realised that she must have been talking to Miss Devine only a few hours before she died. She frowned as she reached the end of the article. It seemed to imply that she had killed herself by taking an overdose of 'a substance as yet undisclosed'. Replaying the events of the previous evening in her mind, she gave her head a shake. They must have made a mistake.

She left the office, but instead of taking the usual omnibus to Bloomsbury, she waited for one to take her to Haymarket, at the heart of the city's West End. However, when it pulled up, the conductor stood at the entrance blocking her way.

"Oh no. I'm not having you on here, dressed like that, causing all sorts of trouble," he said jabbing his finger towards her.

Glancing down, Dorothy realised she was still wearing Raymond's clothes and must look rather odd. She opened her mouth to explain, but the conductor hadn't finished.

"You're one of them suffragettes, aren't you?"

"Yes, I am," admitted Dorothy. "I'm a member of the Women's Freedom League and I can assure you, sir, we have never done anything to disrupt public transport."

"Pah!" he snorted. "I'm not taking any chances with you lot. Now clear off."

Knowing it would be hopeless to argue, she stepped back on to the pavement. As the bus pulled away, she glanced up and down the road. There wasn't a taxi or hansom cab in sight. Despite her sore ankle, she'd have to walk to the West End. Her progress was slow, but it gave her the chance to make sure everything was clear in her head before she spoke to the police.

At the end of the performance, after the second curtain call, the rest of the audience began to leave the auditorium, but she had made her way to the front of the stage where Jean Bagster's niece was waiting for her. Miss Bagster was the theatre's wardrobe mistress and had agreed to take Dorothy backstage. Nervously she had knocked on Miss Devine's dressing room door and had been shown in by a petite, pale, fair-haired maid dressed immaculately in a black-and-white uniform, complete with gloves and pinafore. The room was so full of flowers it looked like Covent Garden.

Edith Devine herself had changed out of her costume into an embroidered silk dressing gown and was sipping a glass of champagne. The actress had been charming, gracious and even more beautiful close-up. She was clearly in high spirits following her performance. She had chatted excitedly to Dorothy about the play and asked about Raymond, before signing the programme with a flourish. Then the maid had returned and announced that Edith had another visitor, a Mr Muller. At this news, Miss Devine had giggled and said, "I could set my watch by him." Then she'd checked her reflection in the mirror.

Dorothy had assumed that Mr Muller must be an admirer and quickly thanked the actress again and left. On her way out, she passed an extremely large man with a shiny bald head and an extravagant moustache. She couldn't imagine for one moment that the beautiful Miss Devine would find him attractive.

As she stepped out of the stage door, she almost bumped into a short young woman carrying a large basket, who scowled at her despite Dorothy's polite apology. That had all happened at about half past ten. What on earth could have occurred to make the happy, vivacious, beautiful woman want to take her own life?

Half an hour later, she arrived in the West End. As she had expected, there were several police officers standing outside the entrance of the Theatre Royal, Haymarket, as well as a small crowd of journalists and photographers. Dorothy quietly made her way to the stage door where she found another police constable standing next to a tall man wearing a long navy overcoat and leaning on a walking stick.

"May I help you, miss?" asked the constable when he spotted Dorothy.

"I do hope so, Constable. Would it be possible to speak to the officer in charge of the investigation into the death of Miss Edith Devine, please?" she asked politely.

The man with the walking stick turned to look at her. He was about forty years old with dark hair, bright blue eyes and a neatly trimmed moustache. Dorothy thought his face would have been considered handsome if it was not for the ugly scar running across his left cheek. It made him look rather intimidating.

"I am Inspector Derwent," he said in a deep but quiet voice. He slowly looked her up and down and for the second time that evening Dorothy regretted still wearing her brother's clothes. Despite her embarrassment, she tried to sound confident.

"Good evening. I wanted to talk to you because the reports in the newspapers seemed to be suggesting that Miss Devine took her own life, and I simply find that impossible to believe. You see, I visited her in her dressing room after last night's performance and she was in very good spirits," she began to explain.

Inspector Derwent raised an eyebrow. "Is that so? Do I take it you were an admirer of Miss Devine?"

"Yes, or rather no, but my brother Raymond is. I wanted to ask her to autograph my programme, so I could give it to him as a gift. He'd given me his ticket because he's been so busy at work so he hasn't had the chance to see the play himself, and with all this talk of war who knows what might happen."

She paused and took a deep breath. She was gabbling as she often did when she was nervous.

"At what time did you visit Miss Devine?" asked the inspector, who she noted wasn't bothering to write anything down.

"The performance finished at half past ten, so not long after that. Mrs Bagster's niece is the wardrobe mistress here and a fellow member of the League. She managed to get me backstage."

"The League?" enquired Inspector Derwent.

"The Women's Freedom League," explained Dorothy. The young constable gave a snort of derision. The inspector shot him a silencing look but didn't reprimand him.

"We believe Miss Devine died at around half past eleven, so unless you were still in her dressing room then, I don't understand how you can be so sure of her state of mind, or indeed know what may have occurred in the hour leading up to her death."

"But she was so happy when I saw her," insisted Dorothy. "She didn't seem to have a care in the world. She was laughing, vibrant, full of life and obviously well loved. Her dressing room was absolutely crammed full of flowers. In fact, her maid brought in another huge bouquet while I was there. I think they must have been from Mr Muller, a large gentleman who was also visiting her. Oh, and there was a blonde lady arriving as I left. She was carrying a basket. Have you spoken to them and the maid?"

"We shall be speaking with all relevant witnesses, miss. As for her mood, Miss Devine was an accomplished actress and could easily have been disguising her true emotions."

Dorothy paused to consider this for a second and was about to reply when Inspector Derwent raised his hat.

"I shall be sure to pass on your observations to the coroner, miss," he said as he turned away.

"Miss Peto. My name is Miss Dorothy Peto," Dorothy called after him as he limped towards the waiting police car, but he didn't look back.

Patronising fool! thought Dorothy as she watched him being driven away. She turned away from the smirking constable and began to trudge home towards Bloomsbury. She was as angry with herself as she was with the policemen. She had wanted to get her point across, but she'd become flustered and rattled on like an out-of-control sewing machine instead. The ridiculous outfit she was wearing didn't help. No wonder they hadn't taken her seriously.

DOROTHY LIVED WITH Raymond in a small flat in Bloomsbury. It was on the top floor of a modern red-brick building opposite the British Museum. She unlocked the front door, collected the post lying on the doormat and lit the oil lamp in the hallway. Fortunately, Raymond still hadn't returned from the Foreign Office, so she hurriedly hung up all the items she had borrowed in his wardrobe and hoped he wouldn't notice his hat was missing before she managed to replace it.

She ate her supper of bread and cheese alone then went to bed and began to read her book. A little before eleven o'clock she heard the front door close and Raymond's heavy footsteps make their way down the hallway to his room. A few moments later, he'd changed into his dressing gown and put his head round her door to wish her a good night.

"You're awfully late. Is there more news from the Balkans?" she asked.

"Not that I can share with you I'm afraid," he replied shaking his head with a wry smile. When he'd joined the Foreign Office, he'd been required to sign the Official Secrets Act.

"Do you think there will be a war?"

"Not if Grey has anything to do with it. He called 'the cousins' in to meet him today. All at the same time, so they had to wait in the same room. It was quite amusing watching them so puffed up with self-importance, trying to ignore each other."

Dorothy grinned. 'The cousins' was what the Foreign Office called three of the most important foreign diplomats in London. Not only were the king, the kaiser and the tsar related, so were the ambassadors for Germany, Russia and the Austro-Hungarian Empire. She hoped her brother was right and this business in Sarajevo turned out to be nothing more than a family spat between the royal dynasties of Europe.

"What about you? What have you been up to today?" asked Raymond, stifling a yawn.

"Reporting on Mead's cases, but not for long. They threw me out," she admitted.

Raymond shook his head in mock despair and tutted. "Despite being disguised in my clothes! Dear me!"

Dorothy stared at him in surprise. "How did you know?"

"You put my coat back in the shirt section of my wardrobe," he replied with a good-natured smile.

Dorothy groaned. She should have paid more attention. Of the two of them, Raymond was far neater and more organised.

"I'm sorry and I owe you a trilby. Do you mind?"

"No, I just hope Ma and Pa don't get to hear about it or they'll blame me for not keeping you in check. As if I could. But do be more careful, old girl."

Dorothy grinned at him. He had been very good about her moving in to his flat, but she didn't want a ticking-off from her brother. She decided to change the subject.

"Did you hear about Edith Devine?"

His smile faded. "I did. What a terrible waste. And to think you only saw her last night too."

"It must have happened not long after she signed the programme. I went to the theatre to speak to the police there, but they didn't seem very interested in what I had to say."

Raymond yawned again. "Never mind, Dorothy. I'm sure they know what they are doing. Try not to let it upset you. Sleep well." With that he blew her a kiss and closed the door behind him.

Dorothy continued to read until midnight, but when she finally extinguished her lamp, she found she couldn't sleep. She tossed and turned but feelings of fear, anger and helplessness at being dragged out of the court wouldn't leave her. Whenever she closed her eyes and began to drift off, the little girl's pale face came into her mind and then merged into Edith Devine's beautiful smiling image, and she would wake with a start. She threw back the eiderdown, climbed out of bed and quietly made her way over to the window.

She pulled back the heavy drapes and peered out into the street. The moon was full, but there was no sign of life except for a solitary policeman on patrol. He looked up as he drew level with Dorothy's building and she took a quick step back, not wanting to be seen. She'd had more than enough of policemen for one day.

She turned towards her dressing table and picked up the silver photograph frame glistening in the moonlight. It held a photo of her and her brothers and sisters. It had been taken the previous summer when they'd visited her aunt Emily, who ran an English school in Liguria.

Aunt Emily was sitting in the middle with Dorothy and her sisters—Ruth, Audrey and Katherine—either side, while her brothers—Francis and Raymond—stood behind with the mountains in the background. It had been this trip that had first made Dorothy question the role of women in society.

Those weeks in Italy had changed Dorothy's life forever. Aunt Emily was Dorothy's father's older sister and had been living in northern Italy for almost thirty years. Her father usually referred to her as his 'bohemian' sibling, giving Dorothy the impression that he didn't consider this a good thing to be. Apart from the occasional, fleeting visit to England, her nieces and nephews barely saw Emily, so the invitation to spend the summer with her in Liguria had been quite a surprise.

"Why did you never marry, Aunt Emily?" asked Dorothy boldly, one afternoon as she and the others sat with their aunt on the terrace overlooking the lake, sipping small cups of strong coffee and nibbling on the little almond biscuits she always served.

"Don't be so rude, Dorothy," hissed Audrey, looking horrified, but Emily had merely laughed before replying.

"Because, my dear, I had no desire to hand over the money your grandfather left me to a man, or give up the right to own my own house in exchange for a ring on my finger. Then, when the law eventually changed in 1882, I was too old and stuck in my ways to think of marriage, not to mention too busy running this place," she said, gesturing to the lovely villa behind them where she had established her school, teaching Italian and art to English young ladies.

As she listened to her aunt speak, it was the first time Dorothy had thought about her rights as a woman, or lack of them. Although she had complained bitterly that her brothers were allowed to go to school, while she and her sisters remained at home with a governess. She remembered begging her parents to let her go too, but they had only laughed at such a silly suggestion. The thought she might be something other than a wife and mother had never occurred to her. Her father had two other unmarried sisters. Her mother always referred sympathetically to them as 'your spinster aunts', as if they should be pitied, yet here was Emily, living an independent and what seemed to be a very happy life.

It wasn't that Dorothy didn't want to marry and raise a family, but she wanted more. She wanted to make a difference. Her first idea was to become a writer, something her parents had been happy to encourage. When she had declared her intention to move to London, her parents had reluctantly agreed, but only on the condition she lived with her brother. Although both her mother and father had supported her initial ambition to become a novelist, they were less keen on their daughter's decision to join the suffragettes.

"Darling, I know you said the experience of living in London would help your writing, but I really don't see what you hope to achieve by associating with women who get themselves arrested on a regular basis," her mother had complained.

Dorothy had tried to explain that after hearing Nina speaking at a public meeting, she knew she wanted to be part of the campaign for women to be treated equally. She'd been convinced that by joining the Women's Freedom League and drawing attention to how unfair the whole justice system was, she could help bring about change. Now, after today, she wasn't so sure.

Chapter Three

LATER THAT WEEK, Big Ben was striking four o'clock as Nina and Dorothy hurried along Palmer Street together. Since Dorothy had been forcibly removed from the courtroom, so much had happened. The Prime Minister, Mr Asquith, had finally made the announcement everyone had been waiting for. Dorothy still couldn't quite believe it. The whole world had gone quite mad. A month ago, she'd never even heard of Sarajevo, then Raymond had come home full of talk about how an archduke had been assassinated and now look at them. At war with Germany.

Patriotic red, white and blue bunting seemed to have appeared overnight, fluttering from almost every building and, with an increasing sense of panic, people had begun stockpiling food. Young men were rushing to enlist at the army recruitment offices that had sprung up on every street corner, and her mother had sent at least a dozen, increasingly desperate telegrams, begging Raymond not to join up too.

Despite what was happening on the international stage, Dorothy had also been keeping a close eye on events closer to home. She'd scanned the newspapers each day, but there was barely a mention of Miss Devine's death, except for a few inches stating when the coroner's hearing would take place.

However, she had spotted a photograph of the man she had seen heading towards Miss Devine's dressing room that night. It turned out that Mr Muller was a very wealthy German industrialist, who was now living and working in London. Dorothy had telephoned Scotland Yard to make sure Inspector Derwent knew the man's identity. A weary-sounding sergeant had taken her message and promised to pass it on to the inspector, but as yet she had heard nothing.

She had also read in anger and frustration the official court reports. Archibald Abbey, the man accused of molesting the young girl, had been found not guilty and was now free to roam the streets. Her own account of the proceedings had appeared in *The Vote*. She had been pleased with the interest it had generated and today Nina was going to incorporate some of the points she'd made into her speech. She was due to speak at a WFL meeting in Caxton Hall, but they were late, as was so often the case. Nina was a terrible timekeeper, and Dorothy was forever having to nag and chivvy to get her to leave her desk and arrive at appointments on time.

This afternoon, they were delayed still further, as their usual route through St James's Park had been blocked. The army had already taken it over as a space to begin training new recruits. Dorothy had been quite shocked to find the gates were now locked, and the manicured lawns and flower beds, covered with makeshift tents and marching soldiers.

Slightly out of breath, the two women finally turned the corner on to Caxton Street only to see yet more men in uniforms, police uniforms. At least a dozen officers were standing at the entrance to Caxton Hall in front of a large group of WFL members who were protesting loudly.

"Oh, what now?" exclaimed Nina, hurrying forward to investigate, but before Dorothy could follow her, she found her way blocked by a tall, athletic woman of about forty, dressed in tweeds.

"Good afternoon. Miss Peto, I presume. My name is Miss Mary Allen, former organiser of the WSPU Hastings branch," she said, grasping Dorothy's hand firmly and shaking it with great vigour. "I am extremely pleased to meet you. I enjoyed your recent article in *The Vote* immensely and I'm very much looking forward to hearing Miss Boyle speak today. Your organisation has been involved in some wonderful work, highlighting the many flaws in the way women are treated in our courtrooms."

Dorothy was taken aback by Mary's enthusiasm. She smiled politely, although she was always a little wary of any members of the Women's Social and Political Union. She and Nina both agreed that the tactics Mrs Pankhurst's group used to draw attention to their cause were far too aggressive and violent, often causing more harm than good.

"Thank you, Miss Allen. That's very kind," replied Dorothy as she finally managed to extract her hand. "I too was looking forward to today's meeting; however, there seems to be some sort of problem. Please will you excuse me."

Dorothy turned and began to walk towards the crowd, only to find Mary was striding along beside her.

"It looks like we're in for a spot of trouble. I hope Miss Boyle is prepared," she said ominously, making Dorothy feel even more nervous. When the two women caught up with Nina, she was being greeted by her members with loud cheers and applause as they waited outside the hall.

"What's happening, Nina?" asked Dorothy.

"The police have locked the doors of Caxton Hall and refuse to let us in," explained Nina, gesturing to the line of uniformed constables standing at the entrance to the hall. Mary stepped forward and held out her hand to Nina.

"If I can be of any assistance at all, Miss Boyle," she offered.

"Nina, this is Miss Mary Allen. She came to hear you speak today," explained Dorothy quickly. Nina shook Mary's hand and nodded politely, but she was distracted by a stocky police sergeant pushing his way through to the front of the crowd. He approached Dorothy, Nina and Mary.

"Is there a problem, Sergeant?" Nina enquired, calmly.

"No problem at all, Miss Boyle, but your meeting here today has been cancelled," the sergeant replied to a chorus of boos from the women in the crowd.

"Oh really? And for what reason this time?" asked Nina.

The sergeant folded his arms and scowled at the touch of sarcasm in Nina's voice. Dorothy felt a growing sense of fear and unease. She knew Nina wouldn't back down and would continue to antagonise the sergeant. This sort of confrontation never ended well.

"In order to prevent a civil disturbance," said the sergeant. "We understand a large group of medical students are marching against the anti-vivisection league this afternoon. We believe they may target this meeting, as in the past, the Women's Freedom League has shown support to the anti-vivisection cause."

His statement drew more boos and shouts of shame, as

Nina threw up her hands in a dramatic gesture of despair.

"Then why cancel our meeting and not their march?" asked Dorothy, trying to sound reasonable, although she doubted there was such a march planned at all. Most young men were now too busy answering Kitchener's call and enlisting to care about such things as experiments on animals anymore. It was just an excuse. She and Nina should have known the authorities would want some sort of revenge for their little boat trip to the Houses of Parliament.

"Precisely! Surely that's more of a civil disturbance than our meeting. Cancel the march," demanded Nina.

The sergeant shook his head. "Miss Peto, the decision has been made. Miss Boyle, please ask your members to disperse," he said firmly.

"Certainly not! Ladies, the meeting shall go ahead!" Nina announced loudly to the waiting crowd. Her declaration was met with wild cheers and applause from her followers. Then suddenly, one eager young woman—wearing a purple and white sash—broke away from the group, dashed through the police line and, despite the chains, managed to yank the doors to the hall open a few inches. She got her foot in the door, but didn't get any further, before two officers quickly grabbed hold of her and dragged her back. She shouted and screamed in protest.

"No! Let her go!" Nina yelled, rushing forward to assist the younger woman. She began pummelling one of the officers on the arm as Dorothy watched in horror.

"No, Nina! Don't! This is what they want," she cried out, as the sergeant clapped his huge hands round Nina's narrow shoulders with a certain amount of relish.

"Nina Boyle, you are under arrest. You do not…" he began.

"I know, I know," interrupted Nina, as she furiously tried to wriggle free.

"On what grounds do you arrest her?" demanded Mary, stepping forward as a group of burly constables encircled Nina and the young woman, who was also being forcibly restrained.

"Disturbing the peace! Now the rest of you stay back," shouted the sergeant, in response, as he tried to avoid Nina's flailing hands and kicking feet, and the crowd of women surged forward. Another police officer grabbed hold of Nina's ankles and her hat fell from her head as she was lifted clean off her feet. Dorothy couldn't bear it any longer, but as she was about to run forward to help her friend, she felt Mary's hand firmly grip her arm and hold her back.

"No, don't! Stay back. There is no point in you getting arrested too, Miss Peto," Mary urged her. "You will better serve Miss Boyle by remaining free and working for her release."

At that moment, a police van arrived. Dorothy's first thought was that it had appeared suspiciously quickly, but it convinced her to reluctantly do as Mary advised. She and the others could only shout in protest and watch from behind the line of officers, as several more constables jumped out of the van. Dorothy stood on her tiptoes and strained her neck to see what was happening to Nina.

When the rear doors of the van were flung open, she could see it was already full of men, who were also under arrest. As Nina and the other suffragette were bundled inside, they were greeted with whistles and lewd catcalls.

"Stay strong, Nina!" called Dorothy helplessly as the doors were slammed shut and the van disappeared down the street. When it had gone, she bent down to retrieve Nina's hat that had been knocked off in the scuffle and trampled on. She tried her best to brush off the dust and dirt, blinking back tears of frustration as the remaining police officers continued to disperse the now shocked and more subdued crowd.

"Chin up, Miss Peto. She'll be out in no time. They don't have much to charge her with and I always take it as a sign we've managed to rattle them, if they make a point of arresting one of us."

Dorothy turned to see Mary was still standing behind her with an encouraging smile on her face and holding out a handkerchief. Gratefully, Dorothy took it and wiped away her tears.

"That's very true. I'm sorry you didn't get to hear Nina speak, Miss Allen," she said.

"So am I, Miss Peto. I wanted very much to hear more about the ideas you and Miss Boyle have regarding changes to the policing and justice system, but I'm sure there will be plenty of other opportunities in the future. Right now, we need to formulate a plan to secure the release of Miss Boyle and the other young lady."

"We?"

"Absolutely. I'm rather a veteran when it comes to this sort of thing, been in Holloway several times myself. Between us we'll have her out in no time," she declared, grasping Dorothy's arm and leading her along Caxton Street, following the route the police van had taken.

Unfortunately, Mary's optimism was misplaced. They eventually managed to track Nina down to Charing Cross Police Station, but neither of them were allowed to see her despite Dorothy's pleas and Mary demanding so forcefully that she had been threatened with arrest herself. Finally, after several telephone calls, a solicitor arrived. He was allowed to speak with Nina, and he had reassured them that she and the other young lady were in good spirits but had been charged with public order offences and would be appearing in front of the magistrates the next morning.

On hearing this, Dorothy reluctantly agreed with Mary that there was no point in remaining at the station any longer. The two women went out into the now much cooler evening air.

"Thank you for all your help today, Miss Allen," said Dorothy.

"Not at all," replied the other woman, shaking her by the hand and presenting her with a crisp white calling card. "I'll see you at tomorrow's hearing and do call me Mary."

"Thank you," repeated Dorothy weakly as she watched Mary stride away and hail a cab. She tucked the card into her pocket and glanced over her shoulder at the police station, feeling terribly guilty about leaving Nina behind. How typical that at the very time she was due to speak out against the legal system, the powers that be had arrested her yet again.

THE FOLLOWING MORNING, Dorothy found herself back in Marlborough Street Police Court. She and other members had to watch helpless and angry from the public gallery as Nina and the other young woman were sentenced to two weeks in Holloway for disturbing the peace.

The lawyer she and Mary had found was competent enough, and Nina had argued their case as passionately as ever. She'd even joked, "Here we are again, gentlemen," when she'd arrived in the dock. However, as soon as Dorothy heard that Mead was the magistrate hearing the case, she knew all hope was lost. He'd clearly taken great delight in passing his sentence, the maximum available to him, after a long lecture about the many dangers of the suffrage movement. She was sure he'd only lifted his ban on the League being allowed to attend, to teach them a lesson. Dorothy and the other women shouted out words of encouragement to their friends, while Lucy burst into tears and had to be comforted by Jean.

Feeling incredibly frustrated, Dorothy stomped down the steps of the court and almost bumped into a red-faced and breathless Mary, who immediately apologised for being late to the hearing. When she told Mary about the verdict, the older woman had snorted loudly in disgust.

"I suppose we shouldn't have expected anything more from Mead. However, let us not waste the time Miss Boyle is spending at His Majesty's pleasure. Why don't you come for tea this afternoon, Dorothy? You have my card. Margaret and I shall be expecting you at three o'clock."

With that she marched back down the steps before Dorothy had a chance to respond. She retrieved the calling card from her pocket and read the address: 10 Cheyne Row, Chelsea. Dorothy knew the street. It was a terrace of elegant houses close to the river, terribly smart and not at all the sort of place where she would have expected the enthusiastic, slightly odd Mary Allen to live. Feeling intrigued, Dorothy decided to undertake some research before her visit. After all there was nothing more she could do for Nina, and Mary had already proved herself to be an eager ally.

She returned to Bloomsbury and entered the main building of the British Museum, which was also home to the British Library, and began searching through their archives.

It turned out that Mary had not only been a member of WSPU but had also been arrested several times for smashing windows at the Inland Revenue and Home Office. Each time she was imprisoned she had gone on a hunger strike, but the last time she had been subjected to force-feeding. Dorothy recalled the discreet pin badge on Mary's lapel. Mrs Pankhurst awarded the same badge to all her members who had endured this brutal treatment. She shuddered at the thought of being tied down while a tube was forced down her nose and throat. There was clearly no doubting Mary's bravery.

As for the owner of 10 Cheyne Row, Dorothy recognised her name immediately. Margaret Damer Dawson was a well-connected, wealthy philanthropist known to support charities that helped children and animals. As well as her home in Chelsea, she owned a large country house in Kent where she had created a refuge for tired horses. There was a photograph taken at the opening of this animal sanctuary. It showed Mary standing next to Margaret. Dorothy peered closely at the image. Margaret was a plump woman, who looked to be in her mid-forties with a kind, soft-featured face and spectacles perched on the end of her nose. Seeing her next to the lean, trim Mary, Dorothy was immediately reminded of the nursery rhyme about Jack Spratt and his wife.

Reading on, Dorothy discovered that Margaret had also used the money she had inherited from her father to set up a home for foundlings, or as the newspaper put it: 'babies who have been abandoned by their unfortunate mothers'. In addition to this, Margaret appeared to be a keen supporter of anti-vivisection charities and had campaigned for animals not to be bred for food or be allowed to perform in the circus. Dorothy carefully closed the newspaper article she had been reading and leant back in her chair. What could Mary and Margaret possibly want to talk to her about?

Chapter Four

Later that afternoon, Dorothy made her way to Cheyne Row. As she approached number ten, she could hear the faint sound of someone playing Chopin's piano concerto inside, and she remembered reading that Margaret had studied at the London Academy of Music. The front door was opened by a uniformed maid, who gave her a slightly wobbly curtsy. Dorothy stepped into the imposing hallway, taking in the French impressionist artwork on the walls and well-polished mahogany furniture. The longcase clock was striking three, as the maid took her upstairs and showed her into the drawing room. She was immediately greeted enthusiastically by the two women and three dogs.

"Excellent, exactly on time," said Mary, dropping the copy of the *Telegraph* she was reading and striding over to shake her hand.

"How lovely to meet you, Miss Peto. Mary has told me so much about you," said Margaret hurrying over from her position at the piano and kissing Dorothy on the cheek.

"Thank you and do please call me Dorothy."

"How kind, Dorothy. Now let me make the most important introductions. These two adorable creatures are Topsy and Skip," she said, trying and failing to push away the two cocker spaniels who were excitedly jumping up at Dorothy. "And our elder statesmen here, is Herbert," she continued, pointing to the basset hound, who was barking loudly.

"How apt." Dorothy laughed. With his stocky build and grumpy expression, the dog did rather look like Herbert Henry Asquith, the Prime Minister.

"At least our Herbert occasionally does what we ask of him." Mary snorted, then turning to the maid, who was still hovering by the door, said, "Would you bring us some tea please, Annie?"

"Yes, sir," replied the maid before disappearing.

Dorothy wondered if she had misheard as she took her seat on the sofa, but when the maid returned a few moments later with the tea tray she bobbed another uncertain curtsy and said, "Will that be all, miss? Sir?"

"Yes, thank you," replied Mary handing Dorothy a plate as Margaret began to pour them each a cup of tea.

"Did you have a pleasant journey here, Dorothy?" asked Margaret, offering her a sandwich, then sharing a scone between the three drooling canines.

"Yes, thank you. As it's such a nice day, I walked. Everywhere seemed so peaceful, it really is difficult to believe we are at war."

"If only the same could be said for the poor Belgians. I can't imagine how terrible it must be to see your country invaded and then be forced to flee with your family. Mary was just reading about it in the newspaper. Apparently another five hundred arrived this morning."

"Margaret is terribly worried about the Belgians," explained Mary with an indulgent smile. "I'm off to a meeting later of the London Society for Women's Suffrage, to see what can be done to help them."

Margaret looked up from dividing a fish paste sandwich into three, her face full of concern.

"Oh do be careful, Robert dear. Even with everything that is happening, the police are still targeting these meetings. Look what happened to Dorothy's friend, poor Miss Boyle."

As Dorothy nibbled on a cucumber sandwich, she wondered if Nina's current predicament was the reason she had been invited to tea. After all Margaret was extremely well connected. When her father had died, her mother had married Thomas de Grey. He had been a Conservative member of parliament for many years and now he sat in the House of Lords as the 6th Baron Walsingham. Perhaps Margaret could ask him to use his influence to help Nina. She also wondered if Margaret really had addressed Mary as Robert.

"You must not fret so. With so many of their number joining the army, I doubt the police have enough men to target our meeting. Besides, I put up such a struggle the last time I was arrested, I doubt the Metropolitan's finest will want to tackle me again." Mary proudly touched her hunger strike medal and turned to Dorothy. "Actually, it was the police that we wanted to talk to you about, Dorothy."

But before she could say another word, the harsh jangle of the front doorbell interrupted her, and the three dogs all began barking furiously.

"Good Lord! She's early—I'm sure she does it on purpose. I'll make myself scarce," said Mary, suddenly unfolding herself from the sofa and tucking her newspaper under her arm.

"I wish I could," sighed Margaret. Mary grinned and blew her a kiss.

"Good luck, old girl," she whispered, before striding out of the door in the corner of the drawing room and carefully closing it behind her. Dorothy watched in confusion, wondering who this other visitor could be and if she was expected to follow Mary out of the room. A second later, the main door swung open and Annie announced the arrival of Margaret's new guest.

"Lady Walsingham to see you, miss." Annie curtsied yet again, as Lady Walsingham glided past her in a cloud of lavender lace and an impossibly large hat. Dorothy thought she looked like one of the wisteria blossoms that hung around the window of her father's studio. Although she must now be in her late sixties, she was a striking woman and had clearly once been very beautiful. Margaret rose slowly, to greet her.

"Hello, Mother," she said leaning forward to kiss the well-powdered, proffered cheek. Her mother arranged herself on the sofa, recently vacated by Mary. She firmly shooed away the dogs, who were excitedly yapping around her ankles, and Margaret settled into the chair opposite her. Dorothy watched as Lady Walsingham's pale blue eyes scanned the room, absorbing every detail. They rested for a second on the pair of reading glasses Mary—in her hurry—had left behind, before flicking to the door in the corner. She then turned her attention to Dorothy, looking her up and down coldly.

Margaret gave a small cough. "Mother, may I introduce Miss Dorothy Peto. I'm sure you were acquainted with her grandfather, Sir Morton Peto."

Lady Walsingham's expression softened a little. "Who could possibly forget the man responsible for building the Houses of Parliament and Nelson's Column? And your father is quite the talented landscape artist, too. I attended his exhibition at a gallery on Cork Street last summer. You must be very proud of them both."

"It's kind of you to say so, Lady Walsingham," replied Dorothy meekly, feeling as if she'd passed some sort of test.

"Your people live in Hampshire I believe, Miss Peto?"

"That's correct, Lady Walsingham, although I am currently living with my brother in Bloomsbury."

"Very proper. I don't believe an unmarried woman should live alone, unchaperoned."

Margaret poured her mother a cup of tea and coughed again. It seemed to be a nervous tick.

"I wasn't expecting to see you until this evening, Mother," she began. "Although naturally I was very pleased to receive your note saying you were coming to town for a few days."

Lady Walsingham arched an eyebrow. "Well, Margaret, as you refuse to visit us in Norfolk, the mountain has come to Mohammed. However, it took forever to escape the station—the place was so busy—so I decided to come straight here before you disappear off to one of your wretched committees."

"Actually, I am due at the Animal Defence League in an

hour," Margaret replied.

Lady Walsingham raised her eyes to the ceiling. "Oh not those strange anti-vivisection people again, darling! They are such a nuisance! So unreasonable—and why are so many of them Swedish?" she asked, her large hat shaking with indignation.

"Lizzie Lind is perfectly reasonable. Her grandfather was Chamberlain to the King of Sweden. You'd like her if you met her," Margaret explained patiently. "And our ideas are not at all strange. We are more than happy for scientists to practise vivisection, as long as it's on themselves, rather than causing unnecessary suffering to animals," she added. Dorothy thought this description of what their cause stood for did indeed sound quite reasonable, but Lady Walsingham tutted loudly in response.

"Really, Margaret! That ridiculous brown dog affair! Your friends caused nothing but trouble—protests, riots, not to mention the court case."

Margaret's smile faded and to Dorothy's horror her eyes began to fill with tears, but Lady Walsingham didn't seem to notice. "I'm sure Miss Peto here agrees with me."

Dorothy shifted uncomfortably in her seat. Although she had never been actively involved with the anti-vivisection movement, she vividly remembered the brown dog affair. It concerned a poor little terrier, who had been operated on without being properly anaesthetised. Dorothy had grown up in a house full of dogs and for weeks after reading the reports, she'd had nightmares about his tiny body twitching and struggling in agony, supposedly in the name of science. All Margaret, Lizzie and the others had done was erect a simple statue in Battersea to honour him and other defenceless animals like him, but the medical students had taken offence. They were the ones who caused all the trouble, trying to knock the bronze figure down. Not content with watching the poor helpless creature suffer when he lived, they had wanted to destroy his image after his death. Dorothy opened her mouth to speak in support of what Margaret had done, but Lady Walsingham was clearly not interested in anyone else's opinion.

"It was only thanks to Thomas that we managed to keep you out of prison and more importantly, the newspapers," she continued, helping herself to a cucumber sandwich. "He is as eager as I am, that you stop these silly pursuits."

Dorothy watched as Margaret took a sip of Earl Grey, blinked back her tears and frowned at the mention of Lord Walsingham's name. Thanks to her research, Dorothy knew they had married quite recently and that Margaret's mother was his lordship's third wife. Her reaction did not go unnoticed by her mother either.

"Please don't scowl in that unbecoming way, Margaret," she snapped, sharply. "Your stepfather has always shown the utmost regard for you. I do wish you would spend more time together. The two of you have so much in common. You know he loves animals too."

Margaret couldn't stop herself producing a snort of derision that Mary would have been proud of. Dorothy was very much wishing she had followed the other woman's example and left mother and daughter alone. It was bad enough listening to her own family squabbles, listening to those of someone she barely knew was excruciating. However, her mother mentioning animals seemed to have triggered Margaret's fighting spirit.

"He loves putting pins through dead butterflies and blasting innocent birds out of the sky," she argued. "What's his record again? One thousand and seventy grouse in one day? He supports murdering animals, not defending their rights."

"Really, Margaret, the rights of grouse and butterflies—such nonsense! Good heavens, what will you think of next? It was vexing enough when you chose to turn beautiful Danehill into a sort of refuge for horses," Lady Walsingham continued, "then you spend a small fortune on a home for the offspring of silly girls with no morals. When do you think you may find the time to attend to the rights of your own poor mother?"

"Your rights, Mother?" enquired Margaret sounding surprised.

"To be a grandmother!" Lady Walsingham replied, calmly. "You're not quite forty; there could still be time. Although you may never have been a great beauty, you are still a handsome woman. Perhaps if you dressed a little less severely, or did something different with your hair? If all this talk of the war continuing into the New Year turns out to be true, then there could soon be fewer men to choose from."

Dorothy cringed. She was sure her own mother shared some of Lady Walsingham's opinions, especially when it came to finding a husband, but she would never dream of voicing them so bluntly and in front of a stranger. The colour rose to Margaret's cheeks as she self-consciously smoothed down her navy skirt over her slightly too-round stomach and hips. She certainly hadn't inherited her mother's ballerina-like figure.

"For a moment there, I actually thought you meant your right to vote!" retorted Margaret. Lady Walsingham tutted again and shook her head as she placed her cup and saucer on the table.

"Oh, I couldn't think of anything more tedious. And what would be the point? Whom should I vote for now Thomas is no longer in the House? Don't you agree, Miss Peto?"

Margaret saved her from having to answer.

"And what would be the point in me marrying?" She bristled. "Thanks to Daddy, I have more than enough money of my own."

Lady Walsingham rather pointedly waved away the slice of Madeira cake, Margaret offered her. Dorothy did the same. She had completely lost her appetite and was wishing she'd never accepted Mary's invitation.

"Yes, well not only was your father a talented surgeon, but he also had a very kind heart, especially where you were concerned. Unfortunately, it was also a very weak heart. Have you really never considered children of your own? Surely you must want company if nothing else…" she left the slightest pause "…living in this house all alone?"

Margaret refused to meet her mother's piercing gaze. Instead, she bent down to ruffle the silky ears of one of the cocker spaniels, who was waiting expectantly for a slice of cake. Dorothy was now starting to understand the reason for Mary's sudden departure.

"I enjoy my independence and I love darling Skip here,

and Topsy and Herbert, as much as I could love any offspring of my own."

With an exaggerated sigh, Lady Walsingham rose from the sofa and pressed the bell for the maid. She looked down in disdain at the three drooling canines. "Are you trying to tell me, these dogs are the nearest thing I shall ever have to grandchildren?"

"Well, you may struggle to teach them bridge, but I'm sure they'd love to be taken to tea at The Ritz," said Margaret with a smile, obviously relieved to see the visit would soon be over.

Dorothy had to stifle a giggle. Lady Walsingham shook her head, as Annie entered with another wobbly curtsy.

"Really, Margaret, you are quite impossible. Now I must go. Do come to dinner while I am in town and consider what I said about a new hairstyle. It could work wonders. Good day, Miss Peto. It was a pleasure to meet you."

"The pleasure was mine," murmured Dorothy in response, but Lady Walsingham had already wafted out of the room. As Annie closed the door, Margaret flopped back down in the armchair with a groan and raised a hand to her head. Dorothy glanced at the clock on the mantelpiece. Lady Walsingham's visit had lasted only twenty minutes but it had clearly exhausted her daughter. The door in the corner creaked open and Mary slipped back into the room.

"Is the coast clear?" she asked with a grin.

"Yes." Margaret sighed. "The HMS *Walsingham*, the battleship that is my mother, has sailed away. No doubt to bombard some other poor, unsuspecting harbour into submission. Did you hear?"

"Well, her voice does carry rather." Mary wrinkled her nose. "And that awful perfume she wears does linger."

It was true. The heavy scent of violets hung in the air and was clawing at the back of Dorothy's throat. Mary went to the window, pushed it wide open and leant out. From the street came the noisy clatter of horses' hooves.

"There she goes back to Mayfair. I swear, if she lives to be a hundred, she'll never give up her coach and four for an automobile."

"She seems to have renamed me 'Really, Margaret!'" Margaret sighed as she closed her eyes.

Mary laughed and helped herself to several of the remaining sandwiches. "I'm awfully sorry to have abandoned you, Dorothy," she said through a mouthful of bread and cucumber. "I'm afraid Lady W and I have never seen eye to eye."

"I'm sorry too, Dorothy. My mother can be a little overwhelming. We would never have invited you if I'd known she was going to call early," apologised Margaret.

"Not at all," replied Dorothy politely, hoping they could finally get to the point of her visit. "Erm, why did you invite me exactly? Did you want to talk about Nina, perhaps?"

"Well in a way yes," began Mary, but Margaret held up her hand to silence her.

"I do hate to be a bother, but my head is absolutely pounding. I don't think I'm up to discussing anything right now. I really feel I should go and lie down."

Mary bent down to look at her, her face full of concern. "You do look rather peaky, dear. We can arrange another meeting, can't we, Dorothy? And with any luck Miss Boyle will be able to join us next time," said Mary as she stood up and brushed the breadcrumbs from her tweed jacket. Dorothy rose to her feet too, feeling a combination of relief and confusion.

"Yes of course, I hope you feel better soon, Margaret," she said. The older woman, who did look rather pale, gave her a weak smile in return. Mary pressed the bell to summon the maid, then gently took hold of Margaret's hand and pulled her to her feet.

"Come on, old girl, best haul anchor or you shall never be ready for your meeting with Lizzie. Remember you're needed to keep those trouble-making Swedes in check."

"Ha bloody ha!!" chuckled Margaret whilst still clutching her brow.

"Really, Margaret! Such language!" Mary laughed in a perfect imitation of Lady Walsingham, and Dorothy couldn't help grinning too.

After saying goodbye, she followed Annie out of the drawing room. At the top of the stairs, she paused and watched as Mary—with her arm firmly around Margaret's waist—made their way down the corridor with the three dogs at their heels.

When she stepped outside and began walking back down Cheyne Row, she gave a sigh of relief. That had to be one of the strangest meetings she'd ever attended, and she still had absolutely no idea why the two women had wanted to see her. She was even more confused about the precise nature of their relationship. Were they just good friends or something more? Dorothy was well aware that having spent most of her life in rural Hampshire, she could be naïve. Nina and

Raymond were always teasing her about it. As she turned on to the path that ran along the river, she shrugged her shoulders. Mary and Margaret might be a little unconventional, but she rather liked them.

Chapter Five

ALTHOUGH IT WAS summer, the streets of London were still chilly early in the morning. A damp fog from the river clung to the air and refused to lift. Dorothy pulled her coat more closely around her, as she walked briskly towards the offices of the Women's Freedom League. She stifled a yawn. Goodness, she was tired. Last night, she had been working until after ten on the latest edition of *The Vote*, knowing that Nina would still want this issue to be printed on time, even if she wasn't there to oversee it. Hopefully, she should be released in the next few days. Dorothy and the other members of the League had spent every day writing letters and sending telegrams in protest at their comrade's treatment but to no avail. Now the country was at war, it seemed that those in power weren't interested in anything else.

The previous evening, Dorothy had been redrafting her account of Nina's arrest and imprisonment yet again, but she still wasn't happy with it. The article and lack of response to their pleas wasn't her only cause of frustration. Yesterday's newspaper had reported that the inquest into Edith Devine's death had been brought forward. It was now due to take place at the end of the week, but she still hadn't been asked to make a formal statement.

Suddenly, Dorothy stopped in her tracks. There was a light on at the WFL's office window. Nobody had a key except for herself and Nina. Her first thought was a police raid. It had happened several times before. She hurried across the road and cautiously pushed open the unlocked main door. Their office was on the first floor. She tiptoed quietly into the hallway and up the stairs, wincing as each step creaked. If it was a raid, the police were being awfully quiet. With a pounding heart, she paused in front of the office door, her hand on the handle. She took a deep breath but as she pushed it open, she heard a familiar voice call out.

"Good morning, Dorothy."

"Nina, you're back!" Dorothy dashed across the room with relief and hugged her friend, who was calmly sitting behind her desk, smoking a cigarette. "When did they let you out?"

"About an hour ago. Apparently, now we are at war, they have better things to do than keep me incarcerated." Then she grinned. "Well, it was either that or my good behaviour."

"That would be a first!" Dorothy laughed, then looking more closely at her friend, saw that she was very thin and rather dishevelled. She was still wearing the clothes they'd arrested her in. She must have come from the prison, straight here to the office.

"Shouldn't you be at home resting?" she asked.

Nina shook her head. "No! I have done nothing but rest for the last two weeks. Now is the time for action," she declared, raising her hand defiantly and scattering ash from her cigarette across the desk.

"Then at least let me make you a warm drink," said Dorothy with a smile. It was so good to have her friend back. She disappeared into the anteroom they jokingly called the kitchen. It contained little more than a sink and a stove, and the cupboards were usually empty. After much rummaging, she returned a few moments later with two mugs of black tea and a plate of slightly stale ginger biscuits. Nina was bashing away at her typewriter.

"What are you writing?" Dorothy asked, as she carefully placed the tray down on the desk.

Nina didn't look up as her fingers tapped vigorously at the keys. "First an article for *The Vote*, then a letter outlining my latest proposal to Mr McKenna," she replied.

"The Home Secretary?" asked Dorothy in surprise.

"Is there any other?"

"Goodness, I hope it's not a marriage proposal. Reginald McKenna would make the world's dullest husband. Outside of politics his only interests are bridge and golf. I'd even take Asquith over him."

Nina laughed at the look of disgust on Dorothy's face.

"My proposal," she explained, briefly pausing to take a sip of tea and a drag on her cigarette, "is that he should appoint female special constables to the police force."

Dorothy stared open-mouthed at her. "You want him to let us join the police force?" she asked, incredulously.

"Yes. They insist on arresting us, yet they don't have the resources to deal with us," replied Nina in a matter-of-fact manner. "A man arrested me and shoved me into a van full of violent, lewd, drunk men. Then at the police station, a man cautioned me, a man charged me, then another man sentenced me. I didn't see another woman until I arrived in Holloway, over twenty-four hours later, and we know mine is not an isolated case. If we want to achieve true fairness in the justice system, we must change the whole male-dominated process, and this is our perfect opportunity. With the outbreak of war, men are leaving the police force to enlist. We and the other suffrage groups have agreed to suspend our campaign for the duration, but our members are desperate to be useful."

Nina's eyes were shining, she'd obviously thought of little else while she was locked away. Privately, Dorothy thought the idea was insane, but as always when Nina was passionate about something her enthusiasm became infectious. After all, strange things happened during wars. Maybe it could be possible.

"We could carry out basic duties, like give directions or help control traffic?" she suggested.

Nina beamed at her. "Precisely! Allowing us to join the force as special constables would be the perfect solution for everyone."

"You've almost convinced me, Nina," said Dorothy, picking up a biscuit, "but I think McKenna might take a bit more work."

SHE SPENT THE rest of the morning helping Nina draft a letter to the Home Secretary, then having made her friend promise she would go and get something to eat, she dashed over to King's Cross. She wanted to say goodbye to Raymond before he left.

Like almost all the young men she knew, he had desperately wanted to enlist, but thanks to his flat feet, he had been declared unfit on medical grounds. Dorothy had watched him grow more and more quiet and despondent each day, as he watched his friends sign up to do their duty. Finally, it was the Foreign Secretary himself who found a solution. Grey recommended Raymond to Vernon Kell, who was looking for intelligent young men to recruit to his newly formed military intelligence operation where no marching was required. It seemed Raymond's experience at the Foreign Office made him an ideal candidate.

That was as much as he had told her, and that was only after she had begged. She only knew he was leaving today because she'd overheard him ordering a taxicab.

DOROTHY DIDN'T THINK she'd ever known King's Cross station to be so busy. The place was heaving. Whichever way she looked, there seemed to be a sea of people. Troop trains packed with soldiers were departing every few minutes, watched by sobbing and handkerchief-waving wives, mothers, daughters and sweethearts. On other platforms, carriages were arriving and depositing disorientated refugees, clutching two, three, sometimes even four suitcases. Her heart sank as she scanned the crowds. Dressed in his uniform, it would be almost impossible to find her brother. Then suddenly there he was, standing on the other side of the concourse, at least a foot taller than most of the other soldiers around him.

"Raymond!" she shouted as she ran towards him. Her brother turned and smiled at first, then frowned.

"Dorothy! What are you doing here?"

"I wanted to come and see you off. I couldn't let you go without saying goodbye," she replied breathlessly flinging her arms around him.

"We said goodbye this morning and you know I can't tell you where I'm being sent," he said, briefly hugging her back, before untangling himself.

"But what shall I tell Mother? She's already cross with me for not stopping you from joining up. She'll be furious I didn't find out where you are being sent."

"If you don't know, you won't be able to tell Mother or anyone else who asks." He planted a quick kiss on her cheek, then took her firmly by the shoulders and turned her around so she was facing the other way. "Now close your eyes and don't open them again until you've counted to ten. Promise not to look, and I'll be back before you know it."

With a sigh of resignation, Dorothy did as she was told and counted to ten. When she opened her eyes again and turned around Raymond had gone. She felt a pang of fear and sadness. Although he wouldn't be on the front line, it didn't mean he might not be in danger. If he was sent abroad, would she even know? She turned away from the departing trains and was about to leave the station when she spotted two familiar figures on the nearest platform.

Margaret and her basset hound were hovering next to Lady Walsingham, who seemed unperturbed by the other travellers all around her and was busy instructing a harassed-looking porter, who had been tasked with loading her vast collection of luggage on to the train. Margaret waved as soon as she saw Dorothy.

"Good afternoon, Dorothy. How nice to see you again. What brings you here today?"

Dorothy made her way over and greeted Margaret and her mother.

"I came to see my brother off. I had no idea it would be so busy."

"Oh it's utter madness!" declared Lady Walsingham. "All these refugees everywhere. They're flooding the place. I hear it's even worse in all the Channel ports and stations. I honestly don't know where we are expected to put them all."

"Mother has had enough of London and is heading back to Norfolk," explained Margaret cheerfully.

A train pulled in at the next platform and yet more displaced Belgians spilled out. Margaret and Dorothy turned to watch them, as Lady Walsingham continued to harangue the hapless porter. The new arrivals looked totally confused. Dorothy couldn't imagine how they must be feeling. To have to leave their home, their country, with only the possessions they were able to carry. Some family groups began to move away, but about half a dozen teenage girls remained rooted to the spot.

"That group looks completely lost. They can't be more than sixteen," said Dorothy.

"They do," agreed Margaret. "I wonder if they are travelling without a chaperone. Hello there, can I help?" she called across. A couple of the girls in the group looked over. Margaret sighed. "Oh dear, I don't think they speak English. Do Belgians speak French?"

"*Puis je vous aider?*" Dorothy called out, but to no response.

"Jolly good try, Dorothy," said Margaret. "They must be the Flemish ones. Perhaps I should go over."

"Please don't get involved, Margaret," chided Lady Walsingham, who seemed to have an inbuilt distrust of all foreigners. At that moment, a woman wearing a green hat with large feathery plumes approached the girls.

"Oh look, Mother, there's a lady going to talk to them now. I wonder if she's from the Red Cross."

Lady Walsingham briefly gave the group her attention, before glancing away again.

"Really, Margaret, don't be silly," she said, dismissively. "No member of a Red Cross committee would ever dye their hair that unnatural shade of red or wear such a ridiculous hat."

A shrill whistle from the guard distracted them all. Lady Walsingham allowed the porter to assist her as she stepped aboard the train and into the first-class carriage.

"Now, darling, please promise me: no more lost causes," she called through the open window.

"Goodbye, Mother. Do have a safe journey!" Margaret called back. She smiled, blew Lady Walsingham a kiss and continued to wave as the engine puffed away, then when it was finally out of sight, she turned to Dorothy. "Why does she always make me feel like I'm a gauche, inky-fingered schoolgirl?" She sighed.

Dorothy nodded in sympathy. "She's your mother—that's her job."

"Well, she's very good at it. It was so nice to see you

again, Dorothy, but now you must excuse me. Poor Herbert simply hates crowds."

"Of course," replied Dorothy, bending down to stroke the basset hound, who didn't look remotely concerned. She watched Margaret and her dog trot away down the platform, then turned her attention back to the refugees, but they had disappeared. She stared up and down the platform, utterly perplexed. It was as if they had simply vanished into thin air, yet she had only been distracted for a moment or two.

She began to walk back towards the main station concourse, occasionally stopping and straining her eyes to see if she could spot the green feathery hat through the crowds. When she came to a halt the fourth time, she almost bumped into a soldier, who was leaving his table outside the station café in a terrible rush. They both apologised and without thinking why, she quickly took his place. Something told her that what had happened with the Belgian girls was strange. There were so many terrible stories swirling around about how the refugees, particularly unaccompanied young women, were being preyed on by criminal gangs. She'd heard stories of some being forced into unpaid work or, worse, prostitution. Surely it was her duty to try to find out what was happening here at King's Cross. She ordered herself a pot of tea and waited.

About fifteen minutes later, another train crammed full of refugees arrived on the same platform as before. Again, a group of teenage girls, only five this time, remained on the platform, looking around as though they were waiting for someone. Dorothy stood up and watched closely. Sure enough they were approach by a woman, but this time she had blonde hair, and a straw boater had replaced the plumed hat. However, Dorothy was positive it was the same woman. She was the same height and same build and was wearing the same navy coat. Quickly, the woman ushered the girls away. They passed by Dorothy, but rather than follow them she decided to remain where she was and see if the strange woman returned again.

Twenty minutes later, when three girls were waiting on the platform, the woman appeared again. Now she had dark hair and a red felt beret. This time Dorothy decided she would follow them. It wasn't easy. The woman herded the girls through the crowds with remarkable speed. Dorothy hurried after them, apologising as she pushed past people on her way. The mysterious woman led the girls outside to a where a hansom cab was waiting. As they began to climb in, Dorothy finally caught up with them. She was out of breath and flushed, but she politely tapped the woman on the shoulder. The woman spun round in surprise and glared at her.

"Madame, please excuse me for…" Dorothy began, but before she could say another word, the mysterious woman shouted something rapidly in a foreign language and jumped into the cab too. The driver cracked his whip and the horse trotted away at speed, leaving Dorothy standing alone and puzzled on the pavement. She'd seen the woman's face before but she couldn't for the life of her remember where.

Chapter Six

REGINALD MCKENNA—THE HOME Secretary—had a thin face, was clean-shaven and wore an expression of almost permanent melancholy. However, as Dorothy sat opposite him, she was unable to see any of these features, only his shiny bald head. She and Nina had been announced and ushered into the office by a secretary. McKenna had briefly glanced up, motioned for them to sit in the chairs across from him, then returned to whatever it was he was reading.

According to the loudly ticking longcase clock, that had been five minutes ago. Dorothy felt like a naughty little girl again, summoned to her father's office for a telling-off, but she tried to remind herself how she was lucky to be here. She and Nina were surprised he had agreed to a meeting at all. Nina had only written to him a few days ago. When his reply arrived, they had hoped that perhaps he was finally going to see sense; now she wasn't so sure. Nina had asked Dorothy to come with her and take notes. However, the fact that the secretary had not remained in the room made Dorothy think McKenna didn't consider it was worth doing the same.

On the chair next to her, Nina was leaning forward and had begun quietly drumming her fingers on the desk.

Dorothy gave her a small nudge with her elbow to make her stop. But impatient by nature, Nina was unable to sit in silence any longer.

"It is very good of you to see us, Home Secretary," she began.

McKenna slowly raised his head. He peered intently over his half-moon spectacles at them both and gave a wry smile. "Miss Boyle, members of the Women's Freedom League have an unfortunate habit of chaining themselves to the railings outside my office and hurling bricks through my windows when your requests are denied. In order to avoid this, a meeting with you, their leader, and your assistant, Miss Peto, seemed the more sensible option."

Nina attempted to return his smile, as she raised a finger. "If I could correct you, Home Secretary. The WFL do not advocate violence and none of our members have ever been convicted of criminal damage. When it comes to brick hurling, perhaps you are thinking of the WSPU?"

"Ah yes, Mrs Pankhurst's organisation," the Home Secretary replied, "which I believe you were a member of until two years ago. As for convictions, there is quite an extensive list against your name. Should I assume you thought up this latest proposal during your most recent period of detention at His Majesty's pleasure, Miss Boyle?"

"So you have read my proposal?" asked Nina not rising to the bait. Dorothy could tell she was eager to move the conversation on. So far, it wasn't going in the direction they had hoped.

The Home Secretary glanced down at the papers on his desk and read out loud. "To allow women to join the

Metropolitan Police Force as special constables."

"Yes," Nina replied as Dorothy began scribbling down his acknowledgement.

"In the hope that you may become one of these special constables yourself, Miss Boyle?"

"Possibly," agreed Nina.

"And no doubt others in your organisation have the same desire?" continued McKenna. He fixed his eyes on Dorothy and she was relieved that they had agreed Nina would do all the talking.

"The Women's Freedom League have always believed that women should take an equal role to men and my members are keen to help our country in this time of peril," said Nina, repeating one of the lines they had worked on for this meeting.

McKenna leant back in his leather chair and turned his head towards the window that overlooked King Charles Street. Nina gave Dorothy a questioning look, but she could only shrug in return. The man was inscrutable. After a brief pause, he turned back to face them.

"Forgive me, but I am a little puzzled, ladies. Miss Boyle, since becoming leader of the Women's Freedom League, you have encouraged the non-completion of taxation forms and censuses, you have led demonstrations and protests against His Majesty's government. In short, you have incited others to break the very laws which you now think you are fit to enforce."

"It is precisely because I have been on the other side of the law and know first-hand how women are treated when under arrest that I am qualified to…"

McKenna held up a hand to silence her. "Miss Boyle, this country is now at war. A war, I may add, you have also spoken against. With more men joining our armed forces, the police will find themselves dealing with an ever-increasing workload."

"And female special constables could help ease the burden," insisted Nina, determined to make her case.

"And you and your followers could also ease the burden if you behaved appropriately and stopped acting in such a way that leads to you being arrested." He paused and placed his hands in front of him on the desk. "Allow me to be blunt, ladies. As you very well know, women may not sit on juries or vote in parliamentary elections. In fact, in the eyes of the law you are not a proper person and so cannot be given the power to arrest. Therefore, it is not possible for me to agree to your request."

Dorothy paused with her pencil in mid-air. Forget all the rude jeers from men when Nina made a speech, or the abominable pronouncements from Mead, this was possibly the most shocking thing she'd ever heard. This powerful, intelligent man, sitting calmly at his desk, honestly believed that she and Nina were not real people. He may as well have slapped her across the face. If the man in charge of law and order in this country thought they were some sort of subspecies, what hope did they have?

"But if you…" began Nina, her voice rising in anger.

"No, Miss Boyle. The answer is no."

McKenna stood up, making it clear the meeting was over. He walked to the door and held it open for them. Nina stood up, scraping her chair back in frustration. She had no choice but to leave. With one last look at McKenna, she stormed through the outer office—startling several clerks—and then down the stairs and out into the street. Still feeling stunned, Dorothy stood up too and followed her friend at a slightly more sedate pace.

She caught up with Nina in the street outside. Her friend had already lit a cigarette and was pacing up and down, her face full of fury.

"How dare he call himself the Right Honourable Gentleman? He isn't any of those things! It would have been easier begging Asquith himself. McKenna was every bit as pompous, pig-headed and unreasonable as his boss. I think he only invited me there, so he could tick me off. We cannot possibly join the police because we are not proper people. We are proper enough to cook their meals, tend to their wounds when they are injured and give birth to their children. Why can't they see that we simply want to be useful? If we can put our differences to one side and try to do what's best for the country, why can't they? And he had absolutely no right to get our hopes up like that! If he was going to say no all along, he could have put it in a letter," Nina demanded loudly, attracting enquiring glances from passing strangers. Dorothy linked her arm through Nina's and steered her away from the Home Office.

"Come on," she suggested, "let's leave Whitehall behind and go somewhere a little friendlier."

Fifteen minutes later, they arrived at Alan's Tea Rooms on Oxford Street. Dorothy was feeling much more composed, but Nina was still ranting. Alan's was a popular place with suffragettes. The owner, Marguerite Alan Liddle, greeted them warmly. She was sympathetic to their cause and often let them hold meetings in the upstairs room, free of charge. In fact, her own sister—Helen—had recently been on hunger strike in Strangeways.

As they made their way to their regular corner table, Dorothy waved to another table of WFL members that included Charlotte Despard and Alice Schofield. Nina sank into the chair and immediately lit a cigarette as Dorothy placed their order with a waitress. Nina didn't stop complaining about McKenna until their Earl Grey arrived.

Dorothy waited for her friend to take a drink and hopefully calm down. The walk over here had given her time to think. In her handbag was a letter from Mary Allen outlining the subject she and Margaret had wanted to discuss with her before their meeting was cut short by Lady Walsingham's visit. She had refrained from telling Nina about it until they knew what McKenna's response would be, but now she wasn't sure if this was the right time to mention it. She knew Nina could very well spend the rest of the afternoon brooding over her encounter with the Home Secretary. As Nina began nibbling on a piece of shortbread, she decided it was worth a try.

"I know it's terribly disappointing, Nina, but really it would have been a miracle if McKenna had agreed to the proposal so easily," she said carefully, placing a calming hand on her friend's arm. "Look, I've been thinking. If we acted as volunteers rather than members of the regular police, how could they stop us? If we aren't using public money, then…"

"We would still need permission," Nina replied with a frown, but Dorothy took the fact she didn't dismiss the suggestion immediately, as an encouraging sign.

"Then we should go directly to Scotland Yard. The Metropolitan Police are the ones under pressure, with so many constables leaving to enlist and hundreds and hundreds of refugees from across the Channel arriving every day."

Nina took another sip of tea and a long drag on her cigarette. "If we were volunteers, we would still need private funding of some sort. We'd need to advertise, supply new recruits with whistles and torches, that sort of thing. Then there would be the administration costs. Who do we know with that kind of money?"

Dorothy smiled as she came to the most important part of the plan.

"Margaret Damer Dawson. The animal rights activist. She's got pots of money and is always throwing it at some good cause or other. Do you recollect she set up a foundling hospital?" asked Dorothy, then noting Nina's blank expression, added, "The two of you met at the Criminal Law Amendment Committee, a few months ago."

Recognition slowly dawned on Nina's face.

"I remember! Miss Double D! She seemed to have a whole pack of dogs running around her feet wherever she went." Nina laughed, and Dorothy could tell she was slowly warming to her scheme.

"That's her. Well, anyway her companion, Mary Allen, has been in contact with me. She's very keen on the idea of female police volunteers too. We want to try to arrange a meeting between yourself and Miss Damer Dawson as soon as possible."

"Mary Allen?"

Again, Nina showed no sign of remembering. Dorothy sighed in despair. Nina was amazing when it came to memorising speeches, but utterly hopeless when it came to recalling names and faces.

"The rather imposing lady we were speaking with before you were arrested outside Caxton Hall. She's kept in regular contact with me since then and she's been very supportive. She and Miss Damer Dawson live together in Chelsea." Then knowing how much her friend enjoyed a piece of gossip added, "Miss Allen is known as Robert by her friends and likes the servants to call her 'sir'."

Nina grinned mischievously, her previous bad mood having evaporated completely. She raised her cup and clinked it against Dorothy's in salute.

"Very well then. I'll get the better of McKenna if it kills me. Let's go to see Miss Double D and Sir."

They spent another hour discussing how to approach the meeting, then Dorothy left a much happier Nina chatting with Charlotte and the others. On her way home, she picked up that evening's edition of *The Times* to read on the bus back to Bloomsbury. Tucked away on the inside pages was the coroner's verdict on the death of Edith Devine. Misadventure was the ruling. Apparently, Edith was a regular user of cocaine and had taken a larger dose that night. Apart from Inspector Derwent, the only person called to give evidence was Edith's maid, Nan Lambert. It was reported that 'the young woman had a shy and nervous disposition on the witness stand'.

Dorothy tutted quietly to herself. The maid had reported that her mistress had been distraught after an unnamed gentleman friend had visited her dressing room and ended their relationship. Nan's comment that "she sobbed so violently that I was afraid for her", seemed enough to convince the court that a heartbroken Edith had killed herself accidentally. Surely Muller couldn't have been the male visitor who had upset her so. She'd seemed almost dismissive of his visit.

Dorothy closed the paper in disgust. What sort of hearing didn't call all witnesses? It was bad enough that her evidence had been ignored, but there was none from Muller either and no mention of the woman Dorothy saw at the stage door. Although Edith was of course only a woman. Perhaps the coroner and the inspector agreed with their boss, McKenna. Edith's death wasn't worth a proper investigation because she wasn't a proper person.

A FEW DAYS later, Dorothy was once again perched on the edge of the sofa in the drawing room at 10 Cheyne Row. This time Nina was sitting next to her. She could tell her friend was trying very hard not to kick either of the yapping spaniels, who were avidly sniffing her shoes. Herbert, the rather flatulent basset hound, had already coated the hem of her own skirt with drool. Margaret, however, seemed quite oblivious to her dogs' behaviour as she chatted away happily and poured out four cups of tea.

"We always read your articles in *The Vote* with great interest, Miss Boyle," she said.

"I, for one, particularly enjoyed hearing all about that

stunt the two of you pulled on the Thames," added Mary, who was standing in front of the fireplace with her arms clasped behind her back. "I wish I could have been there. I bet McKenna's face was a picture, not to mention Asquith's. He must have looked as grumpy as our own Herbert, eh boy?" She bent down to stroke the basset hound, who looked up at her with sad, drooping eyes.

"I was so sorry to hear of your dreadful ordeal in prison," continued Margaret.

"Thank you, Miss Damer Dawson," replied Nina. "It wasn't my first experience of being held in custody, but it was definitely one of the most unpleasant."

"I can only imagine. Poor Robert was in Holloway only a few months ago. The whole experience was incredibly brutal." She smiled up at Mary. Dorothy nodded politely in agreement, although she was still finding it quite strange to hear Mary being referred to as Robert. She was pleased she had forewarned Nina, who was inclined to find such things amusing. However, today her friend looked deadly serious, focused on the point of their visit.

"Brutal and degrading, Miss Damer Dawson," she agreed, "but fortunately women like Miss Allen and myself have the fortitude to cope with such an unpleasant experience. Imagine how terrified the more vulnerable women in our society must be."

"Not to mention the children, who are often still held in the cells at police stations," added Dorothy.

"Oh it simply breaks my heart to think of the little ones being imprisoned. They must be so alone and frightened," agreed Margaret with a shudder. "And the way they are treated by the courts is quite appalling."

"Precisely. How much more humane would it be to have a female police officer present to speak to these scared creatures and reassure them when they are being questioned or to accompany them to court, if necessary," said Nina. Dorothy took a sip of her tea and watched Mary and Margaret nod their heads in unison. The meeting seemed to be going well; even the dogs had settled down.

"Exactly what we think, Miss Boyle," continued Margaret, "and speaking of frightened creatures, I can't tell you how worried Robert and I are about the plight of the Belgian refugees too. There are young girls arriving here without a chaperone, not speaking a word of English. They are so vulnerable. We're sure they are being preyed upon by criminal gangs who force them into heaven knows what."

"I fear you may be correct be. Do you recall the group of girls we saw at King's Cross?" asked Dorothy. She then quickly recounted what she had witnessed at the station.

"Good Lord!" exclaimed Mary. "No doubt the poor creatures have been dragged into the white slave trade." Nina lowered her head and took a quick sip of her tea, while Dorothy managed to look concerned, although this explanation did sound a little far-fetched. Over the last couple of weeks, Dorothy had discovered that one of Mary's pet theories was that gangs of white slavers lurked around every corner ready to spirit away any unsuspecting, defenceless female. However, now wasn't the time to indulge her. The conversation was beginning to drift off course. It was time to steer it back.

"The refugees' plight is yet another example of how overstretched the police are and how we women could help," she said.

"Members of the Women's Freedom League could be patrolling stations and ports, assisting and advising the refugees as they arrive and making sure they don't fall prey to anyone with criminal intentions," added Nina. Dorothy watched closely as Margaret and Mary exchanged a brief glance.

"Forgive me, Miss Boyle, but I understood the Home Secretary turned down your proposal?" queried Margaret.

Nina took another sip of her tea. The fingers holding her saucer were twitching, a sure sign she was desperate for a cigarette. Dorothy had warned her that Margaret did not approve of smoking indoors. They couldn't risk upsetting her, not now they had reached the crux of the meeting. They must tread delicately. Dorothy had also warned Nina not to be too forceful. Margaret was a generous philanthropist rather than a campaigning suffragette. She was used to committees not confrontation.

"For us to become special constables yes," began Nina, "but not a voluntary force patrolling the streets, using our common sense to defuse situations before there is any need for arrest. How could anyone object to that? We would still need permission of course. I thought, if you are in agreement, we could jointly try to arrange a meeting with Sir Edward Henry, the Metropolitan Commissioner, and tell him of our plans."

"Excellent idea!" agreed Mary quickly. "The commissioner is a man of action and intelligence, not a pale-faced pen pusher like McKenna. Look at his amazing work using fingerprints to solve crimes. He's a forward thinker. We're bound to get more sense out of him."

"And I also hear he's very fond of dogs," added Margaret as she fed Topsy a small piece of Madeira cake and ruffled the spaniel's ear. Dorothy carefully placed her cup of tea back on its saucer. Now was the time for her to raise the most delicate issue, but the one that for her was the whole point of this meeting.

"As a voluntary organisation, it would of course need to be funded." She hesitated for a second. "Nina and I have worked out a few initial figures for premises, training, uniforms and so on. All the things we would need to begin with."

She reached down and removed the neatly typed estimate from her handbag and discreetly slid it across the table. She and Nina had been up half the night going over the numbers again and again, trying to keep costs down, but it was still going to be a terribly expensive enterprise. She held her breath, but Margaret barely glanced at the sheet in front of her. Dorothy exchanged a quick questioning look with Nina. Was this a good sign or not? Mary didn't seem interested in the figures either.

"Any ideas on uniform?" she asked instead.

Dorothy gained the impression that this issue was going to be very important to Mary. "We were thinking as close to the police uniform as the commissioner will allow. A useful blue serge skirt, a Norfolk jacket, a hat of some sort," she suggested.

Mary nodded enthusiastically. "Jolly good idea. I'll get on and draft some designs."

Next to her, Nina gave an almost inaudible sigh of relief.

"Wonderful," said Margaret beaming at all three of them. "Well we seem to be in agreement on everything. Now let's see what the commissioner has to say about our idea. What do you say, ladies?"

"Wonderful!" replied Dorothy and Nina in unison.

Chapter Seven

ALMOST THREE WEEKS later, Dorothy, Nina, Mary and Margaret were sitting together on a hastily arranged row of chairs in front of the desk of Sir Edward Henry, the Commissioner of the Metropolitan Police. It was a little after nine o'clock and the man himself had not yet arrived. The four of them had expected him to be late this morning and planned their visit for that very reason. In fact, thanks to Dorothy, they knew almost every detail of his life.

When Margaret had complained that her second letter to Sir Edward, requesting a meeting, had gone unanswered Dorothy decided to take matters into her own hands. She remembered that Ruth, a fellow member of the WFL, was employed as a governess to Sir Edward's youngest daughter. Although she only had one Wednesday off each month, she spent much of her precious free time working in the League's offices. When Dorothy approached her, she immediately agreed to help by passing on information about her employer.

Thanks to Ruth, Dorothy had discovered that Sir Edward had been having a difficult week. The number of police officers leaving the force to enlist in the army was growing every day. The young men clearly believed the recruitment posters that were plastered all over the city and thought there was more excitement and glamour to be found on the other side of the Channel. This combined with the huge number of soldiers and refugees arriving in London was placing an enormous strain on his remaining officers. The capital's crime rate was rising and during a particularly tense meeting, the Home Secretary had informed Sir Edward that he expected the situation to be remedied and quickly.

Ruth had heard Sir Edward loudly explain all this to his wife over dinner one evening and in turn had relayed the information to Dorothy early the next morning.

The two of them had arranged to meet early each morning by the servants' entrance before the rest of the household was awake. This morning Ruth had exciting news. The previous evening, Milly—Sir Edward's favourite Labrador—had given birth to a litter of six beautiful puppies. Sir Edward hoped that at least one of them would be good enough to join his newly formed dog section, an achievement he was particularly proud of. "Men and dogs working together to fight crime is a joy to behold" he had declared several times.

Ruth assured Dorothy that this meant not only would he be in an unusually good mood, but that he was also bound to be running late as he was sure to want to spend time with Milly and her brood before leaving for Scotland Yard. Dorothy had immediately flagged down a hansom cab and sent a note to Cheyne Row, then hurried to Nina's flat to wake her up and tell her the news. This was the day they had been waiting for.

Now as the four of them sat in silence, Dorothy only

hoped Ruth knew her employer as well as she thought. She nervously twiddled the pencil she was holding, then paused and listened. She smiled to herself. In the distance she could hear the sound of cheerful whistling and brisk, heavy footsteps. Ruth had been right. Suddenly both footsteps and whistling stopped outside the door.

"Good morning, Sergeant. Is something wrong?" the deep voice of Sir Edward asked.

"Good morning, Sir Edward," replied the sergeant sounding nervous. The poor man hadn't looked at all happy when Margaret had insisted they would wait for Sir Edward. "Not exactly, but there are four ladies who are waiting to see you in your office."

"Ladies? Do they have an appointment?"

"No, sir, but they were very keen to speak with you. There is a Miss Dorothy Peto, a Miss Mary Allen, then there is a Miss Nina Boyle, who is the leader of the—"

"Yes, I am aware of Miss Boyle and Miss Allen. I recall that both have been arrested and held in this very building several times. What on earth possessed you to let a delegation of suffragettes into my office, Sergeant?" snapped Sir Edward. Inside the office, Dorothy cringed, Nina rolled her eyes and Mary folded her arms defiantly.

"I am very sorry, Sir Edward," they heard the unfortunate sergeant stammer, "but well, the fourth lady, who to the best of my knowledge we've never arrested, is Miss Damer Dawson. She's the stepdaughter of Lord Walsingham," he added in hushed tones.

Dorothy glanced over to where Margaret was sitting serenely with the confidence that came with being wealthy and well connected. She might not be fond of her stepfather, but he was an important man who had served under Disraeli and now sat in the House of Lords. Sir Edward wouldn't risk offending one of his relatives.

The door swung open and Sir Edward entered his office with the look of a man who knew he had been ambushed. He had a thick grey moustache and hair that he wore brushed back. He was a tall man but walked with a slight stoop. Thanks to Ruth, Dorothy knew this was due to the scar on his abdomen, from an assassination attempt two years earlier. Apparently, it throbbed during times of stress.

"Good morning, ladies," he said, greeting the four expectant faces reluctantly as he took his seat on the other side of the desk. Mary half stood up and reached over to shake his hand firmly, while the other three remained seated, smiling and echoing his greeting. Dorothy wondered if he had ever had so many females in his office.

He cleared his throat. "Miss Damer Dawson, thank you for your recent correspondence. If I recall correctly, I have received four letters from you in the past two weeks, outlining a proposal where women are allowed to join the police in some sort of voluntary capacity. I assume that is the reason for your visit today."

"It is, Sir Edward," replied Margaret.

"Then, I fear you may have had a wasted journey. As I am sure you are aware, I have made my opposition to women joining the police force quite clear."

"I understand completely, Sir Edward," replied Margaret, "However, the organisation we proposed would be quite separate from the force, privately funded and only there to assist your hardworking officers where we are able."

Sir Edward looked slightly mollified, then he glanced at Nina and Mary and frowned. "That may be the case, Miss Damer Dawson. However, I still struggle to see how it would work, particularly in view of the strained relationships between the sexes in connection with the agitation over the suffrage question…" He paused mid-sentence as Nina raised a gloved finger.

"Sir Edward, excuse me, but the Women's Freedom League have agreed to suspend all campaigning and to call a truce as it were, during our country's time of peril."

Sir Edward's cheeks flushed red. He was clearly not a man who was accustomed to being interrupted.

"If I may speak plainly, Miss Boyle, I find the request for you to lead this band of police volunteers quite mystifying. I have always viewed you as an intransigent individual who is in total opposition to constituted authority."

Dorothy felt her heart sink. Nina opened her mouth to protest again, but Mary spoke first.

"Sir Edward, what if Miss Damer Dawson was to lead the volunteers instead of Miss Boyle?" she enquired.

Nina shot Dorothy a look of surprise. Over the past two weeks the four of them had held many meetings to prepare for presenting the commissioner with their proposal, but this suggestion had never been raised. Nina looked like she was going to say something, but Dorothy gently touched her arm to silence her. She could see Sir Edward was now beginning to nod his head thoughtfully. If there was a chance he was about to agree to their plan, did it really matter who was the figurehead? After all it was Margaret funding the whole thing.

"Naturally, I am aware of Miss Damer Dawson's excellent work on the Criminal Law Amendment Committee," Sir Edward began, "as well as her many charitable endeavours. I would find her a more than acceptable commandant."

"Thank you, Sir Edward, that's very kind," Margaret replied, demurely. Dorothy studied her and Mary. Was this really a spur-of-the-moment thought, or had they privately agreed between themselves to promote this idea?

"Would we then have your approval, Sir Edward?" Nina pressed. Sir Edward stroked his moustache pensively. Dorothy wondered if he was thinking about his difficult meeting with the Home Secretary earlier in the week. She hoped he would see their proposal as a way to solve his problem of policing levels in the capital. Perhaps he might also rather enjoy the thought of annoying McKenna by accepting a proposal he had rejected. After a few agonising moments he finally spoke.

"With Miss Damer Dawson as your leader, I would have no objections to you and your group of volunteers organising patrols. During these patrols, you may offer advice and support to those you come across who may be in need. However, you may not use the buildings, vehicles or any other resources belonging to the Metropolitan Police Force. I must also stress that as volunteers you will not have the power to arrest. Do I make myself clear?"

"What about a uniform, Sir Edward?" enquired Mary.

The commissioner raised an eyebrow. It was clear he felt he had already been more than generous with his offer.

Seeing his reaction Dorothy quickly intervened. "It

would be so much more reassuring for the people we approach, especially those from foreign lands, if we were to be dressed in a uniform, Sir Edward. It would of course be subject to your approval."

Sir Edward appeared mollified once more. "Very well, I do not have any objections to a uniform. However, I do want you each to give me your solemn promise that you understand your role as a volunteer will be to advise and assist in upholding the laws of this land. That means all the laws, ladies, not your interpretation of them, or only the ones you happen to agree with." He fixed his eyes pointedly on Nina, who gave him her most charming smile.

"Of course, Sir Edward," she replied, trying to sound as sincere as possible.

"Yes, absolutely," Margaret agreed.

"Yes, Sir Edward," said Dorothy.

"You have our word," insisted Mary.

"And what shall this new group be called?" he asked.

Out of the corner of her eye, Dorothy saw Mary open her mouth to respond, but this time Nina was quicker.

"The Women's Police Volunteers, or WPV," she replied, briskly.

Sir Edward nodded his head in resignation rather than agreement as he rose to his feet. "Then, ladies, I wish you and the WPV good luck."

The four of them shook his hand, then hurried out of his office and Scotland Yard before he could change his mind.

"Good heavens! I can't believe we did it!" exclaimed Mary as they spilled out into the street. "I thought it was touch and go in there for a moment."

"But what a stroke of luck that you thought to suggest Margaret as leader, Mary," said Nina, with a slight edge to her voice.

Mary's face reddened a little and Margaret gave a small cough.

"It was rather a surprise, but it seemed to do the trick, dearest," she said looking at Mary rather than Dorothy or Nina. "Not that it matters one jot. You'll still be second in command, Nina. After all it will be your WFL members who will make up the majority of our new volunteers."

As they headed towards Oxford Street to celebrate at Alan's Tea Rooms, Dorothy really wanted to believe Mary and Margaret. She thought they had been working well together as they plotted how best to win Sir Edward over and made plans for their new organisation. To Dorothy it had seemed that the four of them had been acting as one, and she really didn't want to be proved wrong at the very moment it appeared they had achieved their goal.

A FEW WEEKS later, the offices for the newly formed Women's Police Volunteers were a hive of activity. Several new recruits were being measured and fitted for uniforms, while another line of volunteers waited patiently to enrol. All had responded to Nina's hastily designed poster that she and Dorothy had plastered around the city.

Mary and Margaret had found, leased and furnished a small suite of offices on Little George Street, in the heart of Westminster. To Dorothy the place felt like a cross between a schoolroom and a Bloomsbury tea salon. One large room contained a blackboard and several small writing desks, while at the other side, three comfortable sofas upholstered in floral fabric were arranged in a U-shape. There was an office with a large window that Nina and Margaret shared complete with their own telephone. Next to it was a smaller anteroom for Dorothy and Mary to use as an office. There was also a decent-sized washroom and kitchen. She had to admit the kitchen here was far better equipped and stocked than the WFL's.

This morning Nina was proudly showing Mr Harkin, a journalist from *The Times*, around their new accommodation. She was keen to promote the WPV and Mr Harkin had agreed to write an article about the organisation. Dorothy was taking some of the latest volunteers through their basic training and explaining what was expected of them, but she kept one ear on what Nina was saying.

"As you can see, we have no shortage of volunteers, Mr Harkin, and I am proud to say many are my fellow members of the Women's Freedom League, including Mrs Bagster and Miss Peto, here. Our volunteers will be instructed in first aid, signalling, police court procedure, even self-defence, and Miss Peto is in charge of enrolling and training the new recruits."

They stopped close to where Dorothy was standing in front of the blackboard. Nina gave her an encouraging nod and she tried not to feel embarrassed as she addressed the group of eight women with the journalist watching.

"It's very important," she began, "that when we are patrolling at the railway station, you remain in pairs. You will each be supplied with whistles in the event you require assistance. The refugees should be relatively easy to spot as they leave the trains, and we will be holding signs up in their own language. We will of course be focusing on those trains arriving from Dover, but so will the criminal gangs whom we believe operate in the area, so you must be vigilant at all times and if necessary be prepared to move quickly."

Dorothy's eyes scanned her audience. All were elegantly dressed and looked as though they were on their way to a luncheon party, not to give chase to suspects. She glanced across to Mr Harkin, who was busily making notes, and wondered if he was thinking the same thing. As she began to hand out sheets of written instructions, the interview continued.

"The plight of the Belgian refugees was one of the main reasons for wanting to form the WPV," Nina explained.

Mr Harkin nodded. "Yes," he agreed, "and something that is of great concern to many of our readers, but forgive me if I am wrong, isn't another reason you are on patrol at stations because they are places where, how shall I put this, women of loose morals loiter?"

"You mean prostitutes? Yes, Mr Harkin, we are aware they congregate at stations and part of our work will be to assist in their protection and welfare."

Mr Harkin raised an eyebrow. "And assist in their arrest if necessary?" he asked with his pencil poised.

Nina smiled brightly. "We do not have the power to arrest, but naturally we'll do whatever we can to help."

Dorothy was relieved her friend was being so diplomatic. Nina had strong views on whether prostitutes should be treated as victims rather than criminals, but for once she wasn't voicing them.

"I see," continued Mr Harkin, "and is it true you and your members of the WFL have abandoned the campaign for women to have the right to vote?"

"As I said, the WFL are keen to provide assistance in any way we can in this, our country's greatest hour of need. The energy and determination we brought to our campaigning will now be focused on our work with the Women's Police Volunteers instead."

Mr Harkin shook Nina's hand.

"Thank you for your time, Miss Boyle. I'll wait for my photographer to finish and then we'll leave you to your work."

As he moved away, Nina came over to join Dorothy while the new recruits went to collect their whistles and torches. Over in the far corner of the room, a photographer and his assistant were busily arranging a suitable background for the picture. The original idea had been to take the photograph in Parliament Square Garden, but an unexpected downpour had brought them inside.

Waiting patiently in a formal pose, as large plants in urns and velvet drapes were manoeuvred around them, were Margaret and Mary. They were dressed in the new WPV uniform. It was exactly the same shade of blue that the regular police wore and consisted of a long skirt, shirt and tie, and a short, neat jacket. The look was completed with sturdy riding-style boots, peaked cap and belted overcoat. They were also modelling their matching, new cropped hairstyles. Margaret's hand kept fluttering, self-consciously, up to where her tresses had once fallen. She had confided in Dorothy that she still wasn't used to how cold and exposed her neck felt, but Mary had convinced her this new, sensible style would ensure they were taken more seriously when out on patrol. Dorothy couldn't help thinking this new look wasn't quite what Lady Walsingham had had in mind when she'd suggested Margaret change her image.

"Aren't you going to be in the photograph too?" asked Dorothy thinking about the other members of the WFL. She knew many of them had been surprised and a little disappointed to hear that Margaret would be in charge of the WPV with Nina acting as her deputy.

"No, I said I'd take care of the interview if Mary and Margaret posed for the photo," replied Nina evenly. "Besides," she added with a grin, "you know how keen Mary is on the uniform."

Chapter Eight

FOR THEIR FIRST patrol, a dozen members of the WPV arrived at Waterloo station. Margaret had wanted them to go to King's Cross, following Dorothy's report about the woman they all now referred to as Madame Chameleon. However, when she ran this idea past Scotland Yard she was told politely but firmly that they would prefer them to go to Waterloo. Nina had offered to remain outside the station, where prostitutes were known to congregate, with half the group, while Margaret and Mary led the others, including Dorothy inside.

To the public, not used to seeing women in uniform, they caused quite a stir as they strode purposefully across the concourse. Some people pointed and laughed, a couple of soldiers gave shrill whistles and others simply stared. Dorothy was determined not to let it bother her. The WPV placed themselves on the platforms where the trains from Dover and Folkestone were due to arrive. As the first tired and confused Belgian refugees began spilling out, Dorothy took a deep breath, then started walking up and down announcing first in her basic French, then English.

"Ladies and gentlemen, welcome to London. We are the Women's Police Volunteers. If you would like to go to the

Red Cross, please follow Miss Allen. If you require the Belgian Embassy, please follow Mrs Bagster."

Mary and Jean each held signs carefully written in both languages. As Dorothy kept repeating the message, the refugees soon began to congregate around the destination they needed. They were then shepherded by other members of the WPV to where they wanted to go. Dorothy had taught them the phrase "*On y va*", or "let's go", which Mary in particular kept repeating enthusiastically as she led her group through the station.

When outside the station, they put their charges in taxis they had arranged to wait for them. Unfortunately, they had underestimated demand. Dorothy, who was leading a family with three small children, arrived on the pavement to find the taxis had all gone. Waiting a little farther away was a hansom cab. The two black horses were swishing their tails and the driver had his feet up on the front rail while he flicked through a newspaper. Dorothy approached him.

"Excuse me," she asked politely, "please could you take this family to the Belgian Embassy?"

"No," he replied without looking at her.

"May I ask why not?"

"I don't want them. I'm waiting for another fare."

Dorothy felt herself flush. The driver wasn't only being rude to her but to this poor exhausted family as well, who they had been trying so hard to welcome to London. She stepped forward and lowered her voice. "What's wrong with this fare?" she hissed at him.

He finally looked up from his newspaper and scowled down at her. "I don't like foreigners," he hissed back. "And I don't like trouble-causing, bossy women."

Dorothy opened her mouth to argue, but just then Mary shouted over.

"Dorothy, bring your group over here. We have room for them."

Giving the cab driver the fiercest look she could, Dorothy turned on her heel and ushered her little family to the waiting taxi.

Before returning to the arriving trains, Dorothy paused for a moment and watched Nina and her group. They were meant to be patrolling the streets surrounding the station, but they didn't look to be having much success. Although many of the volunteers were members of the Freedom League and were used to and unconcerned by gaining attention from the public, the group Nina was leading were mostly volunteers who had responded to her recruitment poster and were not part of the suffrage movement. They ranged from looking a little self-conscious to utterly terrified. The situation wasn't helped by the number of soldiers, prostitutes and drunks standing outside nearby pubs all pointing, staring and shouting at them in their new uniforms.

"Come along now, ladies, let's get to work," Nina said encouragingly, but her request was met with blank faces. Dorothy caught her friend's eye and Nina raised her hand in acknowledgement.

"What are we meant to do exactly?" asked Lucy Summerton, the pretty blonde League member, who was the youngest volunteer and looking paler by the second.

"Lucy, I did try to explain. Our work won't simply be

directing any passing vicar to a Promenade concert," replied Nina, who was trying her best not to sound impatient. "Look, watch me."

Nina took a deep breath and confidently approached two women standing in the doorway of a boarded-up house, sharing a bottle of gin and loudly soliciting any man who passed by. "Ladies, you must move along," she stated firmly.

Two pairs of dark angry eyes turned to look at her scornfully.

"Says who?" asked the one nearest her in a strong cockney accent.

"I do."

"You and whose army?"

"As a member of the Women's Police Volunteers…"

Both women burst out laughing.

"What's that when it's at home?"

Nina stood her ground. She wasn't embarrassed or intimidated. Dorothy remembered her talking about all the times she had shared a cell with women who sold their bodies to earn a living. They may put on a veneer of hardness and act as though they didn't care, but underneath she knew they weren't so different to her and her fellow suffragettes.

"Look," she said, bluntly, "you are clearly causing a public nuisance by being here, so you can either listen to me and move along or you can wait for a male police officer to arrive, arrest you, throw you in the back of the Black Mariah and cart you both off to Holloway. I don't know if that has happened to you ladies before, but it has happened to me and it's not an experience I recommend or would want to repeat."

The women exchanged a look and nodded.

"We were done here anyway," said the second one and with that they stepped out of the doorway and made their way towards the nearest pub. As they left, Nina's group began clapping as if they'd watched a piece of street theatre.

Nina glanced at Dorothy and shrugged. Dorothy smiled back. More training was definitely required.

Returning to the station platform, Dorothy found Margaret holding her clipboard and overseeing the arrival of the latest batch of refugees. She beamed when she saw Dorothy.

"Isn't it amazing, Dorothy dear! Everything is going so smoothly." She checked her watch. "We've only been here an hour, but we seem to be making a real difference to all these poor souls. It isn't nearly as chaotic as when we were at King's Cross." Before Dorothy could agree, Mary marched over to join them.

"Margaret, I've just spoken to one of the porters. He told me two more trains are due to arrive from Dover in the next hour. Do you think we should draft some of Nina's group in to assist us? They don't seem to be doing much outside."

Margaret frowned. "I think we should check with Nina first. I don't want her to think we are treading on her toes."

Mary put her hands on her hips. "Margaret! You are the commandant. What you say goes."

"What do you think, Dorothy? Would Nina mind? Dorothy?"

But Dorothy didn't reply. She had been distracted. A flash of green on the next platform had caught her eye. There it was again, a green feather. She strained her eyes to follow it as it seemed to dance along among the khaki uniforms, appearing then just as quickly disappearing. She edged along the platform trying to keep it in sight.

"Do you see that green hat, Margaret? I think it's the lady we saw at King's Cross. The one I watched." Margaret fished a pair of opera glasses out of her handbag and focused them where Dorothy was pointing.

"I can't see anyone," said Mary. Then a large group of soldiers boarded a waiting train and suddenly they all saw her.

"Good Lord, it's her! Madame Chameleon!" Margaret gasped.

"Are you sure, Margaret?" asked Mary.

"Absolutely. It's the same hat, coat, red hair, everything."

"Right then, Dorothy, come with me," Mary shouted over her shoulder, as she began striding towards the bridge that led over the tracks to the next platform. Dorothy hurried after her, not at all sure what they were going to do if they caught up with the woman.

"I'll keep an eye on her from over here," Margaret called after them.

Mary and Dorothy were soon on the same platform as Madame Chameleon, but their way was blocked by the arrival of yet more troops. From the other side of the tracks, Margaret began frantically gesturing.

"She's getting away," cried Dorothy.

Mary raised her whistle to her lips, gave three shrill blows and in her loudest voice shouted, "Hey, you there in the green hat, stop! Stop in the name of the law!"

Most of the platform including the woman, turned round in surprise. When she saw Mary was staring directly at her, she began backing away through the crowd. Mary gave another piercing blast of her whistle, then she and Dorothy pushed their way through after the retreating woman, ignoring the shouts and puzzled looks of passengers leaving the train. The woman moved surprisingly quickly, but thanks to her ridiculous hat they could easily keep her in view. They had almost caught up with her at the station's main entrance when she sprinted outside towards a waiting hansom cab. Dorothy realised it was the same cab driver who had refused to help them. He must have been paid to wait for this mystery woman.

They chased after her. Dorothy leapt forward and firmly held the horse's bridle, despite the driver's shouts of complaint, while Mary grabbed the woman by the shoulders. There was a scuffle and both the green hat and red wig ended up on the ground. The woman, her naturally light brown hair scraped into a bun, continued to struggle and swear in both French and English as Mary gripped her arms tightly. The shouting and whistle-blowing had caught the attention of two passing police constables, who came running towards them.

"Oh thank heavens you are here, officers," cried Dorothy, as the large horse whinnied loudly.

"You must arrest this woman immediately," demanded Mary. "We suspect she is involved in the trafficking of refugees into the white slave trade."

Dorothy cringed as she saw the two constables exchanged a sceptical look. They no doubt thought Mary was overreacting. One reached out, took over holding the horse from Dorothy and told the complaining drive to be quiet, while the other addressed Mary.

"If you could let the lady go please, miss," he said. Reluctantly, Mary released the woman, who immediately spun round and slapped Mary across the face. She raised her arm to strike the policeman as well, but he was too quick for her and grabbed her wrist, before deftly clapping a pair of handcuffs on her. The second constable stepped forward to assist his colleague.

"Thank you, ladies. We'll take it from here," he said, before they led away the woman who was still cursing Mary and protesting her innocence loudly in heavily accented English. As they disappeared, the cab driver cracked his whip and quickly drove away. Dorothy turned to Mary and winced when she saw blood pouring from her lip where the woman's sharp nail had scratched her.

"Gosh, Mary! Are you all right?"

"Injured in action on my first day—not bad, eh?" Mary replied with a grin as she dabbed at her face with a handkerchief. She looked quite exhilarated after the chase.

"So what shall we do now?" asked Dorothy, who was still trying to catch her breath.

"Report to the commandant, then back to escorting refugees. Come along." Mary marched away, but Dorothy remained where she was. She bent down and retrieved the woman's wig and hat. Both reeked of her perfume. She really should make sure they were returned to their owner. She made her way over to the police desk. The incident had been quite overwhelming, but at least after seeing Madame Chameleon without her ridiculous wig and hat, Dorothy now knew why she seemed familiar. She was the woman entering the stage door on the night Edith Devine died.

AT FIVE O'CLOCK that Friday evening, the new recruits were returning to the WPV offices after their first week on patrol. Many had never worked, let alone held a full-time position and most looked tired and more than a little crumpled. Several had collapsed on to one of the sofas, removed their boots and stockings and were now rubbing their sore feet. They had walked for miles each day. Quite a few of their number could drive and indeed owned their own automobiles; others relied on their husband's chauffeurs to transport them around. Tramping along the city's pavements had come as quite a shock. The last to arrive were Mary and a tearful Lucy.

"Oh, do pull yourself together," Mary snapped at the distressed young woman, causing her to cry even more. "You'll hear far worse than that when you are out on patrol, believe me."

"What happened?" asked Dorothy, looking up from the newspaper she had been reading.

"A prostitute we were trying to move on told her, rather crudely, to go forth and multiply," explained Mary, bluntly. Some of the other women in the room gasped. As the week had gone on, the differences between the WFL members, many of whom had been arrested themselves, and the other volunteers had become even more apparent. Some, who had clearly thought they would be required to do little more than give directions, had left after only a day or two on patrol.

"She's been blubbing all the way from Euston," complained Mary gesturing impatiently towards Lucy. All the volunteers were beginning to learn that sympathy was not Mary's strong point.

"It was such a shock. I have never been spoken to that way before. I've never heard such language." Lucy sniffed. Several of the older women came forward to console her.

"Well perhaps you could stick to working with refugees from now on," suggested Nina, patting Lucy on the shoulder, but Mary immediately shook her head.

"Now don't pander to her, Nina! She'll have to learn. Your advert clearly stated you wanted volunteers who were 'healthy, reliable and self-reliant'. There was no mention of dissolving in a puddle at the first harsh word."

Lucy's lower lip began to quiver again, but then Margaret appeared at the doorway of her office wearing a huge smile and totally oblivious to what was being discussed.

"Oh, you're all here, that's wonderful!" she began, clapping her hands together. "Sir Edward just telephoned. He wanted to thank and to congratulate us. His officers believe Madame Chameleon, or I should say Clara Fleurot—the woman Mary and Dorothy chased and apprehended at Waterloo station—is known to Scotland Yard. She's been preying on vulnerable young women arriving from Belgium, first at King's Cross then Waterloo. She kept changing her appearance to avoid detection. Apparently, she is half Belgian and pretended to be from a charitable organisation. The poor girls thought they were going to be well cared for. Anyway, officers from the Met were able to locate the girls and free them. Isn't that wonderful!"

"White slavers! I knew it!" declared Mary. "Those poor girls were probably due to be shipped out to Arabia any day, destined for some dastardly sheikh's hareem."

"Actually, Robert dear, I think they were being used as unpaid labour in various laundries throughout the city," explained Margaret.

"Oh," said Mary sounding disappointed, "anyhow, well done to you and Dorothy for spotting Madame Chameleon in the first instance, Margaret."

"Nonsense, nonsense," continued Margaret blushing a little. "I'm sure the police would have caught up with her eventually. You were the one who put yourself in danger giving chase like that."

Dorothy frowned. She'd been thinking about Madame Chameleon a lot since their encounter with her at the station and what she was doing at the theatre that night. As she had when she'd recognised Mr Muller in the newspaper, she had wanted to let Inspector Derwent know that she was the woman entering the stage door that fateful night, even if Miss Devine's death had been ruled as misadventure. This time she had visited Scotland Yard in person, but the harassed sergeant manning the front desk had merely thrust a form at her to fill out. She would be amazed if it ever arrived on the inspector's desk.

"What about the Belgian girls? Who's taking care of them?" she asked.

"Oh, the Belgian Embassy, I believe," replied Margaret, airily. "But that's not all my news. Sir Edward also wondered if we would be able to accompany his constables when they patrol Hyde Park this evening."

"Good heavens!" exclaimed Nina. "Are they actually taking us seriously?"

"So, it would seem. I say three cheers for Miss Allen and Miss Peto," declared Margaret, then she noticed Lucy's tear-stained face and fished a large white handkerchief out of her pocket. "There now, don't cry, my dear, it's an emotional time for us all."

Chapter Nine

AUGUST TURNED INTO September, leaves began to fall from the trees and the jubilation that had accompanied the outbreak of war turned to shock when the first injured soldiers returned to London from the front. The Women's Police Volunteers had got over the excitement of their first week, and after a few teething troubles settled into a routine of patrols and assisting the regular police force. People were getting used to seeing them on the street and the numbers in their ranks were growing steadily.

One morning, Dorothy was in the small anteroom filing away the latest raft of enrolment forms. From her position, she had a perfect view of the office Margaret and Nina shared. Both women were sitting at their desks, facing each other. Nina's was covered in piles of paper and an overflowing ashtray. Margaret's was far more orderly with photographs and potted plants arranged in neat rows. Unfortunately, the office-sharing arrangement wasn't exactly running smoothly, particularly as both women were used to having their own way. Dorothy had borne the brunt of both their complaints.

Nina preferred to work alone and had the distinct feeling she had been put in the office so Margaret could keep an eye on her. Margaret, for her part, found the almost constant tapping of the typewriter very distracting and objected to Nina's smoking. Then Nina in return complained about Margaret's three canine companions and argued that the smell of smoke at least covered their odour. The result was a window left permanently open. It was autumn now and no matter how well stoked the fire was, the room was always chilly.

Margaret, her cashmere shawl draped over her shoulders, was humming quietly to herself as she read the paper and shared a square of tiffin with her dogs. Nina opened the top drawer of her desk, retrieved an envelope and tossed it over on to Margaret's desk.

"Take a look at this. It's a letter I received from a Mrs Smith of Grantham. Apparently, she read my interview in *The Times* and saw your photo and is keen to join the WPV. She wants to know how she can obtain a uniform. I was thinking of going up there to give her some advice and support."

Margaret wiped the crumbs from her fingers, placed her glasses on her nose and began reading the letter.

"Really? I wouldn't have thought a little rural town like Grantham would require the assistance of the WPV."

"It seems there is a large army training camp nearby," explained Nina.

Margaret looked up, her forehead creasing as she thought for a moment. "Gosh, you're right. I'm sure Mother mentioned my cousin has been sent there. Wouldn't Dorothy be the perfect person to send? She's been so good at training all the volunteers."

In the outer office, Dorothy lowered her head, knowing perfectly well her being sent to Grantham was not part of Nina's plan.

"But it's not only Grantham," she heard Nina reply, ignoring Margaret's last comment. "According to my correspondence, Hull, Liverpool and Aldershot are all wanting the assistance of WPVs and some councils are even offering to pay them a wage."

She leant over and handed a bundle of letters to Margaret, who quickly flicked through them, taking note of each of the postmarks.

"Oh, I see what you mean, all ports and army towns," she said.

"Quite," agreed Nina. "The sudden increase in soldiers and sailors has led inevitably to an increase in 'the unfortunate trade' as our politicians love to say. Just think, if we equip every district in the country with a body of women able and willing to do this class of work, it will be very difficult for the authorities to refuse to employ women after the war."

Margaret held up her hand. "Let's not run before we can walk." As was often the case, she sounded slightly alarmed by Nina's enthusiasm. "It's an awful lot of women we need to find and realistically they probably can't all afford to be volunteers. Look, this town in Northumberland is only willing to offer a living allowance of twenty-five shillings a week. How on earth can they expect an educated woman to work for that?"

Nina shrugged and cleared her throat. "I did wonder if you thought I should embark on a little tour. You know to raise awareness of our organisation and funds of course. It could help ease the financial burden on you. I could offer encouragement and help with training."

Dorothy grinned to herself. She knew Nina had been biding her time, waiting to broach this subject. A campaigner by nature, she was much more suited to going out on the road, encouraging others to join the WPV rather than spending her days telling prostitutes to move on.

"Oh, what a good idea!" agreed Margaret as she dropped another piece of tiffin into Hubert's drooling mouth. "I shall ask Mary to accompany you. Many hands make light work and all that."

"Excellent," said Nina. Dorothy saw her smile tightening a little. "I'll begin making arrangements."

Back in the anteroom, Dorothy chuckled quietly to herself as she tried to envisage Nina travelling around the country with Mary. This had most definitely not been part of her plan. Although she and Nina had worked well with Mary and Margaret at first, it was becoming clear that their priorities were sometimes quite different. She knew Nina often found Margaret frustrating and Mary too bossy, and they both thought Nina was inclined to be reckless. It didn't help that occasionally Nina made fun of her two colleagues. Twice she'd publicly referred to them as 'Sir and Miss Double D'. Dorothy only hoped they could put their differences to one side and continue working together. She loved her new job, even filing away enrolment forms. It felt so good to be doing something useful and it stopped her worrying about Raymond and all the other young men she knew who were serving 'King and Country'. Apart from the occasional telegram from her brother, she hadn't heard from him and the flat felt horribly empty. The more the WPV occupied her time, the better.

THE FOLLOWING WEEK, Dorothy found herself once more in the Marlborough Street Police Court. Sitting next to her on the wooden bench outside Courtroom Two was a very anxious Lucy. Dorothy was trying to provide moral support. For the previous six weeks, the WPV had been accompanying the regular police as they patrolled the city streets. Despite some of the male officers' initial scepticism and occasional hostility, everyone involved agreed that the joint patrols had been a huge success. The dwindling number of men could be spread further, and the women volunteers proved themselves to be sensible and useful, particularly when dealing with female offenders.

It was on one of these patrols through Hyde Park, that Lucy and Margaret had assisted their male colleague with two arrests for indecency. Now the case had come to court, two witness statements were required to obtain a conviction. The first was to be provided by the arresting officer and the hope of the WPV was that the second would come from either Margaret or Lucy.

"I do hope Miss Damer Dawson's evidence is accepted and I'm not called. I'm so nervous," whispered Lucy. Jean, who was sitting on the other side of her, patted her hand reassuringly.

"Now don't worry, dear. Remember what Margaret said.

Try to be as clear and concise as possible. Don't go off at a tangent or get flustered. Frederick Mead never allows women to sit in on indecency trials. If you make your statement in a professional manner, you might actually change his mind."

"And if I don't, Miss Allen might kill me," the younger woman muttered.

Dorothy patted her on the shoulder. Fortunately for Lucy, Mary was still away with Nina, but the two of them were due to return to London that night. It sounded like their trip had been a success and miraculously they had managed not to murder each other. Despite Jean's optimism, Dorothy couldn't imagine today would turn out so well. Not if Magistrate Mead was involved. Getting him to accept a witness statement from a woman would be nothing short of a miracle.

"You wait here. I'll go and see what's happening," she said standing up and making her way towards the courtroom. She slipped inside just in time to see Margaret calmly taking her seat in the witness box. She was the only other female in the room and Mr Mead couldn't stop glowering at her. He was clearly furious that he might be forced to accept evidence from a female, particularly in a case of indecency.

Margaret, however, seemed unperturbed. Unlike most of the women who appeared before him, Margaret was an educated woman of independent means. She was used to addressing large gatherings and socialising with politicians and lawyers. She also knew how important her role was today and had told Dorothy of the many times she and Mary had read accounts of the appalling way Mead treated women in this very courtroom. If her statement was accepted today, it would be a huge step forward for their cause and it would hopefully save Lucy from having to give evidence. She was sure the poor girl would take one look at Mead and, as Mary might put it, 'dissolve in a puddle of tears'.

The clerk, a small nervous-looking man, handed Margaret a Bible. She spoke clearly as she was sworn in and confirmed her name. Then the prosecution lawyer rose to his feet.

"Miss Damer Dawson, for the benefit of the court, can you confirm you are Commandant of the Women's Police Volunteers."

"Yes, I am."

"I understand members of your organisation have been accompanying officers from the Metropolitan Police Force on their evening patrols."

"Yes, we have."

"And on the night in question, you and Miss Summerton, another member of the Women's Police Volunteers accompanied Constable Nelson as he patrolled Hyde Park at approximately ten o'clock. Is that correct?"

"That is correct," replied Margaret ignoring Mead's sneer at the second mention of the WPV. "It was the third time we had been on patrol with Constable Nelson."

"When you came across the couple, the lady and gentleman who are on trial here today, would you agree with Constable Nelson when he states that, 'from their position and the disarray of their clothing, I deduced they were performing an act of indecency'?" the lawyer continued as Mead began to rapidly turn puce.

"Yes, I would and if I may add, also from their movements," replied Margaret.

"Their movements?" queried the lawyer, arching his eyebrow slightly. Margaret nodded and raised her WPV notebook for his benefit.

"Yes, 'backwards and forwards quite vigorously'," she read out calmly. The lawyer bit his lip as Mead who could no longer contain himself, erupted in rage.

"Good Lord, woman! Your peculiar work has clearly sterilised you of any maiden modesty."

Margaret ignored him and peered down at the clerk of the court instead. "But my statement has been recorded?" she asked.

The clerk nodded nervously, and Margaret beamed at him.

"Thank you so very much," she said. "Am I excused?" The lawyer nodded and thanked her. As Margaret stepped triumphantly down from the witness box, Dorothy hurried out of the court with Mead's ranting ringing in her ears. She quickly told a very relieved Lucy that she would no longer be needed to give evidence.

Then she moved a little farther down the corridor to the next courtroom. It wasn't only supporting Lucy and Margaret that had brought her here today. According to the court schedule Madame Chameleon—or Clara Fleurot as they now knew she was called—was standing trial today and she wanted to see what sentence she received. She was about to push the door open when she felt a heavy hand on her shoulder. Turning around, she found Sergeant Munro standing behind her.

"Sorry, Miss Peto. I've been given strict instructions. No

one is to enter the courtroom while the trial is under way."

Dorothy knew there was no point arguing. She certainly didn't want to be thrown out again.

"All right, Sergeant, but can you at least confirm it is Clara Fleurot on trial in there?"

"The Belgian one? Yes, it's her in there."

"I don't suppose you know why she's being tried here and not at the crown court?" she asked.

"Deception is not a crown court matter. I thought you would have known that, what with all the time you've spent here scribbling things down." He chuckled, but Dorothy frowned.

"The charge against her is deception? Why isn't she being charged with abduction or attempted abduction at least?"

"I don't make the rules, Miss Peto," he replied cheerfully. Dorothy opened her mouth but before she could speak, the sergeant raised his finger to his lips and lowered his voice.

"Between you and me, I heard she managed to get a deal. A lesser charge in return for information."

"That hardly seems fair," protested Dorothy. The sergeant shrugged and at that moment, the courtroom door opened and out stepped Inspector Derwent. Even without the scar and walking stick, Dorothy would have remembered him and the dismissive way he treated her. He nodded to Munro, then paused when he saw Dorothy. He looked her up and down, taking in her uniform.

"Miss Peto, what brings you here?" he asked raising his hat slightly.

"I helped apprehend Clara Fleurot," she replied, feeling herself flush. She hadn't expected him to remember her.

"Did you now?"

"Yes. I'm a member of the Women's Police Volunteers."

"So I see."

"I wanted to hear the sentence she'd been given."

"There was no sentence. She was found not guilty due to diminished responsibility."

"Diminished responsibility?" echoed Dorothy incredulously.

"Yes. Her defence was that she was forced to deceive those young girls."

Dorothy remembered how fiercely Clara had fought Mary and the two policemen. She couldn't imagine her being forced to do anything.

"The magistrate believed her?"

"He did. As I'm sure you are aware there is a great deal of sympathy towards Belgians at the moment and she had a very persuasive character witness."

The door opened again and amongst the group of black-gowned lawyers was Clara Fleurot, dressed in a simple navy suit and with her hair in a neat bun. Alongside her was another petite young woman. Dorothy recognised her at once.

"That's Edith Devine's maid. What's she doing here?" she asked quietly.

"Nan Lambert was Miss Fleurot's character witness," explained the inspector. The maid stopped in front of them, her head was lowered and Dorothy half expected her to curtsy.

"Thank you for coming today, Chief Inspector. I felt much braver with you here," she said in such a quiet, timid voice that Dorothy had to stoop to catch her words.

"You did well, Miss Lambert," the inspector reassured her as he shook her gloved hand. She bobbed her head and gave a weak smile. As she walked away, the inspector turned back to Dorothy.

"Clara worked for the company that supplied the theatre with fresh laundry. The two women struck up a friendship while Miss Devine was appearing there. Miss Lambert testified that Miss Fleurot had told her on several occasions that she was scared of the man she worked for and that he threatened her with violence if she didn't do what he wanted."

"So that's what she was doing there?" said Dorothy almost to herself.

The inspector gave her a quizzical look.

"Madame Chameleon, I mean Clara Fleurot, was the woman I saw at the stage door on the night Edith died. I did leave a message for you about it, in case it was important," she explained.

"When you spoke to me, you said the woman was a blonde. Clara Fleurot has light brown hair."

"But she changes her appearance. That's why we dubbed her Madame Chameleon. When we chased after her at Waterloo, she was wearing a red wig. She must have been wearing a blonde one on the night Edith Devine died."

The inspector shook his head and frowned. "That doesn't make any sense. Why would she need to change her appearance, if she was simply delivering clean laundry to the backstage of a theatre?"

"Precisely," replied Dorothy, "and what about the man

she worked for? Have you arrested him?"

Suddenly, there was an angry shout of "*Jamais*". Dorothy turned her head. Clara had joined the maid and they were heading towards the main entrance. Nan Lambert had her head lowered still and seemed to be trying to calm down Clara, who was clearly angry. Dorothy tried to make out what they were saying as they hurried away.

"Well, they don't look like two friends who are happy because one of them has kept the other out of jail, I must say," commented Sergeant Munro as the two women disappeared out of the door, but Inspector Derwent was looking at Dorothy.

"Do you know what she was saying, Miss Peto?" he asked.

Dorothy shook her head. "Not really, she was talking too quickly. I could only pick out a couple of words but she definitely said, '*jamais*' and '*encore*'. Never and again."

"That's not much to go on," grumbled Munro.

"I don't know. I think it might be rather useful," replied Inspector Derwent. "Thank you, Miss Peto." He raised his hat once more and began to limp away.

"What about the man Clara worked for? Will you be arresting him?" Dorothy called after him, but he didn't look back. Dorothy's shoulders sagged. It seemed nobody would pay for what had happened to those poor Belgian girls.

Chapter Ten

Autumn quickly turned into winter and it soon became clear that the war would not be over by Christmas as everyone had first thought. Dorothy saw 1914 turn into 1915 at her family's home in Hampshire. It had not felt remotely festive. Each day the casualty lists in the newspaper contained at least one name of a young man she and her sisters knew—someone's brother, son, fiancé. Raymond had not been granted leave and they still didn't know exactly where he was. Her mother had spent most of the time locked in her bedroom, quietly sobbing.

Dorothy was quite relieved to return to London. However, her relief was short-lived. On the 19th of January, the Norfolk towns of Great Yarmouth and King's Lynn were struck by Zeppelin air raids. Ramsgate and other towns on the Kent coast followed, and the WPV were warned that London could expect to be hit too. Their patrols seemed more important and more dangerous than ever before. Street lighting was restricted, while guns and search lights were mounted on top of prominent buildings and worried Londoners turned their cellars and basements into places of refuge.

Then in May, what everyone had feared happened. London was hit. The monstrous airships loomed over the capital and dropped three thousand pounds of bombs on the terrified people of the East End. That first raid had killed seven people, mainly children, and since then the city's inhabitants had lived in fear. The war in Europe now felt much closer to home and it was impossible to know when the next huge airship would float into view. The Thames, for centuries the lifeblood of the city, was now cruelly used as a reference point by the Germans, as its waters glinted in the moonlight giving them a route to follow. The beautiful lake in St James's Park had been drained so they couldn't use it in the same way to locate Buckingham Palace.

ONE SPRING EVENING, Dorothy was out on patrol with Mary at Charing Cross station. Originally Nina had been scheduled to be on duty with Mary, which had caused more than a few raised eyebrows at the WPV offices. It was no secret that their personalities clashed, and the two women rarely worked together. Their tour of the country had not brought them closer together; in fact, if anything it had only highlighted their many differences of opinion. Therefore, it had come as no surprise to Dorothy when Nina declared she was suffering from a terrible migraine an hour before her shift. Dorothy had volunteered to take her place instead.

That evening the station was busier than ever, but not with refugees or troops departing for the front. Instead, it was crowded with desperate mothers and wives waiting to see if their son or husband was on one of the many trains carrying the wounded back from the second Battle of Ypres. As Dorothy stood and watched them, she remembered when the first trains full of injured soldiers arrived back in London after the Battle of the Marne. Initially, they had been met by cheering crowds welcoming them home, but as stretcher after stretcher was carried off the train, it became obvious just how many brave young men had lost limbs or eyes, or both, and the crowds fell into a shocked silence.

This time it was even worse. The Germans had used poisonous gas against the British and there were almost sixty thousand casualties, many with terrible burns and damage to their lungs.

After an hour or two, the crowds began to leave the station. The last train from the coast had arrived. There would be no more soldiers returning home tonight. Dorothy watched as the last of the sobbing women filed out. They had caused no trouble, but heavens it had been miserable seeing the fear and anguish etched on every face.

They had planned to continue their patrol out on the surrounding streets. However, she was now waiting for Mary who was loudly remonstrating with a prostitute she had spotted soliciting a young soldier, his bandaged arm in a sling. Dorothy didn't have the heart to assist Mary. She was beginning to think the men returning home had been through so much they should be allowed to take comfort wherever it was offered. She would never voice these thoughts to Margaret or Mary though. They took the vow they had made to Sir Edward, to uphold all the laws of the land, very seriously.

While Mary continued to berate the unfortunate woman,

Dorothy noticed two policemen approaching a little girl who was begging close to the entrance of the station. She was a pathetic sight with bare feet, tangled hair, a grubby dress and was clutching a pink rabbit. As the two policemen approached her, she looked utterly terrified and immediately burst into tears. Dorothy hurried over.

"Hello, may I help at all?" she asked politely as she gave the little girl what she hoped was a reassuring smile. The constables exchanged a glance; they were now used to the WPV interfering and had come across Dorothy before.

"That's kind of you, Miss Peto, but everything is under control," replied the older of the two constables as he nodded towards the girl. "We've warned her earlier about what would happen if she kept hanging around here. Now, she'll be arrested for begging."

"Oh my goodness, officers, that sounds like an awful lot of paperwork for such a small child and…" she paused as she glanced down at the paltry collection of coins at the girl's feet "…what looks to be no more than sixpence. Why don't you entrust her to the care of myself and Miss Allen? We'll ensure she leaves here and gets home safely. I am sure you gentlemen have far more important work to do."

The two constables looked at each as they considered her offer. One of the first things Dorothy had learnt was that regular policemen were not fond of paperwork. They nodded in unison.

"Well, if you are sure, Miss Peto…" began the older one.

"Of course," replied Dorothy, smiling brightly, "after all that's what the WPV are here for: to assist you in any way we can, Constable."

The two constables turned and walked away. Dorothy knelt down, took hold of the little girl's tiny hand and waited until the policemen were out of sight.

"Hello there. My name is Dorothy. What are you called?"

Before the girl could reply, Mary arrived at their side.

"Well, I don't think she'll return here in a hurry. I certainly gave her plenty to think about," she said as the prostitute marched out of the station, throwing Dorothy and Mary a furious look over her shoulder. "What do we have here? She looks like she belongs in the lost property office," Mary said pointing at the little girl.

"Those two constables were going to arrest her for begging. I intervened and said we'd make sure she got home safely," explained Dorothy.

Mary pursed her lips and peered down at the still-sobbing little girl. "For heaven's sake, Dorothy! We are supposed to be here to provide assistance, not tell the men patrolling what to do. I hope you haven't done anything to upset them and endanger our cause."

Dorothy struggled to keep her tone neutral. She had come a long way since she'd first met Mary on the day of Nina's arrest. Then she'd been scared and a little emotional, but several months of police patrols and training other recruits had changed her. Mary might be the elder of the two of them, but her habit of constantly talking down to her was beginning to get on Dorothy's nerves and they were only two hours into their shift.

"Not at all, Mary," she replied, calmly. "They were pleased I offered to take her off their hands. Besides this is part of the cause. The WFL have long advocated that there should be a change in policy with regard to how women and children are treated by the police and the courts. Before the war we had built up quite a catalogue of…"

"Yes, yes," interrupted Mary. "I know, and we can discuss all that later. Now let's get this urchin home, then we can return to doing some real work upholding the morals of our city. Where does she live?"

"I don't know," admitted Dorothy looking down at the frightened child. "She hasn't spoken yet."

Mary frowned and, bending down so she was only inches from the girl's tear-stained face, bellowed, "Where do you live, child?"

The girl's lip began to tremble once again, and she wiped her streaming nose with the back of her hand. Mary recoiled in disgust and turned back to Dorothy.

"Perhaps she's deaf," she suggested, "or dumb, or an imbecile."

Dorothy gave the girl's hand a gentle squeeze. "You don't need to tell us if you don't want to. Lead the way and we'll follow—how does that sound? Will you show us where your house is? Where Mummy is?"

The little girl paused as she stared back at Dorothy, then nodded slowly. She reached down and scooped up the few coins she had earned and then began to walk to the station entrance, still holding tightly on to Dorothy's hand. Mary reluctantly followed them accompanied by much tutting and heavy sighing.

"You are being very optimistic if you think she lives in a house, Dorothy. I expect it's more likely to be a single room in a hovel."

The three of them left the station and crossed the Strand. A banner reading 'Quiet for the Wounded' hung outside Charing Cross Hospital where so many injured soldiers were being treated. Several policemen were on duty, slowing down the traffic to try to lessen the noise for the soldiers who were trying to rest or were suffering with their nerves.

The little girl turned on to St Martin's Lane and Dorothy realised they were heading towards Covent Garden, but instead of arriving at the famous piazza, the girl turned on to Little Earl Street, part of the notorious Seven Dials district. This area had been one of the city's worst slums for hundreds of years. It was hard to believe that such poverty and deprivation was only a stone's throw away from the busy market full of beautiful blooms and the elegant opera house. Mary elbowed Dorothy sharply in the ribs and gave her a superior look.

"I might have guessed," she said under her breath. Dorothy ignored her and allowed the little girl to continue to lead them through the maze of streets with their cramped houses and rubbish piled up in the gutters. Although it was now growing dark, children in tattered clothing were gathered outside the rowdy pubs. Women selling themselves were standing on every street corner. To Dorothy, it felt like the whole place had been left behind in the last century; it belonged in a Dickens novel. Suddenly the girl stopped and, looking up at Dorothy, pointed to the entrance to a small courtyard.

Dorothy bent down to speak to her. "Is that your house? Is that where you live, my dear?"

The little girl nodded.

"All right then," said Dorothy, "we'll stay here and watch while you go. Goodbye, and here take this."

She put a coin into the girl's small dirty hand. The girl gave her a small smile then bolted straight off down the street. The two women watched as she ran into the dingy courtyard and through a blue-painted door.

"Honestly, I really do despair sometimes," hissed Mary when the child was out of sight. "We are trying to be seen as part of the police force, not some charity for every waif and stray to come begging to with their grubby paws out."

"Mary, it was only a shilling, barely enough to buy a dozen eggs," replied Dorothy reasonably as they turned and began to make their way back to Charing Cross. Mary gave a snort of derision.

"If you think whoever that child is going back to will spend your money on eggs and not gin, then you are a complete fool, Dorothy Peto."

"I don't see that it matters as long as it makes the poor little thing's life a bit easier…" Dorothy began to argue, but before she could say another word, she was interrupted by the shrill sound of a police whistle being blown, then another and another. A police constable whizzed past them on a bicycle. The two women looked around, slightly bewildered. Then at that moment, all the gas streetlamps were dimmed.

"Zeppelin!" Dorothy and Mary shouted in unison and automatically raised their eyes to the dark night sky. The inky blackness was already being punctuated by the sweep of searchlights trying to find the vast airships for the gunners positioned high on the city rooftops to aim at.

It was a warm evening. Most people had their windows open and soon the street was full of people, many in their nightclothes all swarming around in a panic.

"Where's the nearest shelter?" Dorothy asked urgently, wondering how long they had until the bombs began falling.

"Covent Garden underground station," replied Mary promptly, pointing in the direction of Long Acre. Dorothy nodded and together the two women began to blow sharply on their whistles, trying to get the attention of the growing crowd.

"This way, ladies and gentlemen," shouted Mary in her loud clear voice. "Please make your way to the underground station. Follow us to safety." She began marching towards Long Acre, blowing her whistle as she went. Dorothy started to do the same, then she paused as she watched a man hurrying out of his front door, tucking in his shirt and pulling up his braces. He stopped briefly to put on his shoes and Dorothy immediately thought of the little barefoot girl they had just left behind. She turned and started running back the way they had come.

"Where on earth are you going?" shouted Mary.

"I'll be back soon," Dorothy called over her shoulder.

A few moments later, she was back near the courtyard the girl had disappeared into. Everyone around her was running in the opposite direction and, as she looked up, she could see the unmistakable shadow of the Zeppelin in the distance. She hurried to the blue door and pushed it open. It was dark inside. The only light was coming from the full moon that was assisting the Zeppelin. It took a few seconds for Dorothy's eyes to adjust, then she saw two frightened eyes looking back at her.

"Hello again," said Dorothy quietly. The little girl was huddled next to a figure sprawled on the floor. Dorothy edged forward. She was grateful it was dark; at least she couldn't see how filthy the place must be. There was a heavy smell of perfume in the air as if someone had tried to cover the underlying scent of damp, decay and gin. There was a smashed bottle on the floor. It looked like Mary had been correct. Dorothy knelt down next to the body, which she could now see was a woman. The little girl remained still and silent.

Outside was a loud thud and distant screaming. The first bomb had exploded. Dorothy gently reached out and took hold of the woman's wrist, praying for a sign of life, but there was no pulse. Trying to think what to do, Dorothy turned to the little girl.

"Is this your mother?" she asked.

The little girl nodded as a tear trickled down her face.

"Well don't worry, I'm here now. I'll take care of you," she said sounding far more confident than she felt. Just then there was the sound of running feet and another thud as the door was pushed wide open and Mary appeared in the doorway, looking crosser than ever.

"I might have known. I swear, Dorothy Peto, if you are killed tonight, they'll canonise you and make you the patron saint of lost causes," stormed Mary, as she removed her new flashlight she had attached to her belt. She switched it on, dazzling Dorothy and the little girl and shining a bright beam of light on to the body.

"What do we have here?" she asked stepping forward for

a closer look.

"She's dead," replied Dorothy. Now thanks to the flashlight, she could see that the woman must once have been pretty with high cheekbones and full lips, but her skin was so pale it was almost translucent, and her blonde tresses had come loose from their combs. Beneath her upturned nose were specks of white powder.

"Cocaine overdose," stated Mary bluntly.

"Really? Are you sure? When do you think it happened?" asked Dorothy. She was shocked. The papers were always full of stories of widespread drug use in the capital and as was often the case, prostitutes got the blame. Dorothy had assumed they were simply sensational stories. She knew that in hospitals cocaine and morphine were frequently given to ease a patient's pain, but she couldn't imagine why anyone would use them recreationally. Mary shone her torch around the room.

"By the look of things, she may only have been dead a short while; perhaps the child thought she was only sleeping. Had she spoken yet?" asked Mary gesturing to the girl, who was still sitting motionless by the side of her dead mother.

"No, poor little thing," sighed Dorothy her heart was breaking for the silent child, "perhaps she's in shock."

"Well, she can't stay here, and neither can we," declared Mary.

"Don't you think one of us should stay with the body?" whispered Dorothy. Mary gave her a withering look.

"I am turning my flashlight off now, Dorothy, as—in case I need to remind you—we are in the middle of an air raid. If you want to stay in the dark with a dead body, rather than do your duty and help the living, then that's entirely your choice."

With that Mary switched off the light, plunging the room into darkness, and strode out through the door. Dorothy bit back a retort and instead scooped the little girl up in her arms and together they followed Mary out into the street, which was now eerily empty. To the east they could see an ominous orange glow.

"Where have they hit, do you think?" asked Dorothy.

"The docks by the look of things. Be thankful we aren't in Woolwich tonight," replied Mary. "Come on, let's get the child into the shelter, before they get any closer."

They made slow progress towards the underground station, with the thud of the bombs getting ever nearer. They had to keep ducking into doorways for shelter. Dorothy held the girl close. She felt like a rag doll in her arms.

In the chaos, and not knowing Seven Dials well, they took several wrong turnings. As they passed by the opera house for the second time, Dorothy couldn't help feeling relieved that it was closed. The Ministry of Works had requisitioned it as a furniture depository at the outbreak of war. She dreaded to think what it would be like if they had to deal with a terrified audience spilling out into the night too.

As Mary, Dorothy and the little girl finally approached Long Acre, they joined the queue of people jostling to get down the steps to the safety of the underground. When they eventually arrived on the crowded platform, Dorothy set the little girl down and she and Mary leant against the cold brick wall as they tried to catch their breath. People were crammed in all around them. Babies wailed, and mothers tried to comfort them. Then there was an enormous explosion above their heads. The air was filled with screams, and dust and bits of cement began to rain down on their heads. The little girl turned and buried her face in Dorothy's skirt. Dorothy stroked her hair and was about to try to reassure her, when she was shocked to feel her other hand being gripped very tightly. She turned to see Mary standing alongside her with her eyes screwed tightly shut and her lips trembling.

"Mary, what on earth's wrong?" she whispered.

Mary opened her eyes. She looked pale and terrified. "I've got to get out of here," she said through gritted teeth.

"You can't go outside—it's far too dangerous," replied Dorothy in horror, but it was too late. Mary had let go of her hand and was already pushing her way back up the steps. Although she was too proud to admit it herself, Margaret had confided to Dorothy that since her last time in jail, Mary had suffered from terrible claustrophobia. Dorothy looked around her in a panic. She couldn't let Mary go outside alone. She might be maddening, but they were meant to be on patrol together. On the other hand, she couldn't leave the little girl alone either. Dorothy spotted a Red Cross volunteer handing out blankets. Dorothy waved to her and gestured to the little girl.

"I have to go. Will you keep an eye on her, for a few minutes?" she asked.

The volunteer edged her way over to Dorothy. "Don't worry, I'll stay with her," promised the older woman, immediately unfolding a blanket to wrap around the girl.

"I'll be back soon," Dorothy called over her shoulder before pushing her way through the crowd. She staggered out into the empty street and saw Mary silhouetted against the threatening glow lighting up the dark night.

"What on earth is the matter, Mary?" she asked. "I know it can feel frightening down there—it's perfectly natural to be scared—but it is much safer."

Mary turned around abruptly. The fear Dorothy had seen in Mary's eyes as they sheltered had been replaced by her usual air of unfettered confidence.

"Don't be ridiculous, Dorothy. The air down there is foul. Not surprising considering everyone is squashed together like sardines. A few deep breaths of fresh air is all I needed. You should do the same; you'll feel much better too," replied Mary as she began to inhale and exhale deeply, to prove her point. Dorothy did the same, but soon stopped as her nostrils were filled with the rancid smell of burning.

"I think the wind might be blowing the fires this way. Please come back and shelter with me, Mary," she pleaded.

"Absolutely not! You cower down there if you must. However, our orders were to patrol around Charing Cross station and that's exactly what I intend to do."

"But isn't there a good chance the Zeppelins will target the railways?" argued Dorothy.

"Very possibly, which is exactly why we should be there, in case our help is required. Now come along and do try not to get distracted by any more beggars."

Mary began marching back towards the Strand. Dorothy sighed. There was no point arguing with her. That brief glimpse of vulnerability she'd displayed was the first and probably the last time Dorothy would ever see her less than self-assured. Dorothy glanced back at the entrance to the underground and decided she had to return to the motherless little girl rather than go scurrying after her stubborn colleague. No doubt Mary would be furious with her or call her a coward, but Dorothy didn't care anymore. She would deal with Mary tomorrow. Back down in the underground, the lady from the Red Cross had been as good as her word and was still hovering close to the little girl.

"Has she said anything to you?" asked Dorothy hopefully, but the Red Cross lady shook her head.

"No, not a word." And with that she disappeared through the crowd.

"She's back, is she? Found her, did you? Well, you're wasting your time trying to get her to talk. She doesn't speak no English," said a voice behind her. Dorothy turned around to see an old lady sitting on the floor wrapped in a Red Cross blanket.

"What? Do you know her?" she asked.

The old woman nodded. "She lives opposite me in Seven Dials. Her and her mother. They're foreign, some of them Belgian refugees. Hello, dearie." She raised her hand and gave the little girl a friendly wave. Dorothy watched as the little girl waved back with a shy smile. She thought back to the first patrols of the WPV. They had congratulated themselves on helping save a few of the young refugees, but clearly plenty were still in need.

"What's her name?" asked Dorothy.

"Alice—and her mother's called Ellie or Elsie something like that. Like I said they're foreign. Moved in about a month ago. She was a bit hoity-toity but Alice here seemed like a sweet little thing. She understands a bit of English, but she doesn't speak a word."

Dorothy nodded. That at least explained the lack of communication. She bent down so she was level with the little girl.

"Hello, Alice," she said and was rewarded with another smile, then she turned to the old woman and lowered her voice.

"Her mother is dead. We found Alice next to her body."

Not a flicker of emotion crossed the old woman's face. "Well, I can't say I'm surprised. What was it? Booze or that muck she stuck up her nose?"

"The cocaine, I think. Was she addicted? Where did she get it from?" asked Dorothy.

"One of her men friends I dare say," replied the old woman with a shrug, "There was always some young man hanging around at all hours. Not that I'm one to judge. I expect she needed to do something to support her and her little girl."

"Didn't she have any female friends?"

"Not really. She was one of those Dutch-speaking Belgians you see, and a lot of people thought she was a German. They weren't happy about having her living next door. Some even thought she was a spy."

It briefly crossed Dorothy's mind that if she was a proper police officer, she could investigate the woman's death, but for the moment she must concentrate on her daughter's welfare instead.

"Would you be able to take Alice in?" asked Dorothy. It wasn't ideal, but at least Alice would be with someone familiar, until she could arrange an alternative. The old woman folded her arms and gave a firm shake of her head.

"Oh no, dearie. Sweet as she is, I've got enough on my plate without another mouth to feed. I've raised my children—I'm too old to raise any more."

"Could you at least keep an eye on her while I see if I can find somewhere else for her to go?"

As she spoke there was another thud and more dust fell from the ceiling on to their heads.

The old woman shrugged her shoulders again. "I suppose so. By the sound of things, it doesn't look like I'll be going anywhere else anytime soon."

Dorothy thanked her and turned back to Alice. If her elderly neighbour was correct then she was from the Dutch-speaking part of Belgium, but Dorothy didn't know a word of Dutch. She supposed it was possible the little girl might understand French better than English. Dorothy's own French was a little basic, but eventually she came up with: "*Restez vous ici*, Alice."

Alice nodded and curled up on the floor, wrapping the blanket tightly around her. Dorothy gave her little hand a quick squeeze, then she headed off in the direction the Red Cross lady had gone, stepping over bodies huddled under blankets as she went. People had clearly decided they might as well get some sleep if they were going to be there all night.

Over the next few hours Dorothy kept checking on Alice as she tried to make herself useful helping the Red Cross provide those sheltering with blankets and mugs of tea. She was relieved to see that after a while the little girl had fallen asleep with her head resting on the old woman's lap. Dorothy asked the Red Cross volunteers if they could help with Alice. They were all very sympathetic and suggested several orphanages, but none with any Dutch or French speakers and Dorothy didn't want to take her anywhere if they didn't speak her language. She would be even more scared and confused.

Finally, at almost two o'clock in the morning, a young police constable came down the steps of the underground to tell them all it was safe to leave. Dorothy returned to Alice, who was now awake. She gently picked her up and carried her up the stairs. Out in the street a policeman cycled past blowing a bugle to signal the all-clear. Dorothy looked around her. Slowly, the streetlamps were being turned back on, but it was still quite dark. She decided to go to Charing Cross Police Station. At the very least she needed to report the mother's death and hopefully someone there could help with Alice too.

The desk sergeant didn't look at all surprised to see Dorothy and Alice when they walked through the door.

"You've just missed her," he said.

"Who?" asked Dorothy.

"Your other half, Miss Allen. I thought it was odd she was here on her own. You lot normally travel in pairs. She's been helping two of our lads over at the railway station. They brought in one drunk and disorderly and one for soliciting. Oh, and then she reported finding the body of a dead woman."

"The woman in Seven Dials?" asked Dorothy.

The sergeant glanced down at his notes. "That's right. Miss Allen didn't have a name or much of an address but said we should look for a blue door. It's not much to go on, but I'll pass it over to Holborn. Seven Dials is on their beat."

"The woman's name is Elsie or something similar. She's a Belgian refugee," explained Dorothy. This was typical of Mary. She was so keen to be the one to report the death and have her name next to it, that she wouldn't think to wait and see if Dorothy had any more information about the dead woman. Dorothy looked down at Alice, who was hiding in her skirts again. The burly desk sergeant must seem quite intimidating to her. Dorothy stroked her hair. "This is her little girl, Alice. I don't suppose you know where I can take her, do you?"

"Well, you can't leave her here," the sergeant replied firmly. "We're full downstairs and I'm short-handed. Most of our lads have gone to help over at Stepney and Leytonstone. Bloody Germans, if you'll pardon my French. I'm sorry, Miss Peto, but I'm not running a kindergarten."

"No of course you aren't, Sergeant," replied Dorothy a little impatiently. Did he really think she would leave Alice to wait downstairs with the drunks and prostitutes? She turned to go, then a thought struck her.

"Her mother's death will be investigated, won't it? Miss Allen and I thought it was an overdose of cocaine, but of course we can't be sure."

"Cocaine, eh?" repeated the sergeant shaking his head. "It seems the filthy stuff is everywhere. They're even selling it in Harrods would you believe?"

"What?" asked Dorothy, incredulously.

"In little tins, cocaine and morphine with a syringe and spare needles. They advertise as 'a useful present for friends at the front'." The sergeant pulled a face. "It takes all sorts I suppose. Me? If I was out there, I'd rather have a pair of nice warm socks and some tobacco for my pipe."

Dorothy left the police station, not at all convinced that the poor woman's death would be investigated properly. She had seen it time and time again. The police so often made assumptions if the victim was a prostitute and, on top of that, drugs seemed to be involved. It was unfair, but right now Alice was her main concern. The only other place Dorothy could think to try was the Belgian Embassy. They may at least be able to find out if the little girl had any relations here or at home. However, the embassy was over in Belgravia on Eaton Square about a forty-five-minute walk from where they were. Thanks to the late hour and the bombing raid there wasn't a taxi to been seen. She looked down at Alice's bare feet. Even though it was a mild night, she would never be able to walk all the way there. Dorothy crouched down and gestured to her back.

"Piggyback?" she said, wishing for about the hundredth time that she had learnt some Dutch. Nevertheless, Alice seemed to understand as she climbed aboard and wrapped her skinny arms around Dorothy's neck. Wobbling slightly, Dorothy tucked her arms under the girl's knees and rose to her feet.

"Hold on tight," she said and because she couldn't think of anything else, "*On y va!*"

To keep their spirits up she began quietly singing 'It's a Long Way to Tipperary', the song that had been so popular amongst the departing troops. Dorothy smiled as she remembered how Nina had mischievously changed the words to 'It's the Wrong Way to Tickle Mary'. She yawned as she trudged along. She had been awake all night and was exhausted, but judging by the slow, heavy breathing coming from behind her, Alice may have managed to fall asleep again.

It was beginning to grow light, as they approached the city's largest and arguably grandest square. The two of them received quite a few amused glances from passing milkmen, the only other people who were about at this hour. The Belgian Embassy was located in one of the imposing white houses in the row of porticoed terraces. Dorothy was relieved to see a tall grey-haired man, dressed immaculately in the uniform of the Belgian police standing to attention on the door. She had been afraid it might not be open yet.

She was also suddenly aware of her own appearance. Her uniform was creased, she was covered in brick dust and there was a child dressed in rags riding on her back. If she was refused entry, she had no idea where they would go next. She gave a weak smile as she approached the door. By this time, she was so exhausted her brain wasn't capable of using any foreign language.

"Hello," she said weakly.

The man on the door nodded politely. "Good morning, madame, and—" he peered over her shoulder and grinned "—good morning to you, mademoiselle." He opened the door with a flourish, then stepped to one side. The sound of the man's voice had woken Alice. Still clutching her pink rabbit, she slid off Dorothy's back, took hold of her hand and together they walked into the embassy.

They entered a very grand reception hall, with high ceilings, marble floors, and Belgian flags hanging on the wall. Beneath a huge portrait of Albert, King of the Belgians, sat a man at a highly polished mahogany desk. He looked terribly smart, with slicked-back dark hair and a neatly clipped moustache.

"Good morning, oh I do hope you speak English," began Dorothy.

The man rose to his feet and bowed his head. "Of course, mademoiselle. How may I be of assistance?" he replied, as if a dusty suffragette and a grubby child appearing before him at five o'clock in the morning was the most natural thing in the world. Dorothy could have hugged him.

"My name is Dorothy Peto—I'm one of the Women's Police Volunteers—and this is Alice. She's Belgian."

The man smiled down at Alice. "*Bonjour*," he said.

"Actually, I think she speaks Dutch mainly," explained Dorothy.

"Ah, then, *goedemorgen mevrouw*," he said and this time he was rewarded with a shy smile from Alice.

"We found her in Seven Dials. She lived with her mother there, but unfortunately her mother is dead; in fact we found her with the body," Dorothy began to explain, but the man held up his hand.

"One moment please, mademoiselle. If you will allow me, I should like to make notes." He returned to his seat and, after picking up a silver fountain pen, began to write as Dorothy told him the whole sorry story, trying to include all the details she could remember.

"I'm sorry, but I didn't know where else to take her."

"Not at all, Mademoiselle Peto. You did exactly the right

thing. We will take care of her now." He rang a small brass bell on his desk and a smartly dressed young woman appeared.

"Miss Leblanc works with child refugees and is also a Dutch speaker," he explained.

"Gosh, you all start work very early," replied Dorothy.

"Sadly, these last few months have been busy for us. We have staff working all day and all night."

The young woman knelt down and began talking to Alice in her own language. The little girl started to nod her head vigorously as Miss Leblanc spoke. Then Alice took the young woman's hand and together they walked towards a large white door. Before they disappeared, Alice turned and smiled.

"*Dank je*," she said quietly and gave Dorothy a little wave. Dorothy waved back and felt tears well up in her eyes. The man behind the desk noticed and kindly offered her his pristine white handkerchief. He took her details and promised she would be kept informed about Alice's case.

When Dorothy stepped back out into Eaton Square, the early morning sun was shining brightly. Although she was exhausted, she felt her spirits rise. What had happened to Alice was terrible, but thanks to her, the little girl was now in safe hands. She had made a difference. It had been a good night's work.

Chapter Eleven

WHEN DOROTHY FINALLY arrived home, she almost fell into her bed and slept until noon. She was only woken up by Nina knocking loudly on her front door.

"You'll never believe what she's done now. Honestly, that woman is the absolute limit," she declared before Dorothy even had the chance to say 'hello'.

"Who is?" asked Dorothy yawning and rubbing her eyes as she followed Nina, who had marched past her and into the flat's little sitting room.

"Mary! This morning she stormed into the office and said she wanted to make a formal complaint against you. 'For dereliction of duty'. Something about you staying in the bomb shelter to look after a little girl. I'm sure it was only for my benefit. She must have already told Margaret what happened last night."

Dorothy's heart sank. She knew Mary was cross, but an official complaint sounded serious. What if she couldn't be a member of the WPV anymore?

"What did Margaret say?" she asked.

Nina shrugged. "Not much. You know how she hates confrontation, but Mary wouldn't stop going on and on. In the end, I suggested you write a letter to Margaret explaining your reasons for not going with Mary and an apology to Sir might not go amiss either. Sorry, I know it's a nuisance, but it did at least shut her up. I really think wearing her precious uniform has made her quite power crazed. Now she's quite happy to police the prostitutes she would have been sharing a cell with a few months ago. It's as if she's forgotten whose side she's meant to be on."

"Do you think they'll ask me to leave the WPV?"

"No of course not. You are far too important and work harder than the rest of us put together. Besides, I wouldn't allow it."

After staying for a quick cup of tea and hearing all about Alice and her mother, Nina left, and Dorothy set about writing her letters. She couldn't believe Mary had complained about her. It was so petty, but if a couple of letters kept the peace, so be it. She should probably write to her parents too. The telephone had yet to reach their part of rural Hampshire and they would be desperately worried when they heard about the Zeppelin raid.

However, no sooner had she sat down at the small bureau than she realised she had run out of ink. It was Sunday and no stationers would be open. Perhaps Raymond might have some. She pushed the door open to his room. There was still the faint smell of cigarettes and the cologne he wore in the air. It reminded her how much she missed her brother. It had been over two weeks since she'd heard from him. She went over to his desk and began searching for a bottle of ink. She tried to be careful not to disturb anything. Raymond was far tidier than she was and a great collector of this and that. Each drawer and compartment seemed full of letters, postcards, stamps, shells and all manner of other things.

Finally, she came across an opened bottle of blue ink but as she picked it up, she sent a pile of neatly stacked cigarette cards falling to the floor.

"Oh bother!" she muttered as she knelt down to retrieve them. He was bound to know if she put them back in the wrong order. She didn't want him to think she'd been snooping while he was away. Then she froze. Staring up at her from the floor was the dead woman from Seven Dials. She picked up the card and squinted at it. Yes, it was definitely her. Smiling and lovely, rather than pale and lifeless. Dorothy read the name.

"Elsa Dubois," she said quietly. She looked at the other cards. They were all of famous actresses. There was Phyllis Dare, Mrs Patrick Campbell, Jean Aylwin and even Edith Devine. Did that mean Elsa Dubois was a famous actress too? If that was the case, how on earth had she ended up in that awful place in Seven Dials? Dorothy slipped the card into her pocket and carefully replaced the others. Then she hurried back to her desk, penned a letter to Margaret and the most sincere apology she could muster to Mary. She dressed quickly. She wanted to pass on the information about the identity of the woman as soon as possible. Hopefully, it would help find little Alice's relations. The letter to her parents would have to wait.

Within an hour, Dorothy had arrived at the WPV offices. Although it was a Sunday, both Nina and Margaret were at their desks. Nina gave her an encouraging smile as she walked through the door. Margaret looked up and blushed. Dorothy placed the two letters in front of her.

"I'm sorry if you feel I let you down last night, Margaret. I've explained my actions in this letter. I did what I thought was the right thing. I've also written Mary an apology. However, if the two of you wish to discuss the matter further…"

"No, no, I'm sure that won't be necessary, Dorothy dear. I'm sure the whole thing was simply a silly misunderstanding between friends," said Margaret quickly, flapping her hand at Dorothy and putting the letters, unopened into her desk drawer. "Now why don't the three of us join Mary for a nice cup of tea and we'll put this whole business behind us."

She stood up quickly and bustled out of the door. Dorothy turned to Nina who was shaking her head.

"I told you," her friend whispered, "she hates confrontation. It was all Mary's doing."

The two of them followed Margaret down the corridor. Margaret pushed open the door to the main room and all three of them stopped in their tracks. Lucy was sitting on the sofa wearing what looked like a riding hat while Mary was hitting her over the head with a rolled-up newspaper.

"Good heavens, Mary! What are you doing?" asked Nina.

Mary turned around, her arm poised mid-air. "Miss St John Partridge has designed us a new hat, similar to the helmets the chaps wear. This is the prototype. We're testing it out. It should be able to withstand a fairly hefty blow to the head." She frowned as she noticed Dorothy standing next to Nina. "I wasn't expecting to see you today, Dorothy."

Before Dorothy could reply, Margaret gave one of her small, nervous coughs.

"I've just received a lovely letter and an apology from Dorothy, so I think we can put the matter behind us, don't you, Robert?"

"I suppose so," replied Mary a little coldly, turning back to the job in hand. Dorothy winced as she whacked Lucy again, then put down the newspaper and picked up a book.

"Are you all right, Lucy?" she asked.

"It's fine, Dorothy. Honestly, I can't feel a thing," confirmed Lucy with a slightly anxious smile.

Mary frowned at Dorothy. "Are you only here to deliver your apology? You aren't on duty again until tomorrow."

"I'm not, but I was wondering if anyone from Scotland Yard had been in touch about the body we found in Seven Dials?" replied Dorothy. She had to stop herself from adding: 'You do remember we found a dead woman, don't you?' Mary seemed far more concerned with this perceived slight she'd made Dorothy apologise for, than what had happened to Alice's mother. "I've discovered who she is. Her name is Elsa Dubois. She was a famous Belgian actress."

"Really?" asked Nina in surprise.

"Then what on earth was she doing in that hovel?" asked the still-frowning Mary.

"That's precisely what I was thinking," replied Dorothy.

As they were talking, Lucy escaped from her position of torture and went over to the telephone desk and picked up a piece of paper.

"Somebody from Scotland Yard did telephone earlier. Sorry, I completely forgot to mention it in all the excitement about the new hat. The officer leading the investigation is an Inspector Derwent."

Dorothy's heart sank. "Oh dear," she groaned.

"What's wrong?" asked Margaret.

"I've met him before. He was in charge of the investigation into the death of Edith Devine. When I tried to pass on some information, he was quite dismissive. It was the same when I saw him at Clara Fleurot's trial. I doubt he'll be much more receptive now."

Margaret nodded sympathetically and Nina looked as if she was about to speak when Mary tutted loudly. "Now that's hardly the attitude, Dorothy," she declared. "Inspector Derwent is one of the most well-respected officers at Scotland Yard. Everyone says Derwent always gets his man, or woman, for that matter. He is also one of their most experienced chaps. As a matter of fact, when he was a young constable, he worked on the Ripper case."

"Good heavens! How frightful!" gasped Lucy.

Ignoring her, Mary continued. "He's also something of a hero. He left the force to serve his country during the Boer War and I'm sure he'd have joined up again if it wasn't for his injuries, the poor chap."

That explains the scar and the walking stick, Dorothy thought to herself.

"Perhaps I judged him too harshly," she admitted.

"It certainly sounds like," said Mary sharply. "When you speak to him about the body in Seven Dials, I want you to promise to be respectful. Always remember we are there to assist the regular officers. You mustn't do anything to damage all the good work we have done, so whatever you do, don't…"

"Go ruffling any feathers," Nina and Dorothy said in

unison, exchanging an amused glance and earning themselves one of Mary's filthiest looks. Dorothy didn't care. It was clear that despite what she'd told Margaret, Mary hadn't put the events of the previous evening behind them, but from now on she was going to follow Nina's example and face her pettiness with humour. She turned down Margaret's offer of a cup of tea and instead headed straight to Scotland Yard.

HAVING ONLY RECEIVED the most basic directions from the desk sergeant, Dorothy made her way through the warren of corridors and staircases of the Metropolitan Police's headquarters, until she found herself outside the door bearing the name Inspector Derwent. Following their previous encounters, she was determined not to get flustered again. After all, since then, she had been a member of the Women's Police Volunteers for several months, helping members of the public and most importantly assisting regular police officers, and after her encounter with Mary, she was well and truly tired of people talking down to her. She took a deep breath, then raised her hand and knocked loudly.

"Enter," said a voice she recognised. Dorothy pushed open the door and found the inspector standing and staring out of his window rather than behind his desk. He turned around but didn't speak. As he was no longer wearing his hat, she could see he had thick, almost black hair that was greying slightly at the temples.

"Good morning, Inspector. I understand you are in charge of the investigation into the death of the body we found in Seven Dials. I am a member of the Women's Police Volunteers. My name is…"

"Miss Dorothy Peto," he interrupted. "We met several months ago, at the stage door of the Haymarket Theatre and again more recently at Marlborough Street Magistrate's Court. Do you imagine all police inspectors are unable to remember the names of witnesses or just me?"

Dorothy could feel a warm flush creeping up face. "I'm here because I discovered a women's body in Seven Dials last night," she continued, determined to make her point, no matter how rude he might be.

The inspector frowned as he looked down at the piece of paper on his desk.

"It says here, Miss Mary Allen, a Women's Police Volunteer, reported finding the body."

"Yes, she did. You see we were on duty together, but we got separated during the air raid. She went to Charing Cross station…"

"While you took it upon yourself to take the deceased's child to the Belgian Embassy."

"Well, I couldn't very well leave her in a holding cell. There was nowhere else to take her," she protested, then paused. "Wait, how did you know about me going to the embassy?"

The inspector raised an eyebrow. "Strangely, Miss Peto, we haven't been twiddling our thumbs and waiting for you to make an appearance. My officers have been making their own inquiries. Did it not occur to you that this child was an important witness and could well have vital information about the death of her mother?"

Dorothy felt herself flush again. "Actually, no it didn't. I was more concerned with getting her to a place of safety where she could be cared for. Besides, she was so terrified the poor little thing barely said a word. I think she was in shock."

"Is that a medical diagnosis, Miss Peto?"

Dorothy decided to change tack. She hadn't come here for a telling-off. "Have you been able to identify the deceased yet?" she asked.

"We are still making inquiries. Strangely for someone fleeing her country she had no travel documents amongst her belongings."

"Well, I think I know who she is." She removed the cigarette card from her pocket with a flourish and proudly placed it on the desk. "My brother, Raymond, is a great collector of cigarette cards and a fan of the theatre," she explained.

Inspector Derwent picked it up and peered closely at it. "Elsa Dubois," he read aloud. "I agree the similarity is striking."

"It's definitely her," insisted Dorothy, disappointed that he didn't seem to share her excitement. "I could see her face clearly in the flashlight and one of her neighbours I spoke to in the shelter told me her name was Elsie or something similar and that she was Belgian."

The inspector frowned at the notes in front of him. "There's no record here of that information. What was the neighbour's name?"

Dorothy could have kicked herself. The old woman was sheltering with her for hours, but she never thought to ask what she was called.

"I'm sorry I didn't get her name," she admitted, "but I did report what she'd told me to the desk sergeant at Charing Cross." Despite her best efforts she could feel herself getting flustered again.

The inspector looked up and fixed his dark blue eyes on her. "I'm sure you did, Miss Peto. However, I will need to carry out further investigations before we can know who the deceased was for sure. I should be grateful if you didn't share this information with anyone until we are able to confirm her identity."

Dorothy looked quickly away as she remembered she'd already told Mary, Nina and Lucy she knew the dead woman's name. He was right, she should have kept quiet. She'd look an awful fool if she was wrong and what if Elsa Dubois's family heard the news from someone other than the police?

"If there is nothing else, Miss Peto," said the inspector gesturing towards the door, but Dorothy still had something she wanted to ask him. Something she'd been thinking about on the way over here.

"Actually, while I'm here, I also wanted to ask you about the Edith Devine case. I read about it in the newspapers, of course…"

"Then you'll know there is no case. The coroner ruled that she died by misadventure," interrupted the inspector briskly.

Dorothy pressed on undeterred. "Yes, but did you share his opinion?" she asked.

He surveyed her for a second. "Why do you ask?"

"Well, I was wondering if there might be a connection

between her and Elsa Dubois. They were both actresses. They look rather similar. Both died from an overdose of cocaine; at least that's what it looked like when I found Elsa. They even share the same initials: ED," replied Dorothy eagerly.

Inspector Derwent raised an eyebrow. "Forgive me, finding the cigarette card is one thing but I think you may be getting a little carried away, Miss Peto. If you are concerned about everyone with the initials ED, you'll be investigating me next." He gestured to the brass plaque on his desk bearing the name Inspector E Derwent.

"What does your E stand for?" asked Dorothy.

"Edgar."

"It suits you."

"Thank you, although it's a little late in the day for me to do anything about it if it didn't meet with your approval. And I'm afraid you may be disappointed to learn that Edith Devine was merely a stage name she began using when she left Yorkshire and arrived in London."

"Really? What was her real name?"

"Gwen Snicklethwaite."

"Heavens! No wonder she changed it."

Derwent's lips almost twitched into a smile as he rose to his feet and went over to the door and called out for a sergeant, who appeared almost immediately. He handed the cigarette card over to the officer.

"Thanks to Miss Peto, we may have a name for the woman we found in Seven Dials. Find out all you can about Elsa Dubois, a Belgian national, an actress we believe. I'll be with Dr Stirk if you need me. He should have completed the post-mortem by now."

"Yes, sir," replied the sergeant as he hurried away.

"May I join you?" asked Dorothy eagerly as the inspector reached for his hat. He turned and looked at her in surprise.

"I think you may have misunderstood, Miss Peto. I shall be visiting the morgue to discover if the woman in Seven Dials did indeed die of a cocaine overdose."

"Yes, I understand. I thought I might be of assistance. The doctor might wish to speak to me. After all, I did discover her body."

Inspector Derwent shook his head. "I think there is more chance of man walking on the moon than Wilfrid Stirk asking a young lady for assistance, but you may join me if you wish. I trust you aren't squeamish."

"Not at all. Thank you very much, Inspector," she replied gratefully and followed him out of the door, past the busy incident room and down the stairs. "Do I take it the doctor is a little old-fashioned in his views, Inspector?"

"You could say that. Almost all the young doctors have joined up or are busy treating the injured who have returned from the front. Dr Stirk kindly came out of retirement to take up his previous position as our pathologist."

Despite his limp, the inspector walked at quite a pace and Dorothy had to break into a trot to keep up with him. She was a little out of breath when, ten minutes later, they arrived at the morgue. They found Dr Stirk in a white-tiled room that smelt strongly of formaldehyde. He was a tall, thin, grey-haired man with a pipe clamped between his thin lips and the coldest eyes Dorothy had ever seen. He acknowledged their arrival with a grunt and the briefest nod of his head.

"Good afternoon, Doctor," said Inspector Derwent politely. "May I introduce Miss Peto, a member of the Women's Police Volunteers."

"Women involved in policing! I have never heard such utter nonsense! What next? Female judges sitting on the bench passing sentences on us. Ha!" He barked out a laugh at the very idea. Dorothy glanced over to the inspector to see if he was laughing too, but his expression remained as stern as ever.

"We have found the WPV have brought a new dimension to policing, Doctor," he replied. "It was Miss Peto who discovered the body you have been examining. We thought you might have some questions for her."

"There's nothing she could tell me that I don't already know. It's a clear case of suicide."

He pulled back the sheet to reveal the woman's face and pointed to a fierce red rash on her neck that Dorothy hadn't noticed before.

"See this, Derwent? A nasty case of dermatitis. She had tried to cover it up with thick powder, but it was bound to spread to her face and probably scar. She was a pretty enough little thing. I dare say her face was her fortune. No doubt she realised that thanks to the war, single men would be in short supply. She didn't wear a wedding ring. An unmarried woman burdened with a small child would find it almost impossible to get anyone to take her on and if that woman was disfigured. Well…" He shook his head. "With only a miserable future of poverty and destitution to look forward to, in a fit of depression she took her own life."

Dorothy was immediately reminded of the Lady Walsingham's warning to Margaret about the lack of men after the war, but what the doctor was saying didn't feel right. However, the inspector was slowly nodding his head.

"We believe she may have been an actress," he said.

The doctor looked delighted by this news. "That settles it then," he replied as he carelessly dropped the sheet from his hand. "Losing her looks and her livelihood."

As he turned away and went to wash his hands at the huge sink, Dorothy couldn't resist voicing her thoughts. "I'm sorry, but I don't think a mother would kill herself, knowing she was leaving a little child alone in a strange country."

The doctor glanced dismissively over his shoulder but ignored Dorothy and addressed the inspector instead. "Is this the new dimension women are bringing, Derwent? Sentimental claptrap!" He laughed again and continued to lather his hands.

"So, in your opinion she died from a self-inflicted overdose of cocaine?" asked the inspector.

The doctor turned around in surprise. "Cocaine? No, she died from cyanide poisoning. Didn't I say that?"

Dorothy looked at the inspector in confusion. "No, you didn't. What about the white powder around her nose?" he asked.

"Oh, that was cocaine all right, but she hadn't inhaled any. It was cyanide that killed her. Look at that bluish tinge to her skin. Classic sign of cyanide poisoning."

"And how was the cyanide administered?"

The doctor dried his hands and sucked deeply on his pipe before using it to point to the body on the slab.

"Well, it wasn't ingested. I found no trace of cyanide in the contents of her stomach, which amounted to little more than some bread and an apple."

"Don't apple pips contain cyanide? Could that be it?" asked Dorothy recalling something her father had once told her when he'd been sketching in their orchard.

The doctor gave her a withering look. "She would have needed to swallow an entire bushel of apples. Even then I doubt it would have been enough, young lady."

"Could it have been in the gin? There was a bottle next to her when I found her."

"There was no alcohol in her system, otherwise I would have mentioned it," he snapped. Dorothy was about to speak again but the inspector stepped in.

"Do you have a time of death, Doctor?" he asked.

"I would say sometime between five and ten o'clock yesterday evening."

Dorothy had to stop herself rolling her eyes. She had discovered the body at a little before nine o'clock. The doctor clearly hadn't read the report or perhaps he thought women were incapable of telling the time too.

"You can't narrow it down any further?" asked the inspector as if reading her mind.

"I'm afraid not. Got to leave something for you chaps to do. Good day, Derwent."

With that the doctor strode out, puffing on his pipe and leaving Dorothy and the inspector alone with the dead body.

"A year in retirement doesn't seem to have mellowed him at all," murmured the inspector.

"Any chance we could get a second opinion?" asked

Dorothy hopefully.

The inspector almost smiled but shook his head. "I'm afraid not, Miss Peto. As I explained, we are overstretched as it is."

"You don't believe she took her own life, do you?" asked Dorothy.

"I don't know. I'm more concerned about where the cyanide came from and how it killed her."

He stood for a moment in silence, staring down at Elsa, then gently he pulled the sheet back over her face.

"What now?" asked Dorothy.

He looked up at her as if he'd forgotten she was there. "Now, I shall be returning to Scotland Yard, Miss Peto, and I expect you shall do whatever a young woman of the WPV does on a Sunday afternoon."

"Wouldn't you like me to come back with you and make a statement?" she asked, trying not to sound disappointed. The brief glimpse she'd had of the incident room they'd passed by looked far more interesting than their own set of offices. The inspector surveyed her with an expression she couldn't read.

"In Miss Allen's report, she said the body was discovered a few minutes before nine o'clock. That there was nobody in the immediate vicinity and there was no sign of any violence in the deceased's rooms except for the smashed bottle of gin. Is there anything you would like to add to that?"

"There was a strong smell of perfume."

"Perfume," he repeated sounding unimpressed. "Anything else?"

"No, I don't think so," admitted Dorothy thinking back

to the previous night and wondering if she had missed some vital clue.

The inspector nodded and raised his hat. "Then I shall wish you good day." He called out to a passing orderly, "Please be good enough to show Miss Peto out, would you?"

Dorothy reluctantly followed the man in the white coat down the corridor and glanced back to see the inspector disappearing in the opposite direction.

Chapter Twelve

THE NEXT DAY, Dorothy was on patrol alone. Nina was meant to be with her, but her restless friend was becoming increasingly bored with the regular routine of patrols. She'd begged Dorothy to let her spend the morning writing an article she was working on instead. Dorothy didn't mind being on her own. As she walked, she could think about Elsa Dubois. Inspector Derwent had seemed to accept the doctor saying her death was suicide, but Dorothy couldn't believe it any more than she believed Edith Devine would be distraught over Muller. Would anyone choose to end their life because of a skin rash? And if she had wanted to kill herself with poison, surely she would have swallowed it, but that obnoxious man had said there was no trace of cyanide in her stomach. How else could it have happened? And why was there cocaine on her face? Then there was the spilt gin she apparently hadn't drunk. None of it made sense.

The streets were quiet. Despite the time of year, there was a chill wind blowing, shaking the cherry blossom from the trees. It almost looked as though it was snowing. Anyone she passed had their collars up and their heads down as they hurried on their way. On every corner, the newspaper vendors were shouting about the casualties from the Zeppelin raid. The death of three more children in the East End had briefly taken attention away from the hundreds of soldiers who had lost their lives on the other side of the Channel. Death seemed to be everywhere.

As there was little else to keep her busy and she was alone, Dorothy decided to pay another visit to the house in Seven Dials. No doubt Inspector Derwent had ensured the place was secured after his search, but it couldn't hurt to take a look. Perhaps she might even find Elsa's elderly neighbour. It was still bothering her that she hadn't found out her name. She'd been proud of working alongside the regular police and thought she and the other Women's Police Volunteers acted just as professionally, but she'd felt like an utter amateur talking to the inspector.

She walked purposefully through Covent Garden, ignoring the drunken soldiers on leave and the gaudily dressed women plying their trade. She was almost at Elsa's house, when a small man hurrying by caught her attention. She'd recognise that ferrety face anywhere. It was Archibald Abbey, the man she'd seen in Mead's courtroom, accused of abusing the girl from Horseferry Road. She stopped and strained her neck to see where he had gone, but her view was blocked by a cart piled high with sacks of coal. After it had trundled by, he had disappeared. She turned to the two women sitting behind her on the steps of the Royal Opera House, smoking.

"That man who went by just now, do either of you know him?"

"Yes, more's the pity. Filthy creature. They should string him up."

"He won't hang about if he knows what's good for him.

We don't want the likes of him around here," her friend chimed in.

Dorothy nodded feeling slightly reassured. If he was known to the locals perhaps they could protect their children where the law had failed. She began to walk away.

"Is that it then? Your lot usually tell us to clear off," the first woman called after her.

Dorothy turned and smiled. "Not today, ladies. I'm here about something else."

"That foreigner who died in the air raid?"

"Yes. Did you know her?"

"Not really. She kept herself to herself. We used to see her quite a bit. She'd bring her little girl here," explained the woman, pointing to the elegant, boarded-up building behind them. "Every day they walked the same route. Down to Charing Cross station then through Covent Garden market and stopped outside here."

"Although most days it didn't look like she had the strength to put one foot in front of the other," added the friend.

"Did you ever see her drinking in the public houses or on her own? Maybe taking something stronger than drink?"

They both shook their heads.

"Nah, a bit too prim and proper for that I'd say."

"So she er, she wasn't in your line of work?"

"Nah. I never saw her with any men, nor heard nothing. Like I said she kept herself to herself. Word soon gets around if competition moves in—you get my drift?"

Dorothy nodded again and thanked them both but frowned to herself as she walked away. Their description of

Elsa's lifestyle was very different what the elderly neighbour had told her. She continued on her way until she was standing outside the blue door in Seven Dials. In the daylight, she could now see that Elsa and Alice had only occupied the ground floor of the house. There was a flight of steps on the side of the building leading up to the first floor. She approached the door, turned the handle and gave it a push but it wouldn't budge. Inspector Derwent and his team must have found the key and locked it after their visit.

As if reading her mind, a voice called out, "Hello, dearie! You won't get in there. The bobbies locked it after they'd turned the place upside down."

Dorothy turned around. The old woman from the underground was sitting on the doorstep of the house on the other side of the courtyard. She had a thick shawl around her shoulders, some sacking over her knees and was puffing on a clay pipe. Dorothy wondered how miserable her abode must be inside, to want to sit out here in the cold.

"Hello again, er Mrs?"

"Mrs Clayton. Olive Clayton. What brings you here?"

"I'm helping the police. As I was the one who found Elsa, I thought I should take another look at the place in daylight," said Dorothy, hoping that this made her visit sound official without actually telling a lie. The old woman peered at her with heavily wrinkled eyes, then beckoned for her to come closer. Dorothy lowered her head, noticing how broken and stained the woman's teeth were as she spoke in hushed tones.

"There is another key. The previous tenant was always losing hers. She kept a spare beneath the loose brick under the windowsill but never told the landlord."

"Who's the landlord?" asked Dorothy.

The old woman shrugged. "We never see him. He always sends some bossy little madame to do his dirty work."

"He has a female agent?" asked Dorothy in surprise.

The old woman grinned. "Us women are doing all sorts of jobs these days, haven't you heard, dearie?"

She began to laugh at her own joke, but her laughter quickly turned into a coughing fit. Dorothy tried to assist her, but she waved her away and instead staggered to her feet and through her own door.

Dorothy returned to the house with the blue door and just as the old woman had said, found a loose brick under the cracked window ledge and beneath it a key. She unlocked the door and cautiously pushed it open. With the sun streaming in through the window, she could see that the place, although very shabby, was not as dirty as she had first feared. The strange and unpleasant mixture of smells she had encountered that night had also disappeared along with the body. The outline of where it had lain was etched in chalk on the floor. There was a sheet hanging as a makeshift curtain on a couple of hooks above the window. The place was sparsely furnished. Next to where Elsa's body had lain was a faded, threadbare sofa with horsehair sticking out of one arm. A wooden table with two chairs and in the corner was a stove and a small sink.

She tried to remember if there had been any sign of Elsa eating a meal when she'd found her, but it had been too dark and she had been too distracted. Her eyes scanned the rest of the room and came to rest on something peeping out beneath the sofa. She bent down. It was a pair of children's shoes. Black patent leather, a little worn, but very good quality. Yet, on the night she'd found Alice, she'd been barefoot. Had she grown out of these shoes and her mother been unable to afford more?

She peered under the sofa again. There was a pale pink blanket under there too. Dorothy looked up. There was a matching blanket folded on the sofa next to a pillow. Had this sofa been little Alice's bed? Dorothy tried to imagine what might have happened that night. Could Alice have been sleeping on the sofa and then woken up to the sound of her mother falling to the floor? Or could someone or something else have woken her? Dorothy looked around again. The rest of Elsa and Alice's home consisted of only one more room: a bedroom.

This room was even smaller with only a wrought-iron bed and a rickety chest of drawers. On top of the chest of drawers and looking completely out of place was an ornate gilt mirror. Beneath it was a silver dressing table set, consisting of a hairbrush, comb and hand mirror. Pressed into the corner of the mirror was a photo of Elsa and Alice together and in the other corner was the cover of an old theatre programme. Dorothy bent forward so she could read it. It was from May the previous year and was for a production of *Madame Butterfly* at the opera house, featuring none other than the great Caruso. Dorothy had been desperate to go herself, but tickets were like gold dust.

She turned her attention to the large leather travelling trunk next to the dressing table. She lifted the lid and was immediately struck by a strong smell of perfume. It was

Caron's Narcisse Noir, a scent she knew well. Her father bought her mother a bottle every Christmas. Dorothy frowned. Something wasn't right. Carefully, she began to look through the contents of the trunk. There were several silk scarves and cashmere sweaters. Like the child's shoes, all were extremely good quality. Suddenly she froze. She had heard the front door creak open. She held her breath and listened as heavy footsteps got closer.

"Good afternoon, Miss Peto," said a familiar voice and Inspector Derwent appeared in the doorway.

"Oh hello, Inspector," replied Dorothy with a mixture of embarrassment and relief.

"May I ask how and why you are here?" His tone was polite, but as usual he wasn't smiling.

"Well, you see, I felt silly for not noting down the name of Elsa's neighbour, so I thought I'd see if I could find her and I did. She's called Mrs Olive Clayton. She told me there was a spare key hidden under a loose stone beneath the windowsill. So I thought I'd take a look and see if I could remember anything from the night I found Elsa."

"And did you?"

"No, not exactly, but I did find Alice's shoes and blanket under the sofa. Both are good quality—not the sort of thing you would expect to belong to a child found begging. Nor would you expect someone living here to have a silver dressing table set." She gestured to the chest of drawers. "Then there's the perfume. The clothes in her trunk smell of Narcisse Noir."

She bent down and sniffed again several times.

"Do you have a cold, Miss Peto?"

"No, but the perfume that filled the air on the night she died had a heavy scent of violets, but there isn't a trace of it here." She straightened up to look at him. "And I've just remembered where I first smelt it. It was at Margaret Damer Dawson's house."

The inspector raised his eyebrow in that sceptical way Dorothy was beginning to find irritating.

"You aren't suggesting Miss Damer Dawson was here."

Dorothy shook her head impatiently. "No of course not, Margaret would never leave her dogs during an air raid." She was about to explain about Lady Walsingham, but the inspector interrupted her.

"Is visiting Mrs Clayton the only reason you came here?"

"What do you mean?"

"Perhaps you hoped to retrieve something."

He reached into his pocket and produced a silver cigarette case. He held it up for her to see and she stared in disbelief as she realised whom it belonged to.

"Where did you find that?" she stammered.

"On the floor beneath the sofa. It seemed to me rather more important than a pair of children's shoes and a blanket," he replied, then reading the inscription: "*To Raymond, With love, Dorothy.* I assume you are the Dorothy in question and that Raymond is the brother you mentioned."

"Yes. I bought him that as a gift for his twenty-first birthday." She could hear herself stammering as she tried to explain. "What was it doing here?"

"I was hoping you might be able to tell me. Was your brother acquainted with Miss Dubois?"

"No, I'm sure he wasn't," replied Dorothy, not feeling

very sure at all.

"But didn't you say that the cigarette card you found with her picture on it belonged to him?"

"Yes, but that doesn't mean anything. There was a pile of them. He's a collector, you see. As far as I know, the two of them have never met."

"He was also an admirer of Edith Devine."

"Yes, I told you that, but he wasn't at the theatre the night she died. He was working," insisted Dorothy, her mind racing, trying to think of an innocent explanation.

"Look, perhaps the cigarette case had been stolen. Come to think of it, I haven't seen him use it in an age."

The inspector ignored her. "Does your brother live with you?" he asked instead.

"Yes, usually, but not at the moment. He used to work for the Foreign Office, but now he's doing secret war work. I don't know where he is. It's a secret…" She trailed off and the maddening eyebrow shot up again.

"Well perhaps I may be able to ascertain his location. Now I think perhaps I should have a word with Mrs Clayton."

"All right," agreed Dorothy, relieved at the change of subject, although she had a feeling Mrs Clayton wouldn't be very keen on speaking to the inspector. "She didn't say much more except that they don't often see the landlord and that he has a female agent."

The inspector didn't look surprised or impressed by this news. "I'm sure, Miss Peto, but still, I should speak with her myself."

Inspector Derwent locked the door behind them and

pocketed the key, then Dorothy led him to the doorstep where Olive Clayton had been smoking. There was no sign of her, so she knocked on the door. There was no answer.

"She must have gone out," said Dorothy feeling disappointed.

"Or perhaps she saw me arrive and decided she would rather not repeat what she told you, to a real police officer."

Dorothy bridled at this remark. She knocked again on the door, more loudly this time.

"Mrs Clayton," she called out. She turned the handle; the door swung open. Dorothy gasped and recoiled in horror. The old woman's body was sprawled across the hallway. There was a pool of blood from a gash to her head and a broken brick next to her. The inspector knelt down and gently took hold of her wrist.

"Is she?" whispered Dorothy, hardly daring to believe it.

"Dead I'm afraid, Miss Peto," he replied as he rose to his feet and looked up and down the street.

"Did you see anyone else nearby when you were talking to her?"

Dorothy shook her head. "No, nobody. The street was deserted," she stammered.

"At least we know where the brick came from." He pointed to the gap beneath the windowsill of Elsa's house. "Wait here with her, while I go and get help. There should be a telephone I can use at the Royal Opera House. If anyone suspicious should approach you, blow your whistle and don't touch anything," he instructed and quickly began limping away. Dorothy lowered herself on to the step and tried to steady her breathing. Her mind had been fully occupied with trying to think how Raymond's cigarette case could possibly have ended up under Elsa's sofa and now this had happened. It seemed incredible that less than half an hour ago, she had been talking to this woman. Who could have done such a thing to a harmless old woman? Dorothy shuddered. Then Mary's words came echoing back to her.

Derwent always gets his man, or woman.

What if Inspector Derwent really thought she and Raymond were somehow involved?

After what seemed like an eternity, the inspector came around the corner.

"Close the door," he ordered when he got a little closer. "News is bound to spread. Soon we'll have half of Seven Dials here gawping at the poor creature."

Dorothy rose to her feet and did as he said, then turned to face him. "You don't think I killed her, do you?" she blurted out.

"I would hardly have left you here alone if I thought that, Miss Peto," he replied so calmly that she felt rather foolish. "Now are you sure you have told me everything that passed between the two of you?"

"Yes, yes. I think so," she replied although in truth her head was spinning so much she could barely recall her own name. In the distance, she could hear the bell of the approaching police van and shouts of customers spilling out from the pub at the end of the road, wanting to see what was going on. No doubt he would soon send her away, so the 'real' police could do their work.

"You don't think Elsa's death was suicide any longer, do you?" she asked urgently.

"I never did," he replied easily as he raised his stick so his men could see him above the gathering crowd.

"Well perhaps if you thought that way, you should have had one of your men watching the house," said Dorothy, a mixture of tiredness, shock and indignation making her sound more irritable than she meant to, but the inspector didn't taken offence.

He only nodded slowly. "You may be right, Miss Peto. Unfortunately, it seems that someone else was doing precisely that."

AS SHE HAD expected, Inspector Derwent thanked her for her time then made it very clear her presence was no longer required. She didn't argue; instead she jumped on the first bus she could find to take her to the Foreign Office. She needed to get in touch with Raymond and ask him about the cigarette case, before anyone else did. Unfortunately, when she got there, she found talking to the man behind the reception desk was as helpful as talking to one of the pigeons in Trafalgar Square.

"I am sorry, miss, but I am not at liberty to tell you the whereabouts of Mr Raymond Peto," he repeated for the third time.

"I am not asking you to, but it is vitally important I speak to him. I'm his sister. It's an absolute emergency," she insisted. Finally, after much deliberation and consultation with his superiors, he agreed to try to get a message to her brother.

On the bus back to Bloomsbury, Dorothy rested her throbbing head against the window, praying that the officious little man would keep his word.

"Cheer up, love. It might never happen," said the cheery, platinum-blonde conductor who punched her ticket. All the conductors and drivers were women these days. They were every bit as efficient as their predecessors and Dorothy found far friendlier.

She could hear the telephone ringing as she turned her latch key in the lock. Thanks to Raymond's position at the Foreign Office, one of these newfangled things had been installed a few months ago. At first, she'd been a little wary of it, but now she slammed the door behind her and she hurried to answer it. She almost collapsed with relief when she heard the operator telling her it was Raymond. Then she heard his voice down the line.

"Dorothy, what on earth is the matter? Has something happened to Ma and Pa?"

"No nothing like that," she quickly assured him. "Do you know where the cigarette case I bought you is?"

There was a pause at the end of the crackling line and for a second Dorothy thought they might have been cut off. Then Raymond began to speak, and she pressed the receiver closer to her ear.

"Actually, I do, old girl. I hope you don't mind, but I lent it to George. The poor chap had misplaced his, and Aunt Emily had sent me a new one when she heard I'd enlisted, so I said he could borrow the one you gave me. He's always been a bit hopeless, but I'm sure he'll return it as soon as he remembers."

"George Sledmere had it?"

"Yes. You don't mind very much, do you?"

"No, not at all. It's only that it was found by the police in a house where a young woman died."

"Good Lord! How on earth did it end up there? That explains why I also have a message to call Scotland Yard. Now, you mustn't worry, Dorothy old girl. I'll telephone the police first thing in the morning and set them straight about the whole thing. Must dash now. Take care and don't worry."

Dorothy replaced the receiver, relieved that her brother wasn't involved with Elsa Dubois in any way and that he had called her first, but even more confused about what he'd told her. George Sledmere was an old school friend of Raymond's. A good-natured if not terribly bright young man, who had spent so many summer holidays with the Petos, that he almost felt like one of the family.

Although he'd inherited his father's title and vast estate the previous year, George had been one of the first young men she knew to enlist. However, an infected gunshot wound to his right hand had seen him invalided back to England. She glanced at the clock on the wall. It wasn't too late to visit him, and then she might be able to find out what was going on before Raymond told Inspector Derwent about him. She pulled on her coat and hat and hurried out of the door.

Chapter Thirteen

THE SLEDMERES' LONDON home was in a smart white stucco terrace overlooking Regent's Park. An elderly, rather stuffy butler showed Dorothy into the library and informed her that he would tell his lordship she was here.

As she waited for George to appear she studied the silver framed photos lined up on his desk. There was one of him standing next to his mother and the late Lord Sledmere. Dorothy had once attended a house party at their estate in Yorkshire and found them a rather dour and serious pair, compared to their fun-loving son. There were several photos of George and Raymond in their tennis whites, rowing for their college and at the races. Finally, on the back row, there was a large photo of Edith Devine. Dorothy picked it up, assuming that like her brother, George was an admirer. The actress had signed it.

To George, With love, Gwen x

Dorothy frowned. Gwen was Edith's real name and didn't Inspector Derwent say she was from Yorkshire? She was still holding the photo when the door opened and in stepped the new Lord Sledmere. George was a well-built man, with thick blond hair and an open face that was almost always smiling.

"Hello there, Dorothy old girl. It's jolly nice to see you. You look very smart in that uniform. Raymond told me you had joined the police. Good show!"

"It's good to see you too. How's the hand?"

"Mending nicely," he declared confidently, but as Dorothy glanced discreetly down, she thought it still looked badly scarred and misshapen.

He came over and kissed her on the cheek. Then noticing the photo she was holding, his smile faded.

"Poor Gwen," he said with a sigh.

"Was she a friend of yours, George?"

"Yes, although not one that Mother and Father approved of. It was so terribly sad, her dying like that. She was so young and full of life. We'd known each other since we were children. She grew up on our estate. Her mother was one of our parlour maids before she had Gwen. When Gwen turned fifteen, Mother offered her the position of scullery maid. She said, 'Not likely! I don't want to spend my days scrubbing floors. I'm off to London to find fame and fortune'." George grinned at the memory. "You should have seen Mother's face."

Dorothy carefully replaced the photo. "When did you last see her?" she asked.

"Ha! You even sound like a policeman now. I say! Is that why you're here?" he asked looking startled.

Dorothy shook her head. "No, I'm here because of the cigarette case you borrowed from Raymond."

George flushed but he looked quite relieved. "Oh look, Dorothy, I'm terribly sorry, but I seem to have misplaced it.

I'll replace it of course. I know it was a gift from you. I was planning on getting the new one engraved so Raymond might not know the difference. I kept hoping one of the servants would find it, but it seems well and truly lost."

"It isn't lost. The police found it at a house in Seven Dials."

George suddenly grew very pale and he sank down on to the chair in front of his desk. Dorothy watched him closely. She had only ever known him look relaxed and jovial. It was unsettling to see him so worried.

"It was found close to the body of a Belgian national. Her name was Elsa Dubois," she said.

George shook his head slowly. "I should never have gone back," he said so quietly that Dorothy had to step closer to hear him. "But I was worried about her."

"Was she a friend of yours too, like Edith, I mean Gwen?" asked Dorothy.

He shook his head again. "Not exactly, but it's true I was fond of her and little Alice." He paused and ran his hand across his face. "Before I left Belgium, I was ordered to accompany Elsa and her little girl as they crossed the Channel. It was to be a favour to Mr Herman Muller, the German industrialist. My hand was too sore to be able to fire a gun, but I was perfectly mobile and they couldn't really spare anyone else. I don't mind telling you, Dorothy, I was rather taken with her." His face turned bright red as he looked shyly up at her. "She was terribly pretty and so charming. I sailed over with them in Muller's yacht from Ostend to Ramsgate. I tried my best to keep them entertained. I taught Alice how to play The Minister's Cat and I Spy, thought it might help her learn the lingo. When we arrived in Blighty, I escorted them to the Albion, the hotel Elsa had booked rooms in. The Granville is grander of course. I would have preferred to take them there, but it had been requisitioned by the army."

Dorothy frowned as she listened to George unburden himself. Why was Muller, the man who had been wooing Edith before she died, sending his yacht to bring another actress across the Channel?

"So, Muller hadn't arranged accommodation for her when she arrived in England? He wasn't there to meet her?" she asked.

"No. Although I think he may have sent her a gift. There was a silver perfume bottle full of her favourite scent waiting for her when we arrived. She seemed awfully happy about it. She was due to meet him later though." His hand flew to his mouth and he turned bright red. "Gosh, I shouldn't have said that. The whole thing was meant to be hush-hush."

"That's all right, George—I won't tell a soul. Did you stay there with them at the hotel?"

"No. I waited until she booked in, made sure all the luggage was taken to their suite, then I bid them farewell and took the next train to London."

"And you arranged to meet her again when she arrived here?"

"No, I never expected to see her again. In fact, my superior officer had been very clear. I was not to contact her in any way after I left her in Ramsgate."

"Why?" asked Dorothy.

"I don't know," replied George. He stood up and went

over to the mahogany sideboard and with a slightly shaking hand picked up the crystal decanter and poured himself a glass of whisky. She noticed he had started using his left hand since his injury. He silently offered her a drink too, but she shook her head. She was still puzzled.

"It seems rather a strange instruction. Why shouldn't you see her again? A young woman in a strange country would have been in need of friends. Didn't you ask your superior officer the reason?"

George gave her a wry smile. "Questioning an order isn't really the done thing, old girl."

"I suppose not. What happened next?"

George leant against the sideboard and took a large sip of his drink.

"A few days ago, I was walking through Covent Garden, with some chums. It was late. We had been to the music hall. I passed through Seven Dials and that's when I saw her. She was staring out of the doorway of this awfully dingy-looking place. It was dark, but there was a full moon. I recognised her immediately, but I was quite shocked, I can tell you. The place in Ramsgate wasn't grand, but it was respectable. I raised my hand from across the street and she smiled. I went over and asked what she was doing there, and she began to cry. Well, I didn't know what to do. The chaps I was with started shouting and joshing and generally making fools of themselves, so I promised I would return the next evening and see her."

"And did you?"

"Yes, I had this idea of taking her and Alice away from there and letting them stay here or perhaps taking them up to Yorkshire to stay with Mother—not that I'd spoken to her about it."

"What time did you visit her?"

"About eight, I'd say. It was dark. There was a light in the window of her place, but when I knocked on the door there was no answer. It was unlocked though, so I pushed open the door and that's when I saw her. She was lying on the floor. There was a smashed bottle next to her. I was almost certain she was dead, but I knelt down to take her pulse anyway. That must have been when the cigarette case fell out of the pocket in my overcoat. I'm afraid I panicked. I knew I couldn't help and if I said I'd found her, well it was bound to get out. I could have been court-martialled. So, like a coward, I ran away."

"Was Alice there?"

George looked indignant. "No, I would never have left her if she was, court-martial or no court-martial."

"Did you see anyone else as you were leaving?"

"There were a few people milling about. There was an old lady standing on her doorstep, but she was facing the other way, shouting at someone, and there were quite of lot of…" he flushed "…well you know, ladies of the night."

"Prostitutes," supplied Dorothy helpfully as George flushed again.

"Steady on, old girl."

"What was the old woman shouting about?" she asked.

"I don't really remember. 'You stay away. We don't want none of your sort around here.' That sort of thing. Whatever it was, it worked. He soon scuttled away."

After warning George that he could expect a visit from

Scotland Yard the next morning, Dorothy made her way back to Bloomsbury, mulling over everything he had told her. She believed his story, but it had left her with several unanswered questions. How was Muller connected to Elsa? She was sure George had described Olive Clayton, but who was she shouting at? Dorothy had a horrible feeling it could be Archibald Abbey, but poor Mrs Clayton was no longer here to ask.

THE NEXT MORNING, Dorothy was approaching the WPV's offices when she heard someone calling her name. She stopped and saw someone waving at her from the other side of the street.

"Mademoiselle Peto!" the young woman called again. It was Miss Leblanc from the Belgian Embassy. There was a sudden break in the traffic and she dashed across the street.

"Hello again. Is something wrong?" asked Dorothy.

"It's about Alice," Mis Leblanc replied a little breathlessly.

"Is she all right?"

"Oh yes, she is well. She is staying with the Sisters of St Andrew, a community of Belgian nuns near Earl's Court until we are able to reunite her with her family. I visit her regularly. She is eating and sleeping well. She hasn't spoken about her mother or what happened, but…" Miss Leblanc paused as she removed several sheets of paper from the leather satchel she was carrying. "She has been drawing a lot of pictures."

She handed the papers to Dorothy, who began flicking through.

"You see, they are all the same," explained Miss LeBlanc.

Dorothy nodded. It was true. Each childish drawing showed a figure with yellow hair lying down, a smaller figure also with yellow hair, holding something pink, and another figure, upright and drawn in black with a green scribble over their head.

"What do you think they mean?" she asked.

"I thought perhaps the two figures on the floor are Alice and her mother. Alice had a pink rabbit with her when she arrived at the embassy. Do you think perhaps, they might help?" asked Miss LeBlanc.

"I don't know. I hope so. Thank you for bringing them to me."

"Not at all, Miss Peto."

The Belgian woman turned to go, then paused. "There is something else. I don't know if it is important, but the clothes she was wearing."

"Yes?"

"Although they were rather dirty. They were of the best quality. I read the label inside her dress. It was from Harrods. It seemed a little odd to me; that is all."

Dorothy nodded and watched her go. She stood in the street thinking for a moment. The shoes had been good quality too. Had they come from Harrods? If so, then surely they had been bought after Elsa and Alice arrived in England. The question was who had bought them? The sound of tapping on glass interrupted her thoughts. She looked up and saw Nina waving at her from the first-floor window. She waved back and hurried up the steps to the office front door, taking the little girl's drawings with her.

"Hello there! Anything wrong? You looked like you were a million miles away down there in the street."

Dorothy glanced around the offices quickly. The two of them were alone apart from Jean Bagster who had fallen asleep reading the newspaper and was now snoring softly. Then she quickly explained everything that had happened over the last twenty-four hours. From Olive Clayton's death to George and the cigarette case, and now Alice's drawings.

"Good Lord! You've been living in quite the whirlwind," exclaimed Nina. "No wonder Mary couldn't find you yesterday."

"Oh dear, don't tell me she's on the warpath again?"

"Apparently, you were spotted arriving at the morgue with Inspector Derwent. There was much tutting and talk of getting under his feet."

Dorothy groaned. "I was going to take these drawings to Inspector Derwent. Perhaps I shouldn't."

"Fiddlesticks! You go." Nina peered at the pictures Dorothy had laid on the table. "These doodles might be vitally important for all we know. What's this green thing? It looks like a bird to me."

"I've no idea. It might not be anything and I don't want to risk getting kicked out. I love being part of the WPV but this investigation is the most interesting thing I have ever been involved in."

Nina looked unusually serious.

"I've told you it won't come to that. Look, Dorothy, if all these awful casualty figures tell us one thing it's that even when the war ends, life is not going to be how it was before. Women will still be needed, but we don't want to simply do basic policing, ticking prostitutes off and accompanying female prisoners to hospital—we want to do real policing. It may be too late for my generation, but not yours. Make a good impression, show Derwent how useful you can be. It could be the first step to them allowing us to be detectives one day. Imagine how improved our justice system would be if women were involved in investigating crimes, especially against other women."

Nina's eyes were gleaming. Dorothy knew she was probably imagining a day when there were female inspectors in every force in the country.

"Now off you go and don't worry about Sir and Miss Double D. Baggy and I will cover for you," she insisted grinning over to the chair where the older woman was snoozing peacefully.

ONCE AGAIN, DOROTHY found herself making her way through the warren of corridors in Scotland Yard until she reached the incident room next to the inspector's office. The door was wide open. Inspector Derwent was over on the far side of the room. He was on the telephone and had his back to her. There were four other detectives in there too, all either on the telephone or with their heads buried in large files. While everyone was distracted, Dorothy quietly snuck in and made her way over to the large blackboard that dominated one wall of the room.

Stuck in the middle was her cigarette card showing Elsa as well as a far more gruesome photo of her after she'd died. Alongside this picture were photos of Olive Clayton and Edith Devine. Dorothy frowned. What was she doing up there? There were various white chalk lines drawn across the blackboard along with dates and times and a list of names: Herman Muller, Victor Peeters, Raymond Peto (she was relieved to see her brother's name had a line drawn through it) and Lord George Sledmere.

"As you can see your brother has been ruled out of having any involvement in the death of Elsa Dubois, Miss Peto," said a voice behind her. Dorothy jumped and spun around. She'd been so absorbed in the blackboard she hadn't heard the inspector approach. "He telephoned me first thing this morning and explained that he had lent his cigarette case to a friend of his, Lord Sledmere."

"Have you spoken to George?" asked Dorothy.

"Yes, Sergeant Brook and I paid his lordship a visit straight after speaking to your brother. It was rather odd. His family's solicitor happened to be there with him when we arrived. It was almost like they were expecting us."

Dorothy felt her cheeks begin to burn and quickly changed the subject. "Why do you have Edith Devine's photo up there next to Mrs Clayton and Elsa Dubois?"

He paused for a moment before replying. "Do you remember when you brought the cigarette card to me, you said you thought there might be a connection between the two women?"

"I do. You said I was getting carried away simply because they were both actresses with the same initials."

"That is true. However, we have discovered there is another connection between them. Both ladies were…" he looked a little uncomfortable "…how shall I put it, close, to Herman Muller."

"The wealthy German industrialist?"

"Yes, although thanks to his friends in the Home Office, he is now a wealthy British industrialist."

"He's changed nationality already? Gosh, that was quick!" exclaimed Dorothy. Since seeing him at the theatre that night, she had been reading up on Mr Muller. He was a chemist who had made a fortune from his armament factories. The fact that he had moved to England and opened a factory here last spring had made the front pages.

"Quite," agreed the inspector. "Most of his fellow countrymen are in internment camps or have been deported. The only exceptions seem to be the extremely wealthy and well connected. Muller and Edith had been in a relationship. As I'm sure you recall he was the large gentleman you saw as you were leaving her dressing room. At about the same time, he was also arranging for his yacht to bring Elsa to England from Belgium. As well as property in Berlin and London, he also has a house in Brussels. When he lived there, he invested in various theatre productions. That's how he met Elsa."

"Then the evidence from Edith's maid at the inquest was correct. His visit was what prompted Edith to take her own life. She was heartbroken at the thought of him leaving her for Elsa," said Dorothy, wondering if she could have misread the actress's dismissive attitude towards him.

The inspector shrugged and only said, "Perhaps."

When it became clear he wasn't going to elaborate, Dorothy turned back to the blackboard.

"Who is the other man on your list, Victor Peeters?"

This question initiated a heavy sigh from the inspector.

"He is a man who is not only known to us, but also to many other police forces across Europe. For several years, he was one of the most notorious gangsters in Belgium. His activities included running protection rackets, prostitution, illegal gambling and the supply of drugs. A few years ago, he turned up on our shores. The Belgian police alerted us of course, but it seemed that having made his fortune abroad he wanted to go on the straight and narrow here. He bought several nightclubs, laundries and various properties in some of the less salubrious areas of our city. He became something of a slum landlord; in fact he owned the building where Elsa was found."

"Good heavens! Did they know each other?"

"You could say that. Thanks to the young lady I have just spoken to at the Belgian Embassy, I discovered that like Edith Devine, Elsa Dubois was only a stage name. Her real name was Elsa Peeters. She was Victor Peeters's wife. They separated when Alice was a baby. Elsa didn't want to raise a little girl with the threat of her father being carted off to jail at any minute and I think she was probably scared of some of Victor's associates. I imagine she knew the sort of men they were and was frightened they might use Alice to get to him, so she left him in Antwerp and moved to Brussels, changed her name, made a successful career for herself on the stage and won many admirers."

"Including Herman Muller," interrupted Dorothy.

The inspector nodded. "We understand Mr Peeters is a

very sick man. He has been in America these past few months seeking treatment. He was due to return last month on the *Lusitania* but luckily for him he was still too ill to travel. However, we now understand he is sailing back on the *Mauretania*. It's due to dock in Southampton at the end of the week."

"Do you think he could have been behind the death of his estranged wife?"

"That's what I hope to find out. In fact, there are several questions I should like to ask Mr Peeters. Not least why he allowed his only child to be housed in that hovel and end up begging on the streets. Even from a scoundrel like him, I would expect better. I also want to know what instructions he gave to Clara Fleurot while he has been away."

"Madame Chameleon works for him!" exclaimed Dorothy as realisation began to dawn. "That's why you were at the courtroom that day. You wanted to know if Clara would say anything about Victor Peeters."

"Clara is half Belgian and works for Victor Peeters. Amongst other things she has been in charge of running his laundries. However, since he went to America, his business interests have veered off the straight and narrow, the Belgian refugees being used as forced labour and the laundries being used as cover for the supply of drugs."

There was a sharp intake of breath from Dorothy. "You think that's where Edith got her drugs from. Clara delivered them to the theatre along with the clean laundry."

He acknowledged her interruption with a terse nod of the head. "We believe so, but as yet I have no evidence. What I wanted to know was whether it was Clara's idea to take advantage of the war and her boss's absence, or—as was suggested during her trial—was she acting under strict instructions from Victor. However, thanks to her habit of changing her appearance, Miss Fleurot is proving to be extremely elusive, so we may have to wait and speak to Peeters himself."

Dorothy nodded recalling Edith's maid had told the court how Clara was scared of her boss. She turned to the inspector. "You don't think Edith's death was an accident either, do you? That's why her photograph is on the blackboard."

"It was reported that Edith died from an overdose of cocaine. However, that isn't entirely true. She was a regular user of the drug. She kept her supply hidden in a powder compact. On the night she died the cocaine had been mixed with cyanide."

"Good heavens! She died from cyanide poisoning too!" exclaimed Dorothy.

"Yes, although we ensured it wasn't reported in the newspapers. The coroner believed that she was so distressed after Herr Muller's visit, she added the poison to her drugs before putting it up her nose. A supply of cyanide was kept in the caretaker's cupboard; he used it for fumigation purposes. It was next to her dressing room and was unlocked that evening."

"Did you find her fingerprints in the cupboard? Did you check for them?"

"Yes, of course we checked for them," he replied tersely. "There were none except the caretaker's, but he wasn't at the theatre that night. The coroner accepted the explanation that she may have worn gloves. As you know suicide is illegal. If that had been the ruling, the case might have drawn even more attention."

"But I don't understand. Someone else could have added cyanide to her cocaine. Why didn't you continue investigating?"

The inspector didn't reply immediately; instead he drummed his fingers against his bad leg for a moment. Dorothy had noticed that he often did this when he was deep in thought.

"Let me put it this way, Miss Peto. I was informed by my superiors that any case involving Herr Muller should not be investigated too deeply. It wouldn't do for someone who was about to proudly announce becoming a British citizen to have his name connected to the death of an actress."

"My goodness what a web of intrigue," murmured Dorothy.

"Indeed, Miss Peto," agreed the inspector. "Now I have shared some of my information perhaps you would be so kind as to share what you have there in your hand. I assume it is the reason for your visit."

"Oh yes," replied Dorothy quickly. She'd almost forgotten why she was there. "These are some of Alice's drawings. The lady from the Belgian Embassy gave them to me. She thought they might be helpful, as she still won't speak about what happened."

"So I hear. The nuns have refused us permission to interview her until she does. Why didn't the woman from the embassy come here and bring them to me herself?"

"Miss LeBlanc is a respectable young woman. She

wouldn't want to be seen entering Scotland Yard when she could simply pass them on to an acquaintance in the street," explained Dorothy patiently, handing the drawings to the inspector.

"I could have gone to her," he said almost to himself as he began looking at the pictures. Dorothy held her breath half expecting him to scoff, or scrumple them up and throw them in the bin, but instead he studied each one carefully, then went over and tacked them on to the blackboard.

"Listen up please, lads," he said loudly. "Miss Peto of the WPV and cigarette card fame has brought us another piece of evidence. As you know we haven't been able to talk to Elsa's little girl, but Miss Peto here has brought us some of her drawings."

There was a murmur of interest around the room. Dorothy felt embarrassed as the detectives nodded politely to her. They looked to be in their fifties or sixties. Perhaps they even had daughters her age. She briefly wondered if the inspector was married or had children while the other detectives came and crowded around Alice's drawing.

"Over to you, Miss Peto," said Inspector Derwent.

Nervously, Dorothy removed a pencil from her pocket and used the end to point at the picture. "Well, gentlemen, it seems quite obvious that the figure on the floor is Elsa and the small figure with the pink object is Alice herself holding her toy rabbit. I'm not sure about the other figure, but it does look like they are in the room too, not outside. Miss Boyle, one of my colleagues, wondered if this green squiggle above the figure's head could be a bird. Do any of Elsa's neighbours own a parrot or a budgerigar perhaps?" Her enquiry was met with blank expressions and the inspector almost looked uncomfortable.

"We haven't been able to speak to all of Miss Dubois and Mrs Clayton's neighbours as yet. It seems many of them work irregular hours. Taylor, Jones, get yourselves back down to Seven Dials. See if anyone knows anything about a green bird."

"Miss LeBlanc also mentioned Alice's dress was from Harrods," said Dorothy, suddenly remembering the last part of their conversation.

"As were her shoes," agreed the inspector. "Brook, take yourself off to Knightsbridge and find out if a receipt was made out for a child's dress or shoes to anyone linked to our inquiry. Clark, you stay here and man the telephones and keep trying those nuns. The little girl must start speaking at some point."

Following a chorus of "Yes, sirs," the other detectives grabbed their coats and disappeared, except for the oldest one, who returned to his desk. Inspector Derwent turned to leave too.

"Where are you going, Inspector?" asked Dorothy.

"I have an appointment to see Mr Muller or whatever he's calling himself now."

"But all your officers are engaged. Won't you need someone to take notes for you, Inspector?"

He gave her a quizzical look. "Should I assume your previous work reporting on court cases has led to you being a quick and efficient note taker, Miss Peto?"

"Well one doesn't like to blow one's own trumpet, Inspector," she replied giving him her sweetest smile.

"Come along then," he replied with a sigh.

Dorothy hurried after him, thrilled that she had taken Nina's advice and come here. However, her euphoria was short-lived. As the inspector held the front door open for her, he raised his hat and nodded to someone on the other side of the hallway. Dorothy turned to see Sir Edward Henry and behind him Margaret and Mary. The former looked at her with confusion, the latter utter fury.

Dorothy lowered her head and hurried outside before either of them could say anything, but she was sure she'd hear plenty about the matter later.

Chapter Fourteen

Herman Muller looked exactly the same as he had on the night Dorothy saw him backstage at the theatre. He reminded her of a well-fed walrus. He nodded when Inspector Derwent made the introductions but did not invite them to sit down in his lavish Mayfair office. Dorothy held her small notepad in her hand with pencil poised.

"Mr Muller, we should like to ask you a few questions about the Belgian actress Elsa Dubois. She was an acquaintance of yours, I believe," the inspector began.

The walrus puffed out his chest. "My name is now Henry Miller, Inspector. If the king can change his name from Battenberg to Mountbatten, then so can I."

"Very well, Mr Miller. We understand you arranged for Elsa Dubois to leave Belgium on your yacht."

"That is correct. I admired her work on the stage. I had heard she and her daughter wanted to leave Belgium. However, I did not know her well. I have not seen her since she arrived in England."

"Are you aware that Miss Dubois was found dead during the recent Zeppelin air raid?"

Miller shifted a little in his seat and cast his eyes down. "Yes, I was sad to hear so. I was surprised to hear she was in a place such as Seven Dials. I believed her to be living on the coast. At the seaside, as you like to say."

"We believe she may have died of an overdose of cocaine. Can you tell us anything about that?"

Miller's head snapped back up. Dorothy was surprised too. The doctor had said her death was caused by cyanide.

"I hope you are not suggesting I associate with degenerates and criminals, Inspector Derwent. I do not like these questions you ask. Perhaps I should telephone your Sir Edward Henry," said Miller, his face now a deep shade of red. The inspector looked as though he was about to issue a retort.

Instinctively, Dorothy stepped in. "I'm so sorry if we offended you, Mr Miller. It's just that we desperately want to find out what happened to Elsa. For the sake of her young child, if no one else. We should be grateful for any information you have, however insignificant it may seem," she said gently.

Miller inclined his head and appeared mollified. "Very well, young lady, although as I said, I only knew Miss Dubois in a professional capacity. Whatever gossip you may have heard, there was no personal relationship whatsoever, you understand."

Dorothy nodded. The inspector had explained on the way over that Miller desperately hoped to receive a knighthood in the next honours list. Dorothy couldn't imagine what he'd done to deserve one, but she knew any whiff of scandal would put an end to his hopes. She gave the walrus an understanding smile.

"Of course not, Mr Miller but are you positive you did

not see Miss Dubois after she arrived in England?" she asked, remembering what George had told her.

"Absolutely," he replied adamantly.

"Did you ever happen to hear Miss Dubois talk about needing to take medication for her nerves?"

Miller gave a firm shake of his head, causing his jowls to wobble.

"No. She always seemed to be a very sensible, level-headed woman." He glared at Inspector Derwent. "I would be extremely surprised if the inspector's theory about cocaine turned out to be correct."

"You don't think that she was depressed about having to leave Belgium and perhaps that instead of drowning her sorrows, as some might, she turned to something a little stronger?" pressed Dorothy.

Muller made a face as if something unpleasant had been wafted beneath his nose. "Elsa did not drown her sorrows, as you say. Occasionally she would take a glass of champagne on opening night, but never in front of little Alice."

"You're a patron of the arts, I take it, Mr Miller."

"You could say so, young lady," he agreed, seeming to like this description of himself.

"We have a great many talented actresses here in London," she began, wondering if she could get him to mention Edith at all. "Do you go to the West End theatres very often?"

His eyes narrowed. "Not as often as I would like. Now if you will excuse me, I am a very busy man."

It was clear their interview was over. Dorothy slipped her notepad back in her pocket and followed Inspector Derwent out of the door. As they made their way out of Miller's grand office building, the inspector didn't say a word. Dorothy wondered if she had offended him. She glanced across. His brow was creased in concentration and this mouth was set in a thin line. He did look cross, but then he often looked that way. Dorothy decided it would be easier if she apologised, so they could move on to discussing the case.

"I'm sorry if you think I overstepped the mark by interrupting your questions. I only wanted to help."

He looked at her, still frowning. "What? No, not at all. I was pleased you stepped in—he clearly took exception to my line of questioning."

"Why did you ask him about cocaine when we know both women were killed by cyanide?"

"I'm not sure. To see his reaction, I suppose. I was unable to interview him following the death of Edith. I had to make do with a statement from his solicitor, but it was widely reported that she had died of a drugs overdose. I also assume that he may have heard we found traces of cocaine when Elsa died too. He admits to being acquainted with both actresses, yet he appears to be offended by the suggestion that he would associate with drug users. I did wonder if he used the stuff himself. I hear there's a hare-brained theory that it makes you more productive."

"If he did, perhaps he wanted both women dead to stop them saying anything. That would give him a motive. The king couldn't very well knight a rumoured drug user."

"Perhaps."

"What did you think of him?"

"Not a great deal. In my opinion, any man who can

change his nationality so quickly is not to be trusted. Where is his sense of loyalty? If war had broken out while he was in France, I am sure he would now be calling himself Monsieur Henri, and whatever Miller is in French."

"Moulinier," supplied Dorothy. "I think it's obvious he isn't telling the truth about his relationship with Elsa. He said he didn't know her well, but then he was absolutely certain she wouldn't take drugs and he knew she would never drink in front of Alice." She wanted to add that he'd lied about seeing Elsa in Ramsgate, but she didn't know how without betraying George's confidence.

"Also, how did he know she died in Seven Dials, but we didn't release that information to the press? We said she was found in the Covent Garden area," continued the inspector.

Dorothy stopped in her tracks as a thought occurred to her. The inspector stopped too and gave her a questioning look.

"What if Miller is Alice's father? We don't know for sure when they met, do we?" she asked.

"It's a possibility I suppose, but to quote you, why would he kill the mother of his child?"

"Elsa could have been blackmailing him. He needed to keep her quiet. Perhaps he's planning on offering to be Alice's guardian when all the interest around her mother's death has calmed down. Or maybe Victor heard she'd been unfaithful to him and had her killed in a fit of jealousy."

"Perhaps," he sighed, "but rather than dealing in wild hypotheticals, I think we should concentrate on facts. Such as the fact that thanks to Lord Sledmere, your brother's cigarette case was found close to Elsa Dubois's body and that his lordship also visited Miss Devine on the night she died."

"He did?" she asked in surprise. George hadn't mentioned this to her.

"He did," confirmed the inspector. "Thank you for your assistance. Good day, Miss Peto." And with that he tipped his hat to her and walked away. Dorothy stood and watched him go. It was so frustrating. Whenever she thought he was including her in the investigation, he shut her out again.

WHEN SHE FINALLY returned to the WPV offices later that day, she found an anxious-looking Lucy waiting for her.

"Mary and Margaret want to see you. They are in the commandant's office," she whispered urgently.

Dorothy felt her heart sink. She'd forgotten about them seeing her at Scotland Yard. She knocked on the door and pushed it open. "Hello," she said. "Did you want to see me?"

Three sets of eyes turned to look at her. Mary was leaning against Margaret's desk, her arms folded and her mouth set in a stern line. Margaret had one of her spaniels on her knee and seemed almost as anxious as Lucy. On the other side of the room, Nina was smoking a cigarette, looking mutinous.

"Yes, we did. Do you mind telling us exactly what you were doing with Inspector Derwent today? We were told you had a headache," demanded Mary, shooting an angry look at Nina, who simply shrugged and said, "She must have recovered."

Mary scowled and turned her fire back on Dorothy.

"The commandant and I saw you with our own eyes. There's no point in denying it."

"I wasn't going to…" protested Dorothy, but Mary hadn't finished.

"Margaret and I were there to update Sir Edward on how successful our recent patrols of the royal parks had been. Naturally, when he saw you with one of his most senior detectives, he wanted to know what you were doing, and we couldn't tell him. It was most embarrassing."

"I'm sorry, Mary. I was only accompanying the inspector to act as his secretary. He needed someone to take notes when he interviewed a witness. All his own detectives were busy."

"Oh well that seems quite proper," replied Margaret, smiling in obvious relief. "Taking notes is quite harmless and certainly in our remit of assisting, don't you think, Robert?"

"The point is we should have been informed," argued Mary. "After all, you are commandant of the WPV, Margaret."

Behind Mary's back, Nina was rolling her eyes. Dorothy could see she was probably about to say something that would only make the situation worse. Some grovelling and ego boosting was in order.

"Mary, you are quite right—and I'm sorry, Margaret. I should have kept you both informed, but there simply wasn't time. The lady from the Belgian Embassy asked me to take some drawings Alice had done to Scotland Yard. Then the inspector asked for my help, and I didn't want to disappoint him, especially when you had explained how well regarded he is."

Mary began to look slightly mollified, so Dorothy continued with something that had been bothering her.

"Actually, Mary, I think you may be able to assist Inspector Derwent with his investigation too. Do you recall when Madame Chameleon was arrested at the station?"

"Of course."

"Do you remember if she was wearing any scent?"

"I do as a matter of fact. I have an extremely keen nose. I've often thought I would have made an exceptionally good sommelier, if such a thing were allowed."

"Or a bloodhound," Dorothy heard Nina mutter behind them. Fortunately Mary did not hear and continued speaking.

"I remember as I grabbed hold of her, she absolutely reeked of Yardley's April Violets. In fact, she must have drenched her wrists in the stuff because I could still smell it on my hand afterwards."

"You are sure it was April Violets?"

"Absolutely. I can't stand the stuff. Margaret's mother wears it. I thought it would be rather amusing to tell Lady Walsingham that she and a known criminal had similar tastes. A foreign criminal at that!"

Margaret gave a little tinkling laugh, pleased the tension in the room had been broken.

"Oh, Robert, you are dreadful! But you are quite right—Mother would be horrified to think she and Madame Chameleon wore the same perfume. Do you recall when we first saw her, Dorothy? Mother said no member of the Red Cross would wear such an extravagant green feathered hat."

Dorothy stared at her open-mouthed. "Oh my goodness,

Margaret. You are a genius!"

"Am I?"

"Yes! Alice wasn't drawing a bird. That green feathery things was Clara's hat."

"You mean Madame Chameleon could be involved in Elsa's death?" asked Nina.

"Yes, I'm sure I could smell her perfume when we found Elsa's body too. And it's not just Elsa. She was also at the theatre the night Edith died. The inspector told me she worked for a gangster, and she's involved with supplying cocaine. You and I saw how violent she could be, Mary."

"Yes indeed," agreed Mary her hand instinctively travelling to where Clara had hit her on the mouth.

"Margaret, would it be all right if I used the telephone to call Inspector Derwent?" asked Dorothy.

"Yes, yes, no need for permission," replied Margaret cheerfully as she produced a tin from her drawer and opened it to reveal a Dundee cake. "I must say, this is all terribly exciting."

As Dorothy waited for the operator to put her through, she was convinced they had unravelled at least part of the mystery of Alice's drawing, but as she began to explain, the inspector didn't sound so certain.

"I can't arrest a woman because of the sort of hat she wears, Miss Peto."

"But..."

"Or on the strength of a child's scribblings. Or because of the perfume she wears. Or because the WPV have taken a dislike to her because she attacked one of your members."

"What about the fact that she is a known criminal involved in the supply of drugs, that she works for the man Elsa was married to and she was at the theatre on the night Edith died?" pressed Dorothy, aware that the other three were straining their ears trying to hear what he was saying to her.

"I'm sorry, Miss Peto," said the inspector sounding weary. "I appreciate your enthusiasm, but it's not enough."

"No good?" asked Nina, as Dorothy replaced the receiver with a sigh of disappointment.

"Not enough apparently," she said.

"Well, Topsy, Skip, Herbert and I definitely think you are on the right track, Dorothy," said Margaret cheerfully as she shared a slice of cake with her salivating dogs.

THAT NIGHT DOROTHY lay awake in bed thinking about the case. What the inspector had said kept going round in her mind like a broken gramophone recording. *It's not enough.* The more she thought about it, the more convinced she became that Madame Chameleon was involved in Elsa's death. But how could she prove it? They knew she was capable of winning the trust of vulnerable young women, but surely she couldn't be acting alone. What could be her motive? She must be working for someone, but who?

It bothered Dorothy that the inspector still seemed to think George could be involved. Why hadn't he told her he'd seen Edith the night she died? He knew she was trying to help him. Dorothy groaned and kicked her covers off. It was no good. She had too many thoughts running around her head. Perhaps if she wrote them down, they would start to make sense.

She got up and went over to her dressing table. She retrieved a sheet of paper and a pen from a drawer and pushed her vanity set to one side to make room. Then she stopped and stared at the set. Her parents had given it to her as a gift when she left home. It was similar, if not as elaborate as the one she'd found in Elsa's bedroom. There was a comb, a brush, a hand mirror, several silver-topped jars, a compact and a scent bottle neither of which she used, but Elsa did. All the clothes in her trunk had smelt of Narcisse Noir and George had said someone had sent her a silver bottle of her favourite perfume but there was no sign of it on her dressing table. Nor was there a compact, but that awful doctor had said she had tried to hide her skin rash with face powder.

A shiver of excitement went through her. Could a missing compact and scent bottle be the key to solving this case?

There was no possibility of her getting to sleep now and outside it was already beginning to grow light. She quickly dressed and made her way over to Scotland Yard. It was a little after eight when she arrived and she was relieved to hear that Inspector Derwent was already at his desk. Despite the hour, he didn't look particularly surprised when she entered his office.

"How can I help you, Miss Peto?" he asked.

"Good morning, Inspector. It's about Elsa's dressing table," she began.

"Would you like to take a seat, Miss Peto?"

"No thank you. There was no compact," she continued. "The doctor said she used face powder to cover her rash, but there was no compact on the dressing table. Did you find one?"

The inspector placed his pen down and studied her for a second, then he began searching through a pile of papers on his desk. He selected a sheet and ran his eyes down it. "No, we did not."

"What about a silver perfume bottle, quite ornate I should imagine, and containing Narcisse Noir?"

Again the inspector consulted the list and shook his head.

"Well then someone must have taken them. Which means they must be important," declared Dorothy triumphantly. "The doctor said Elsa had been using face powder to cover her skin condition and I smelt perfume in her bedroom."

The inspector nodded.

"Lord Sledmere mentioned Elsa receiving a perfume bottle as a gift when she arrived in Ramsgate." He leant back in his chair and began drumming his fingers on the desktop. "Perhaps she sold them or pawned them. Money or lack of it had clearly become an issue for her," he suggested.

Dorothy felt her heart sink. In her excitement, she hadn't considered this possibility.

"Did you find a receipt or pawn ticket?"

The inspector rose to his feet and went to open the door.

"No, but thank you, Miss Peto. My men and I shall look into it."

Dorothy felt her shoulders droop in disappointment. She had half hoped the inspector would ask her to assist him, but perhaps she was getting carried away with herself. No doubt that's what Mary would say. Reluctantly she left Scotland Yard and made her way back to the offices of the WPV.

That morning she and Lucy were scheduled to patrol Hyde Park. She suppressed a yawn as the two of them set off. She was beginning to agree with Nina about these patrols. Now the tidal wave of refugees coming into the city had ebbed away, her work mainly seemed to involve moving prostitutes on and discouraging courting couples from being overly affectionate in public. Mary and a few of the others had begun to see themselves as some sort of moral guardians. They had begun admonishing schoolgirls they thought were loitering near groups of young soldiers. Mary even reduced one poor little thing to tears when she told her that she should not crimp her hair or wear her hat at a jaunty angle.

Chapter Fifteen

BY FIVE O'CLOCK that evening, Dorothy was quite exhausted and regretting not getting any sleep the previous night. When she returned to her flat, she undressed and collapsed into her bed, but no sooner had her head touched the pillow than the telephone in the hallway began to ring. With a groan she threw back the covers and hurried to answer it.

"Dorothy, what's going on?"

It was Raymond.

"What do you mean?"

"I had another message to call that inspector fellow from Scotland Yard."

"Inspector Derwent."

"Yes, I've just spoken with him. He told me George has been arrested on suspicion of murder."

"Oh no!" gasped Dorothy flopping down on to the armchair next to the telephone table.

"They want me to come back to London to make a statement about the cigarette case. I've cleared it with my superiors, and I've been granted twenty-four hours' leave. I'm catching the eight o'clock train and I should be with you by ten."

"All right. I'll try to find out what's happening. Safe journey."

Dorothy replaced the receiver and stared at it for a second, then picked it up again and prayed the inspector hadn't left for the evening. He hadn't.

"Is it true that you have arrested George Sledmere?" she demanded as soon as she heard his voice.

"Good evening, Miss Peto. I assume you have spoken to your brother, so you already know that to be true."

"But why? Just because he knew Edith and Elsa?"

She heard him sigh heavily.

"There's more, I'm afraid, Miss Peto. When my officers and I conducted a search of Lord Sledmere's home, we found an amount of cocaine and morphine in his bedroom. Were you aware he uses drugs?"

Dorothy was shocked into silence. Not only by this news, but also that he hadn't told her he was planning to search George's house when she'd seen him that morning.

"No," she admitted as she tried to think of an innocent explanation, "but his hand was badly injured. Perhaps he needed them to manage the pain."

"He said something similar," conceded the inspector.

"Well then, there you have it."

"It doesn't change the fact that he was with both women on the night they died. Nor has he been able to explain why he didn't report Elsa's death."

"But it doesn't make any sense. What about a motive? George was fond of both women. Why would he possibly want to kill either of them?"

"That's what I hope to find out. Good evening, Miss Peto."

"But…" Dorothy began to protest, but he'd hung up. Despite all her hopes it was clear he didn't see her as being part of his team. She acknowledged this thought with a pang of disappointment, but then pushed it to one side. She knew George hadn't killed either woman and with or without the inspector she was determined to prove it.

After her conversation with Inspector Derwent, she'd abandoned any hope of catching up on some sleep and instead set about preparing her brother a cottage pie for supper. As she pummelled the potatoes, she tried to think how she could help George. She was convinced Madame Chameleon must be involved, but that she was working for someone. Herman Muller seemed to her the most likely candidate. Dorothy didn't trust him and he had a reason to want both actresses silenced. He could easily have met Clara at the theatre, realised that she supplied Edith with drugs and bribed her to do his dirty work, especially if he knew Clara could get close to Elsa as she worked for Victor Peeters. If only the inspector had arrested Clara as she'd suggested.

As he'd predicted, her brother arrived back at the flat a little before ten o'clock that evening. Dorothy thought how tired and pale he looked. Although he hungrily ate all the food she put in front of him, he barely said a word and seemed irritated when she broached the subject of how they could best help George.

"We both know George is going to be hopeless at defending himself," she began. "We need to find something to push the inspector away from him and towards another suspect, like Muller. George said Elsa coming over on his yacht was meant to be hush-hush. He won't say any more. I don't suppose you know why, do you?"

"I'm sorry, Dorothy, but I can't divulge any information I may have on Mr Muller and we really should be calling him Miller."

"All right, but if we could give Derwent a motive for Miller…"

"For heaven's sake, Dorothy! You know I can't discuss Foreign Office business with you. I've signed the Official Secrets Act, damn it." He stood up abruptly and began pacing up and down.

"Even if it means saving George?"

"Yes," he almost shouted before flopping back down into his chair. "He's my oldest friend and I want to help him, but not if it means betraying my country's secrets."

They were both silent for a moment. Dorothy was shocked at her brother's reaction. He hardly ever raised his voice. Whatever this secret work of Raymond's was, it was obviously exhausting him.

Dorothy was the first to speak again.

"How about if I ask you three questions and if I'm on the right track, you nod your head. That way you don't need to say a word."

Raymond closed his eyes and sighed heavily. "All right. That might work," he agreed reluctantly.

"First question. Why was George asked to accompany Elsa to Miller's boat?"

Raymond rolled his eyes. "How am I meant to nod my head to that?"

"Oh yes, sorry. I'll try again. Was George escorting her

because Elsa was bringing something important with her? Something important to Muller, sorry Miller."

Raymond nodded.

"Did Miller meet Elsa when she arrived in Ramsgate?"

He nodded again.

"That's when she gave him whatever it was she'd brought. That was the secret part George referred to, yes?"

Another nod of the head.

"Then he told her he couldn't see her again because he couldn't afford a scandal?"

Raymond held up his hand to silence her. "That's enough. That's your three questions. We shouldn't discuss the matter any more. I'm going to bed. Goodnight and thank you for supper."

He rose and dropped a quick kiss on top of her head.

"Goodnight. Sleep well," she called after him.

After clearing away the pots, she too went to bed. Her head had been full of George and how best to help him all night, but as she drifted off her thoughts switched to little Alice. Surely if she had been there when George arrived, he would have found her and looked after her, so she must have run away before he appeared. But what or who had scared her so much that she would flee alone into a strange city?

THE NEXT MORNING, Dorothy waited outside Scotland Yard while Raymond went to make his statement.

"Shall I come with you?" she'd asked.

He'd looked horrified. "No. I don't want them to think I

need my big sister to hold my hand. Besides, they might talk more freely if I'm alone."

However, less than ten minutes later, he was back, looking disappointed.

"That was quick," said Dorothy. "What did Inspector Derwent ask you?"

"Nothing. I didn't see him. One of his sergeants took my statement. Clark, I think his name was."

"Is George still being held there? Did they ask you about his character? Would they let you see him?"

"They wouldn't tell me anything. Just thanked me for my time. I'm sorry, Dorothy. I know I've been like a bear with a sore head. I promise to be more cheerful when I'm next home on leave."

He hugged her tightly then hailed a taxicab to take him to the station. Dorothy watched him drive away. He may not be fighting on the front line but this war had aged her little brother just the same.

When he'd gone, she made her way into Scotland Yard. The desk sergeant was speaking on the telephone and had his back to her, so she slipped past and made her way upstairs. As she took the now familiar route to the incident room, she could hear raised voices. They were coming from Inspector Derwent's office. She tiptoed towards the door and listened. It was George who was shouting, "Upon my honour, I never laid a finger on Elsa."

"Your honour?" replied the more controlled voice of Inspector Derwent. "Was it honourable to discover the body of a dead woman and not report it, Lord Sledmere?"

"No, I'm sorry about that, but as I have tried to explain,

you see, I didn't want anyone to know I'd been there…"

"Why? Because you'd killed her?"

"No!"

"What about Edith Devine, or Gwen as you knew her? Did you behave honourably towards her?"

"Always."

"Even when she turned you down on the night she died?"

"I told you, I barely spoke to her that night. I called into her dressing room and offered to take her out for dinner after the performance, but she said she had a prior engagement."

"Yes, with Mr Muller. Did that make you jealous, Lord Sledmere?"

"No, of course not. I have told you a hundred times, Gwen was a childhood friend. We'd known each other for years. She came to my father's funeral for heaven's sake."

"Did you know she regularly took cocaine?"

"Yes, no, I mean, she was always a bit wild. She liked to have a good time."

"Did you introduce her to the drug? Are you responsible for her becoming addicted?"

"No! I would never do anything to hurt Gwen, I swear upon my life."

"A young man like yourself must have found it frustrating that two such attractive young women turned you down for Muller."

"They didn't turn me down. I didn't…"

"You've just admitted Edith did. What about Elsa? After spending time with you alone on the yacht, she was still planning on seeing Muller as soon as she arrived in Ramsgate. She was planning on seeing him, wasn't she?"

"I can't tell you."

"Can't or won't, Lord Sledmere? Is it too difficult to admit Elsa preferred another man?"

"It wasn't like that. Why won't you believe me?"

Dorothy winced at the desperation in his voice. She crept back down the corridor, took a seat outside the incident room and waited, feeling wretched. She should have listened to her mother. She'd always said no good ever came from eavesdropping. No wonder Inspector Derwent had a reputation for always getting his man. He was a fearsome interrogator; controlled and unrelenting. Yet it seemed wrong to her that he was so hard on George, who had been injured fighting for his country, when he had to treat a man like Miller with kid gloves.

The minutes ticked by slowly. The silence was occasionally punctuated by the shrill ring of a telephone or a raised voice from the incident room. Dorothy spent the time organising in her head what she wanted to say to the inspector, so she could help George without betraying Raymond. Finally, the door opened and George walked out. Although he kept his head down, it was clear he'd been crying. He was handcuffed to a uniformed officer who led him down the corridor away from Dorothy and towards the cells. The inspector followed them out and stopped when he saw Dorothy. His expression was inscrutable as he silently beckoned her forward.

"Good morning, Miss Peto," he said sounding a little weary, as she followed him into his office.

"I've had an idea, Inspector," began Dorothy.

"By the tone of your voice, Miss Peto, it sounds as though you are about to share this idea with me."

"I am and when you've heard it, I think you'll realise George isn't your man," she insisted. The inspector leant back in his chair. His expression was sceptical, but it looked like he was prepared to listen, so she hurried on. "I don't think Muller or Miller or whatever he calls himself arranged for Elsa to come over here because of the goodness of his heart. I think he wanted her to bring something with her, something important, something that would ensure his request to become a British national was granted. If Elsa was as close to him as we believe she was, she would have easily been able to access his desk or even his safe at his house in Brussels. That's why George Sledmere was sent. Not to escort her, but to safeguard what she was carrying. When she arrived in England, Muller secretly met her. He collected whatever it was he wanted, perhaps gave her enough money to stay in the Ramsgate boarding house for a few months, but told her he didn't want to see her again. Then when she turned up in London, he killed her or had her killed because he saw her as a liability."

"Do you have any evidence to support this theory, Miss Peto?" asked the inspector.

Dorothy opened her mouth then closed it again. She longed to tell him about her conversation with her brother, but she couldn't betray Raymond's trust.

"No, not exactly, but it seemed to fit in with the rush to make him a British citizen and everything else. Surely you must think it's worth investigating. It could prove George's innocence."

The inspector surveyed her for a moment.

"Not necessarily. Even if there is something in this theory you seem to have come up with since your brother returned home. It doesn't necessarily mean Sledmere didn't kill her; in fact it gives him a motive. If this unknown item she brought across the Channel was so vital, Sledmere could have killed her to ensure her silence."

Dorothy's shoulders drooped. She had been so fixated on finding another suspect she hadn't thought of this and, like Raymond, if George knew what Elsa was carrying and was asked, he would refuse to discuss it, even with the police.

"But I've known him for years. He's a good man and I'm sure you could find a hundred people who would tell you the same."

"Miss Peto, if I had a guinea for every time a man under arrest had a friend swear to their good character, I could have retired long ago."

"What about Alice? Last night I was thinking about her. Someone or something must have frightened her, to make her run away. She knew George. She liked him. He's very good with children. He taught her parlour games on the voyage over here."

"I suppose you are going to suggest a petite young woman like Clara Fleurot is far more frightening."

"Well, I have seen how fearsome she can be first-hand, but actually no, I've thought of someone much worse."

The inspector looked up in surprise. "Who?"

Dorothy pushed a neatly folded paper across the table towards him. "Archibald Abbey. I've written down his name and the date he was on trial for assaulting a young girl. I saw him myself in the area and two local women confirmed that he hangs around the place. Last night, I had the horrible thought that…"

She trailed off as the inspector read her note.

"I'll pass this on to Brook to look into."

"What about the powder compact and the perfume bottle? Have you managed to find them?" asked Dorothy eager to find out all she could before he sent her on her way.

"Yes, as a matter of a fact we have. There was no trace of any receipts or pawn tickets in Elsa's belongings; however, after speaking with you, I sent my men back to Olive Clayton's house. There they found a substantial amount of money under her mattress and a ticket for a local pawnbroker's. When they paid the establishment a visit, they found both the compact and the perfume bottle and the owner gave them a description that matched Mrs Clayton. She pawned them the morning after the air raid."

"Why on earth did she have them?" asked Dorothy in surprise.

"My theory is, she saw Alice run away, hence her comment to you in the underground of 'she's back, is she?', which struck me as an odd thing to say. I believe she went to investigate why the little girl had run away, found Elsa's body and rather than alert the authorities, decided to pilfer her dead neighbour's belongings."

"And to think I felt sorry for her. What a dreadful woman!"

"And cunning too! She made sure to tell you about the spare key. Then if we discovered the compact and bottle was missing, she could tell us she'd seen you letting yourself in."

Dorothy's hand flew to her mouth. "Oh my goodness. I thought I was being clever looking for clues, but in fact I was a total fool."

"Don't take it too badly, Miss Peto. You won't be the first police officer that a criminal has tricked, and it did her no good in the end. I have no doubt that the theft was the reason she was killed." He stood up and Dorothy felt sure he was about to dismiss her again, but instead he said, "Perhaps a visit to Mr Willerby might cheer you up?"

"Who's he?"

"He's the young man who works in our new forensics department. He's been running tests on the compact and perfume bottle."

"He's not like Dr Stirk, is he?" asked Dorothy warily.

The inspector shook his head. "Not in the slightest."

Chapter Sixteen

DOROTHY FOLLOWED INSPECTOR Derwent down several flights of stairs at his usual brisk pace, his cane tapping rhythmically against each step.

"What does finding out Olive Clayton was a thief mean for George?" she asked.

"It's hard to say. Had she lived, Mrs Clayton might have been able to tell us if she'd seen him or not on the night Elsa was killed."

"Surely you don't think he killed her too?"

"No, as a matter of fact, he finally has an alibi. He was having lunch at his club at the time she was killed."

At last, thought Dorothy, *some good news for George.*

Eventually, they arrived in the basement of the building. The inspector knocked on a door before entering a room that looked more like a laboratory. Two well-scrubbed tables were covered in test tubes, petri dishes and glass flasks containing various coloured liquids.

A tall, thin young man in a white coat hurried over to greet them. He had red hair that stuck up at an odd angle and was wearing spectacles with the thickest lenses Dorothy had ever seen. They gave him a wide-eyed almost innocent expression.

"Miss Peto, this is Hugo Willerby. Willerby, I'd like to introduce Miss Dorothy Peto. She's with the Women's Police Volunteers."

The scientist took hold of Dorothy's outstretched hand and pumped it up and down enthusiastically. "Hello there. It's jolly nice to meet you. I have to say I think it's marvellous how all you ladies have stepped up and are keeping the home fires burning, as Mr Novello might say."

"Thank you," replied Dorothy. "I'm looking forward to hearing about your work. It must be fascinating."

The scientist's smile immediately faded. "It is, but if we are to work together, Miss Peto, I want you to know that I would love nothing more than to be able to serve my country. I have tried to enlist on more than eight occasions, but…"

"They won't let you with your eyesight," she interrupted gently. "My brother was in a similar position. He has flat feet."

The young man looked relieved. "So many people don't understand," he said his eyes drifting to a pile of white feathers lying in the corner of his desk. "I've almost stopped venturing outside." Dorothy's heart went out to him. She'd seen the women in the street handing out the same feathers to men who to their mind looked like they should be fighting.

"It's all down to that damn fool Fitzgerald. An admiral should know better," muttered Inspector Derwent in a way that made Dorothy wonder if anyone had dared present him with a white feather too. She stepped forward, scooped up the feathers and took them to the coals that were smouldering in the small grate.

"That's the best place for those," she said decisively, dumping them into the flames.

Willerby beamed at her in admiration. "Gosh! Miss Peto, I say."

"Finally, a use for that fire. I don't know why you keep it lit. It barely gives off any heat," said the inspector, who looked like he was in danger of smiling too.

"I've told you, Inspector, I suffer with my chest. If the air becomes too damp, it can trigger my asthma…"

The inspector held up his hand. "All right enough about your ailments. What can you tell me about the perfume bottle and compact Taylor and Jones brought you?"

"Oh yes, of course."

He led them over to a table where the silver compact and perfume bottle were laid next to each other. Both were extremely elegant. obviously of the highest quality and engraved with the initials E.D.

"May I touch them?" asked Dorothy.

"Please do, Miss Peto. I have already checked for fingerprints, but there's nothing unfortunately. I expect the pawnbrokers gave them a good polish."

Dorothy carefully picked each piece up and turned them over.

"Good heavens! They are both from Asprey."

"I bet Olive Clayton couldn't believe her luck," muttered Inspector Derwent. "Off you go then, Willerby."

The scientist cleared his throat. "Unfortunately, there were only a few drops of liquid left in the perfume bottle, but what I can tell you is that it wasn't pure perfume. It had been mixed with some sort of detergent. Not bleach I don't think because the smell would have been too strong, but something strong enough to dry and irritate the skin. Perhaps flakes of soap powder had been dissolved in it. I'm still working on it. As for the powder in the compact. There's no doubt about it. The face powder was mixed with very finely ground cyanide crystals. So there you have it. The cause and effect as it were."

"I'm not sure I'm following you," admitted Dorothy.

The young scientist adjusted his glasses. "Oh dear, I'm not always the best at explaining things. Let me try again, Miss Peto. The victim must have sprayed the perfume on her neck and wrists as I believe women do. The detergent in the perfume began to cause a rash. The skin would crack and become red and sore. I believe the good doctor commented on this in his post-mortem report. To cover up this rash, the victim applied face powder and the cyanide entered her body through the broken skin."

"You think that's how she was poisoned?" asked Inspector Derwent.

"I'm certainly of it, Inspector. In fact, it reminded me of another case. Do you recall the Yorkshire gardener who died from cyanide poisoning last summer?"

"No," replied Dorothy and the inspector in unison.

Willerby looked disappointed. "Oh well, I think it only made the local papers. What with the assassination of the archduke happening at the same time… An aunt sent me the cuttings. She thought I'd be interested, knowing my line of work. Anyway, this gardener had put a paper packet of cyanide in the top pocket of his shirt. He was going to use it to deal with some sort of pest, wasps I believe. It was a hot day, he began to sweat and the packet became damp as did the cyanide and came into contact with some scratches on his chest that hadn't fully healed. Poor chap keeled over and was dead in a matter of minutes, but because he'd taken his shirt off just before he collapsed nobody linked the two. It turned out he was having an affair with the lady of the house. Her husband was arrested on suspicion of poisoning him and was very nearly hanged for it. Death didn't happen nearly as quickly for our victim though—the amount of cyanide used was much smaller."

"So it was a sort of gradual poisoning," said Dorothy as she tried to follow what he was saying.

"That's right, Miss Peto." Hugo beamed at her. "I'd say it happened over a matter of weeks, perhaps even months."

"Poor Elsa. Whoever wanted her dead must have planned it well in advance."

She glanced over to the inspector, who had been quiet for several minutes. His eyes were fixed on the compact in her hand.

"It also ties quite nicely into another of our lines of investigation. It seems there may be something in your theory concerning Clara Fleurot. One of Sergeant Brook's informants has confirmed what we suspected. She regularly supplied Edith Devine with cocaine when she delivered laundry to the theatre. We've finally managed to track her down. She was arrested this morning."

Dorothy looked at him in surprise. "You're still investigating Madame Chameleon? I'm so pleased. I rather thought you were convinced it was George."

"Hardly, otherwise he would have been charged."

"Do your men have many such informants?"

"Yes, Miss Peto. It may surprise you, but we do sometimes rely on sources of information other than yourself."

Dorothy smiled. His teasing tone reminded her of Raymond.

"Hold on," interrupted Willerby, looking puzzled. "I don't recall carrying out any tests for cyanide on another silver compact, Inspector."

Inspector Derwent shook his head. "No. I didn't think a test was necessary, at the time. It was obvious to me as soon as I saw it lying open in front of Miss Devine. The scent of almonds was unmistakable. After the inquest, Edith's maid sent all her mistress's belongings to her mother back in Yorkshire. I'll write and ask if she still has it. It might be worth you taking a look after all, Willerby. Thank you for your help for now. We'll leave you in peace."

He headed through the door and after thanking the scientist too, Dorothy hurried after him. Being included in the conversation with Willerby made her feel bolder than usual.

"If you are planning on interviewing Madame Chameleon, may I join you?" she asked.

"Are all members of the WPV as keen to help as you?"

"Actually, Margaret and Mary both think we should stick to patrolling the parks and moving along prostitutes who are loitering around the railway stations."

"However, yourself and Miss Boyle feel strongly that there should be a female present when a woman or child is being interviewed by the police or attending court. To make the process less intimidating."

Dorothy stopped in her tracks as he repeated the words she had written months ago. "Good heavens! Do you read *The Vote*, Inspector? Does that mean you are sympathetic to our cause?"

He glanced back over his shoulder. "Perhaps. Or perhaps I believe in the old adage: know thine enemy."

Dorothy couldn't control the tremble in her voice. "You think we are your enemy because we wanted to be treated equally to men?" She was shocked by how much his words had stung. When she'd first met him, she'd hated his dismissive attitude, but since then she'd begun to think that he might value her opinion at least some of the time. Had she been wrong?

He stopped and turned to look at her again. "It was merely a joke, Miss Peto, but clearly not a good one." He sighed. "Very well, I'll agree to you sitting in on the interview and *observing*. You'll notice the stress I am putting on the word 'observing'. You may take notes, but I don't want you to say a word without my permission."

"Of course not. I wouldn't do anything to jeopardise the investigation and I'm certain you'll find Madame Chameleon is involved in Elsa's death somehow."

"There is one more condition."

"What's that, Inspector?"

"You stop calling her Madame Chameleon."

DOROTHY TOOK A seat in the corner with her notepad and pencil at the ready. Clara Fleurot was sitting opposite

Inspector Derwent. There was a uniformed constable and Sergeant Clark on either side of her. She was wearing a dark red velvet dress and matching hat. Her hair was its natural shade of light brown. If she was intimidated, she didn't show it. She held her head high, with her chin jutting forward defiantly. The sneering look she gave Dorothy as she entered the room didn't imply she was grateful to have another female present.

"Your name was entered twice in the poison register at the Covent Garden chemists," began the inspector.

"So what! That is nothing! Victor pays me to collect his rent and keep his tenants happy. Those houses are full of cockroaches. We use cyanide to fumigate. Everyone knows that. If I wanted to kill someone with poison, do you think I would be stupid enough to put my own name in that register?"

"Did Victor also pay you to kill Elsa Dubois?"

"I don't know this…Elsa Dubois."

"You must have met her. She was living in one of Victor's houses."

"Who says I met her? You tell me who has seen me with her."

Dorothy was surprised to see the inspector place one of Alice's drawings on the table.

"Her little girl drew this picture. We believe this figure is you wearing the green hat from when you were previously arrested."

"Pah!" Clara almost spat. "A child scrawls in green crayon and you arrest me!"

With a swish of her hand she swept the piece of paper off

the desk and to the floor. Silently, Dorothy bent forward and retrieved it.

"Olive Clayton might have been able to tell us that she had seen you with Elsa. I take it you knew Mrs Clayton? Was she a good tenant?"

Clara shrugged. "She owed a week's rent, but now she is dead, so it won't be paid."

"Where were you when she was killed?"

"I don't know when she was killed, but whenever it was, I was working."

"We know you visited Edith Devine the night she died. You supplied her with cocaine," continued the inspector.

"I supplied her with clean laundry, nothing else."

Clara's accent was an odd mixture of French and cockney. It became stronger the angrier she got. Dorothy sat spellbound as she watched the interaction between her and the inspector. It reminded her of a tennis match. Each time he served up a new piece of evidence against her, Clara would smash or volley it away.

"Do you know Herman Muller now known as Henry Miller?"

She shrugged again. "Maybe I do, maybe I don't. I know a lot of men, not always their names."

"He's a large man, with a bald head and an extravagant moustache."

"It could be anyone. Some men are large, some bald, some handsome." She narrowed her eyes. "Some are scarred and walk with a limp. I don't care. They are all the same to me."

It seemed clear to Dorothy that without more evidence

they weren't going to get anything else out of Clara. Inspector Derwent must have thought the same, because he nodded to the constable.

"Take her back to the cells."

"Well, she held up better than his lordship," murmured Sergeant Clark to the inspector as Clara was led out of the room. He turned to Dorothy and grinned. "You sure you don't want to go with her, Miss Peto? Make sure she isn't feeling intimidated?"

Dorothy felt herself flush, but before she could reply there was a knock at the door and Sergeant Taylor entered the office.

"Sorry to interrupt, sir, but I've just got back from Asprey's."

"And?" asked the inspector.

"Both the silver compact and perfume bottle were commissioned and paid for by Herr Muller."

Dorothy clapped her hands together in delight. "I knew it was him."

"When was this?" asked the inspector, ignoring her.

"July last year, sir."

"That doesn't make sense. War wasn't declared until August and Elsa didn't arrive here until several weeks later," said the inspector.

"Perhaps he planned to give it to Elsa sooner, but the war got in the way. The perfume bottle was waiting for Elsa when she arrived at Ramsgate, and he could have given her the compact himself. Did he order the things from Harrod's for Alice too?" asked Dorothy eagerly.

The inspector shook his head. "No, we checked. Those

items were all charged to Victor Peeters's account."

"Have you spoken to anyone in Ramsgate about Elsa? I'm sure Muller was lying about not visiting her. Someone might have seen him—he's quite memorable," she suggested hopefully.

"Jones and Taylor here spoke to the manager of the hotel where she was staying," replied the inspector. "He described her as a perfectly charming and respectable guest and said her daughter was enchanting. She received no male visitors; however, he did say that gifts regularly arrived from various London department stores for them, but that some were delivered by hand, including the perfume bottle."

"Whose hand?"

"The manager described a young woman, with dark hair, dressed as a maid, but couldn't tell us any more," said Sergeant Taylor consulting his notebook.

"Could that have been Madame, I mean Clara?" asked Dorothy thinking of all her disguises.

"Possibly," agreed the inspector, "but she can't have been the one who delivered the perfume bottle. If you recall, at the time, she was otherwise detained. She was in police custody after you and your colleague initiated her arrest at Waterloo station."

Dorothy sighed in disappointment. In her head, she had been formulating a theory where Clara was working for Miller.

"It looks like we'll have to question her again," said the inspector.

"Wouldn't it be better to let her go?" asked Dorothy.

All three police officers turned to look at her incredulously.

"Miss Peto, you were the one who insisted we arrest her in the first place. Have you changed your mind?" asked the inspector.

"No, but I don't think you'll get her to say much. I'm sure she is involved somehow, but I'm also sure she must be working for someone. If you let her go, but have one of your men follow her, she might lead us to them."

The inspector's chair scraped noisily across the floor as he rose to his feet and reached for his cane.

"It's a wonder we ever managed to conduct an investigation without you, Miss Peto."

With that he strode out of the room with Sergeant Taylor hurrying after him, leaving Dorothy behind with Sergeant Clark, who was filing away the notes from the interview.

"Oh dear," sighed Dorothy. "Is he very cross with me? Does he think I'm an awful nuisance?"

Clark shook his head and smiled at her.

"Trust me, miss. If that were the case, we wouldn't see you half as much as we do."

Chapter Seventeen

THAT EVENING, DOROTHY and Nina were having supper together at the Eustace Miles restaurant, named after its famous tennis-playing owner. It served delicious vegetarian food, but Dorothy found she didn't have much of an appetite.

"You're terribly glum. What's wrong?" asked Nina as she browsed through the menu.

"Oh I'm sorry if I'm not very good company," apologised Dorothy. "I'm just so worried about George. He's such a nice young man, but not terribly bright, and the way the inspector was interrogating him I'm frightened he might get confused and admit to something he didn't do. I'm absolutely sure he's innocent. He was simply in the wrong place at the wrong time."

"Try not to worry, so. Now Madame Chameleon is under surveillance you're sure to find the true culprit. What about this Muller or Miller fellow? I don't like the sound of him and he's a chemist. Who else could have come up with such an ingenious way to kill Elsa?"

Dorothy nodded her head slowly. "I've been thinking about when we found the body and if that's significant too."

"Do you mean the time of day?"

"No, the fact that it was during an air raid. What if whoever killed her chose that day because they knew the Zeppelin was coming? They could have arranged to increase the amount of cyanide in her powder. In all the confusion of the raid, they thought there would be a delay in finding her body or if Seven Dials was hit, she may never be discovered at all."

"But who would know when the Zeppelin was coming over? One of the watchers on the roof?"

"I was thinking more of someone privy to important information. Someone well connected, who until recently was a German national. Suppose Miller has fooled everyone and he's really a spy for the Kaiser?"

"Heavens! That really would put the cat amongst the pigeons."

"I might be getting carried away, but I just know it's wrong keeping George locked up when the real killer is out there."

"Look, if Inspector Derwent is as good a detective as everyone says, then he won't want to see the wrong man convicted either."

"Perhaps, but it is awfully hard to know what he's thinking. Sometimes he includes me in the investigation like when he took me to meet Willerby, but then he went and arrested George without telling me. I worry he thinks I'm getting in the way."

"Nonsense! You've come up with lots of ideas and leads. I really think you've found your calling. Detective work suits you. I wouldn't be surprised one jot if it's you who finds the killer and Derwent demands that you join his team immediately."

Dorothy smiled at her friend's confidence in her. "Wouldn't that be wonderful! Real detective work. Not that I don't think the WPV aren't making a difference, but…"

"I know, sometimes it feels like we are nothing more than glorified school prefects. It doesn't help that Mary sees our role as the capital's moral guardians. She's taken to following any single women and interrogating them if they dare to approach a man. Did I tell you I caught her stabbing bushes in Hyde Park with her umbrella the other day? If there had been any amorous couples in there, she'd have probably impaled them and told them it served them right."

Dorothy began to giggle. She could just picture the scene.

Nina grinned back at her. "That's better. Being miserable doesn't suit you. Now tell me what you are going to do next to help George."

"I was wondering if I should pay a visit to Ramsgate. The inspector said two of his men had spoken to the manager of the hotel, but they didn't speak to anyone else. I can't help thinking the chambermaids might have been able to tell them more. Think how useful Sir Edward's governess was and it was Edith's maid whose evidence they relied on at her inquest. My mother always says if you want to know what goes on in a house, ask the servants. But I'm due to be on patrol tomorrow. Do you think I should telephone Margaret and ask if I can swap shifts?"

Nina shrugged her shoulders. "You know me, Dorothy. I always tend to think it's easier to beg forgiveness than request permission. Besides Mary and Margaret are away for the weekend. They are in Kent. Margaret thought Danehill would be the perfect place to throw a party to celebrate Denmark giving women the right to vote."

"Gosh have they? I've been so wrapped up in this business with Edith, I've barely read a paper. How wonderful to have some good news at last."

"You are quite right. It seems an awfully long time since we've had something to celebrate."

Nina waved a waiter over and ordered two glasses of champagne. When they arrived, she raised hers in a toast.

"To our Danish sisters. May they be the first of many."

THE SUN WAS shining when Dorothy arrived in Ramsgate the next morning, but her mood didn't match the weather. She'd spent the train journey reading the newspaper. It was full of the latest despicable act by the Germans. They had attacked the British trenches with poisonous gas again. She shuddered as she stepped off the train thinking how the poor soldiers must have suffered. No doubt more weeping wives and mothers would be receiving telegrams with the worst possible news.

The Albion Hotel stood on top of East Cliff overlooking the beach. It was a four-storey white building with a porticoed entrance and black railings at the front. As George had told her, it wasn't especially grand, but it looked well kept and respectable. Due to its size and general staff shortages, she would be surprised if more than one chambermaid was employed there. She spoke to an elderly porter, who confirmed this.

"That's right, miss. Vera is the chambermaid. She'll be taking her break in about ten minutes if you want to speak with her," he said tipping his cap politely.

Sure enough, ten minutes later, a plump young woman, wearing a white apron over her black dress, appeared out of the side entrance. Dorothy followed her as she slipped around the back of the building where the dustbins were stored and lit a cigarette.

"Hello there!"

The young woman spun around looking startled. "Oh, miss, you gave me quite a fright," she said quickly brushing the ash off her pinafore.

"I'm terribly sorry, I didn't mean to." She held out her hand. "My name is Dorothy."

The young woman shook her hand as her eyes looked Dorothy up and down, taking in her uniform.

"Vera. Are you a guest here, miss?"

"No, but I wanted to talk to you about someone who was: Elsa Dubois. Did you know she'd died?"

"Yes, I was very sorry to hear about it. Two gentlemen came up from London to talk to Mr Jackson, the manager, about it."

"But not you?"

Vera shook her head, as if this was a silly idea. "No, miss, not me."

"What was Miss Dubois like?"

"She was sort of private. Kept herself to herself, but she spoke English well enough for a foreigner and Alice was a real sweet little thing. She was a bit shy, didn't say much, but she seemed to understand what I said to her."

"Do you think she was happy here?"

"Oh yes, I would say so. Especially when the weather was good, and they could go down to the beach. Alice loved the donkeys and the Punch and Judy show, but the poor little mite was terribly scared when the Zeppelin came over. We all were."

"Is that what made them leave?"

The young woman's face turned red. "No. I don't want to speak out of turn, but I thought perhaps Miss Dubois couldn't afford to stay here anymore."

"Did she leave without paying her bill?"

"Oh no! Nothing like that!" She looked shocked. "But she always used to be a very generous tipper. There would be a shilling for turning the bed down each night or after I'd tidied her room on a morning, but then it went down to sixpence, then only a farthing, then nothing at all. Not that I expected anything you understand, and I could tell she was embarrassed. She started to make some excuse to leave whenever I arrived."

"But she was sent expensive presents while she was here?"

Vera wrinkled her nose. "I wouldn't say expensive exactly. What I mean is roses and boxes of Belgian chocolates arrived regular like and lots of pretty things for Alice, but nothing she could sell, you know, if money was a bit tight. Oh, except for a very nice bottle of perfume when she first arrived and a lovely silver compact. They were very fancy with her initials on, but I mentioned them to a gentleman friend of mine and he said that would make it harder to sell them."

Dorothy nodded. "Do you know who sent her these things? Did she perhaps write thank you notes?"

"The flowers came with a card that had the name Victor on it. The rest of it wasn't in English. She wrote lots of letters mainly to people back in Belgium; she left them at the reception desk to be posted."

"All of them?"

"Except for the ones she gave to the maid."

"The maid?"

"Yes, the maid who visited her about once a week. She brought the compact and perfume bottle. Everything else was brought by delivery vans."

"What did the maid look like? Did you ever speak to her?"

"She was small and dark, but she didn't speak to me or either of the waitresses. She seemed a bit uppity, like she was too good to speak to us."

"Did Miss Dubois receive any other visitors?"

"No. Nobody. It was a bit sad really."

The young woman dropped the stub of her cigarette to the ground and crushed it under her toe. "I should be going. My break is only meant to last five minutes, miss."

"Please just one more thing. Can you remember if Miss Dubois suffered from a skin complaint at all? Perhaps you saw some cream on her dressing table or in her bathroom?"

"Yes, she did. It started on her neck and wrists but had begun spreading. It bothered her and she blamed our water. Said it was too harsh for her delicate skin. The cheek of it!"

"You've been very helpful. Please take this." Dorothy pressed half a crown into the maid's hand.

She blushed again. "Oh no, miss, I couldn't."

"Please, I'm sure Elsa would want you to have it."

The chambermaid scuttled away, slipping the coin into her apron pocket. Dorothy left the hotel and began to walk along the clifftop path. Down on the beach children were having donkey rides and she thought about what the maid had said. Poor little Alice would never play on a beach with her mother again. Tears began to well up in her eyes and she quickly brushed them away. Sniffing, she searched through her pockets for a handkerchief. Distracted, it took her a moment to realise someone was calling her name. She looked up and to her amazement saw Raymond striding towards her.

"Dorothy, what are you doing here? Are you following me?" he demanded.

"No, don't be silly. I didn't even know if you were in England."

His face broke into a smile and he gave her a hug. "I wasn't until this morning. Sorry if I snapped. Why are you here?"

"I wanted to visit the hotel where Elsa Dubois and her little girl were staying. I talked to the chambermaid to see if she saw or heard anything that might help."

"And did she?"

"Not much. I was hoping she might have seen Miller visit here. We found out that it was him who commissioned the compact and the perfume bottle with her initials on. I understand him leaving the perfume bottle at the hotel perhaps as a sort of parting gift, but why send the compact too, when he said he didn't want to hear from her again? A guilty conscience, do you think?"

Raymond stopped suddenly and laid his hand on her arm. "Dorothy, I know you want to help George. So do I, but I really think you might have to give up on this theory that our German friend is involved."

She looked at him in astonishment. "Our German friend. Since when has Miller been your friend?"

"He's a friend to all of us." Raymond shoved his hands in his pockets and sighed. "Look, I can probably tell you because it will be in this evening's papers. The LZ38, one of the Germans' airships was destroyed last night in Belgium. We discovered it was being stored near Evere and our chaps flew over and bombed it."

"Oh, Raymond! What wonderful news! No more awful raids. I'm so proud of you," she exclaimed throwing her arms around him. He shrugged and looked embarrassed as he untangled himself.

"Well, a lot less at any rate. The point is…our information came from Miller. The map showing the location of the Zeppelin was amongst the papers Elsa brought over with her. He is also helping us develop gas masks for our boys at the front. The king will be honouring him in the next few weeks. He's a good man. He's on our side."

Dorothy tutted quietly, but Raymond continued, "While it's true I've never met him, I honestly don't think he sounds like the sort of chap to kill an actress. He may have been fond of Elsa, but he only agreed to bring her over here if she brought the papers he needed from his house in Brussels and stayed out of the way here in Ramsgate. Their relationship was purely business, but he knew people gossiped about them so her coming over on his yacht wouldn't arouse as much suspicion as if he'd sent one of his secretaries back to Belgium for the papers. When he collected the papers from Elsa, he gave her some money and made her promise never to contact him again. He wanted to ensure there was nothing in his personal life that could embarrass His Majesty when he made him a British citizen."

Dorothy sighed. Raymond was rarely wrong when it came to judging a man's character.

"Then it looks like I am left with trying to prove Victor Peeters arranged to have Elsa killed if I want to save George. Although how he managed that from across the Atlantic, I don't know."

"If anyone can find out, you can. I have every faith in you." Raymond bent down and kissed her cheek. "Now let me take you for lunch and we'll discuss something more jolly."

The two of them spent a pleasant hour in a café overlooking the beach, before Raymond escorted her back to the station. On the train back to London, Dorothy's thoughts strayed to Alice once more and why she had run away from her hiding place under the sofa. Who had scared her? Not George who was her friend, or Olive Clayton, who had only gone to Elsa's house after seeing Alice run away. It must have been the person who had smashed the bottle of gin and placed the cocaine on Elsa's face. She felt sure that person was Clara. She could have gone to Ramsgate dressed as a maid and won Elsa's confidence, but Inspector Derwent had said she was under arrest for the first of those visits. Dorothy closed her eyes and rested her head against the window as the train rattled along. According to Raymond, she was wrong about Miller; perhaps she was wrong about Clara too.

THE NEXT MORNING, when Dorothy returned to the WPV offices, she was relieved to see that Margaret and Mary were both still away. Nina had taken full advantage of the situation. When Dorothy pushed open the office door she was enveloped in a thick cloud of smoke and the ashtray was overflowing.

"Dorothy! You're back. How was Ramsgate?"

"Interesting," replied Dorothy as she pushed the window open. "It's beginning to look like Victor could be our man instead of Miller after all."

Nina clapped her hands together. "Oh that's rather fortunate."

Dorothy frowned at her. "Why? And what is all this?" asked Dorothy gesturing to all the papers Nina had spread over both her desk and Margaret's.

"While you were away, I thought I would do a little detective work myself," said Nina proudly. "First I went to the British Library, to see what I could find out about Victor Peeters. Look, here's a photo of him, after donating a rather large sum of money to the St Andrew's convent near Earl's Court. Didn't you say that's where Alice is now? He's rather handsome, in a roguish sort of way."

"Yes," Dorothy managed to agree between coughs as she wafted the smoke away. She peered at the photo. It was far more flattering than the one in the Scotland Yard incident room. With his chiselled features and slicked-back dark hair, it was easy to see why a woman like Elsa would have fallen in love with him. "You haven't taken these newspapers from the library, have you? I'm sure that isn't allowed, Nina."

"Don't worry about that. I'll return them," replied Nina airily. "Now look, after I'd been to the library, I remembered you said Inspector Derwent had described Victor as a slum landlord, so I paid the Land Registry a visit. He uses the same solicitor for all his conveyancing. It's this chap here in the photo with Victor."

Dorothy looked at the picture again. The second man was short and chubby with grey curling hair and a moustache with neatly twirled ends.

"His name is Claude Pomroy. A Belgian by birth but he's lived here for over twenty years," continued Nina. "Look, I've written the address of his office in Holborn down for you. Why don't you go and speak to him."

"Thank you, I will, but first I want to pay a visit to Alice. I know the nuns have said she isn't ready to speak to Inspector Derwent, but they might let me see her. I'd like to see how she is for myself."

"Good idea! I'm sure she'll be pleased to see her rescuer. Now close that window again, before all my notes are blown away."

Chapter Eighteen

D OROTHY DECIDED TO walk the two miles to Earl's Court. It was a beautiful morning and having spent so much of the previous day cooped up on a train, it was pleasant to stretch her legs and, after ten minutes with Nina, her lungs were in need of some fresh air. When she arrived at the Earl's Court Exhibition Centre, she was amazed to find it seemed to have been turned into a sort of Belgian village. There was an array of small Belgian shops, stalls for various charities and the auditorium of the great concert hall had been turned into the men's bedroom. There was even a nursery for the young mothers to take their children. A member of the Red Cross directed Dorothy to the convent that was situated across the road from the exhibition centre. As she walked towards the large red-brick building, she saw a familiar figure coming out of the front door.

"Miss LeBlanc. How nice to see you again," she called out.

The young woman nodded her head politely. "Good morning, Miss Peto. What brings you to Earl's Court? Are you on patrol?"

"No not exactly, I thought I might visit the convent and see how Alice is, if the nuns will allow it."

"I am sure Alice will be pleased to see you."

"Have you seen her?"

"Yes, I have been there myself just now. Although she still does not say much, her drawings are becoming a little brighter. There are more flowers and fewer black lines. I will return this afternoon. The Sisters of St Andrew are hoping to take the children in their care on a picnic to the Brompton Cemetery. Unfortunately, some of the sisters are elderly and not in the best of health, so they have asked for volunteers to help escort the children there. If you will excuse me, I must return home and change my shoes if I am to be running around after the little ones." With a wave, she hurried away.

Dorothy made her way up the steps and through the front door of the convent. As soon as she stepped inside the wood-panelled hallway, she felt a sense of stillness and calm compared to the hustle and bustle of Earl's Court. It took her eyes a second to adjust to the dim light inside and she almost didn't see the petite figure adding her name to the list pinned to the noticeboard. With a start, she realised it was Nan Lambert, Edith Devine's maid.

"Hello there," she said, brightly.

The maid turned around in surprise then bobbed a small curtsy. "Hello, miss," she replied casting her eyes down shyly.

Dorothy nodded towards the noticeboard. "Are you volunteering for the picnic too? That is kind of you."

"I heard the nuns needed help with the children. I wanted to do my bit. I know what it's like to be alone in the world."

"You must miss your mistress very much. Have you

managed to find any alternative employment?"

Nan shook her head.

"Clara promised to find me a position in one of the laundries she runs, only I haven't seen her for a while. I know it won't be the same as working for Miss Devine and I'm worried about my eczema, but I would be grateful all the same."

She self-consciously pulled her sleeves down over her hands, but not before Dorothy had noticed how red and chapped they were. Poor thing, she thought. Working in a laundry would be a world away from what she was used to.

"It was nice to see you again, miss." She bobbed another curtsy and disappeared out of the front door at the same time one of the nuns arrived in the hallway.

"May I help you, miss?" she asked in a quiet voice with a slight Belgian accent.

"Hello there, Sister. I'm Dorothy Peto. I was wondering if I might be allowed to see Alice Dubois. I was the one who found her and took her to the embassy. I should like to see how she is."

The nun shook her head slowly. "I am sorry, but Alice is having an early lunch then a nap. We do not want the children to be too tired before their picnic and already today, Alice has had two visitors."

"Oh I see," replied Dorothy feeling disappointed. She was about to asked if she could help out at the picnic too, when the nun raised one finger.

"However, if you would care to wait here one moment, I believe there is someone else who would like to see you."

She left as silently as she had arrived, but a few seconds

later she returned with the gentleman Dorothy had seen in the photograph that morning. Claude Pomroy smiled broadly and almost ran to greet Dorothy. He grasped hold of her and despite being a head shorter than her, reached up and kissed her on both cheeks.

"My dear Miss Peto! How good it is to finally meet you. We are all so grateful that you rescued little Alice and returned her to her people."

"Not at all. I'm pleased I could help," replied Dorothy, rather taken aback by his enthusiasm.

"Permit me to introduce myself, mademoiselle. My name is Claude Pomroy, and I am employed to act for Mr Victor Peeters, the father of little Alice." With a click of his heels and a formal bow, he presented her with his business card, bearing the address Nina had already given her.

"Have you been to visit her?"

"Yes, indeed. When I learnt she was here, I promised her father I would visit her every day until his return from America."

There was a small but pointed cough from the nun standing behind them. Mr Pomroy nodded politely to her.

"Forgive me, Sister, I have taken up too much of your time. Miss Peto, perhaps you would like to accompany me back to my office?"

Dorothy took the arm he offered her and together they stepped outside into the bright sunshine. Mr Pomroy hailed a taxicab, opened the door for Dorothy and asked the driver to taken them to Holborn.

"Who told you Alice was at the convent?" asked Dorothy as they set off on their journey.

"I received a telephone call from the Belgian Embassy. They were trying to contact Victor, who as you may know is in America. Although I was deeply saddened to hear of the death of Elsa, I was relieved that Alice had been found. I had lost contact with them when they left Ramsgate in such a hurry."

"How is she?" asked Dorothy.

"She is still very quiet, but her pretty little face lit up when I gave her a large box of the very finest Belgian chocolates on behalf of her father. I tried to explain that he would be here very soon to bring her presents himself, but I am not sure she understood."

"It must be very difficult. Her life has been turned upside down," said Dorothy. "I understand you also sent her things on her father's behalf when she was staying with her mother in Ramsgate."

"Yes, but of course. When Victor heard they were in England, he telegrammed me with instructions. Only the best from Harrods. Clothing, shoes, chocolates, a little pink rabbit that I picked out myself. He knew they would have left Belgium with very little. The last dress I sent was returned unopened with a note from the manager saying they were no longer residing at the hotel. I had been trying to find them ever since."

"How strange that they didn't tell you they were coming to London. What about things for Elsa, perfume and cosmetics—did you send her that sort of thing?"

The solicitor gave a firm shake of his head. "No, only flowers. Elsa was a proud lady. Victor did not want to appear, how shall I put it, presumptuous. I sent a dozen red roses each week on his behalf. Many would not believe it, but Mr Peeters is at heart a romantic. I believe the very reason he, how do you say, changed direction was because he wanted to become a respectable businessman and win her back." The old man shook his head sadly. "Now of course he never will."

"I understand Mr Peeters has been rather ill?"

"Yes, indeed although the good doctors in America have worked miracles. If God is willing, we hope he might still be with us at Christmas."

"I suppose when he found out he was ill, he must have made a will?"

"Naturally. What sort of a lawyer would I be if I had not insisted upon it. And although his business affairs were very complex, the will is simple. Everything is to go to Elsa and Alice."

"And if anything were to have happened to Elsa and Alice?" She left the question hanging in the air.

"That was never a possibility Victor was prepared to consider. Nobody else is named in the will."

"But if something had happened?" pressed Dorothy.

Mr Pomroy shrugged. "Victor's next of kin is his half-sister. They are estranged. Victor hasn't seen her since she was a small child. He wanted nothing to do with her or her mother. He never forgave his father for leaving his own mother for another woman."

"Are you in contact with Miss Peeters?"

He shook his head. "No, and in truth I am not sure that is still her name. I believe her mother married several times after Victor's father died. Little Ettie will be in her early twenties now and well, young women do have a tendency to marry." He chuckled. "We don't even know which country she is in."

At that moment, the taxi came to a halt outside a red-brick building with a brass plaque bearing Mr Pomroy's name on the door.

"Is there anything else you would like to discuss with me, Miss Peto?" he asked as he helped her out.

"No thank you. I should get back to work, but I do appreciate your time, Mr Pomroy."

He raised his hat politely, then after quickly glancing over her shoulder, climbed back in the taxi.

"Not at all. If you will excuse me, I have just remembered I have an appointment in Mayfair."

Dorothy watched him go, wondering why he had left in such a hurry, but no sooner had the lawyer's taxi driven away, than she heard the sound of heavy footsteps and the tap of a cane. She turned to see a slightly out of breath Inspector Derwent approaching her.

"Was that Victor Peeters's solicitor?" he asked without bothering to say hello.

"Yes—Mr Pomroy. He seemed very nice, but he left in rather a hurry."

"He must have seen me coming. I've been trying to talk to him for days, but he's like the scarlet pimpernel. How did you manage to meet him?"

"Oh, we met quite by chance. We were both visiting Alice."

"I don't suppose she's talking yet, is she?"

"No, but I hear her drawings are looking a little more

cheerful, so that's something."

The inspector met this news with nothing more than a grunt. "And Pomroy?"

"Oh he was quite chatty. He confirmed that Victor had asked him to send Alice the clothes and toys, but that he only sent Elsa a dozen red roses. He sounds rather romantic. Mr Pomroy thinks he wanted to become a legitimate businessman so he could win her back."

"A romantic," snorted the inspector. "You tell that to all those working in his laundries and living in his slums. Believe me, whatever Victor Peeters decided to do, it was only ever to benefit his own pocket."

Dorothy didn't bother arguing that. If he insisted on being so dismissive there was no wonder Mr Pomroy didn't want to discuss his client with him.

"Mr Pomroy said he didn't know they had left Ramsgate until a package for Alice was returned unopened. Don't you think it's strange that Elsa didn't tell him that she was running out of money? Although he did say she was a proud woman, so maybe that's why."

The inspector didn't bother to acknowledge her musings, so she continued.

"I also asked Mr Pomroy about Mr Peeters's will. He said that nobody else was named in it except for Alice and Elsa, but Victor does have a half-sister."

"Really?"

"Yes, but they are estranged. She was called Ettie Peeters."

"Ettie?"

"It must be a pet name, but anyway Pomroy doesn't

know where she is now. Apparently, Victor never got over his father leaving him and his mother for another woman."

"A psychologist might say he wanted to take revenge on Elsa for leaving him too."

Dorothy looked at him in surprise. She'd recently borrowed Sigmund Freud's latest book from Nina and had found it fascinating and unsettling in equal measure.

"I didn't know you were interested in psychology, Inspector."

"Mostly I think it's a lot of mumbo-jumbo, but as we are struggling to come up with a motive, I'm prepared to consider it in this instance."

The two of them walked along in silence for a few moments. Like the inspector, Dorothy was stumped when it came to a motive. Did the two women need to be silenced? Could it be jealousy? Or something as mundane as money, an inheritance? Unfortunately, like the rest of the case, it seemed there were more questions than answers. Then she remembered what else had been bothering her.

"By the way, Inspector," she began, "did Sergeant Brook manage to track down the man I told you about?"

"Ah, yes. Mr Archibald Abbey. We traced him through the court details you gave us. A very unpleasant man, but unlikely to be the reason Alice ran away."

"Why?"

"At the time she was heading to the station, he was molesting another little girl. The daughter of the landlord of the Red Lion."

Dorothy's hand flew to her mouth in horror. "Oh no! That's dreadful. If Mead had done his job properly, this would never have happened," she cried. "I hope you have arrested the monster."

"Not yet, Miss Peto. The landlord and his brother caught up with him before we could. Mr Abbey is currently unconscious in St Guy's. If he does wake up again, I doubt he'll be capable of walking or talking."

Dorothy shook her head. "Oh my goodness. This is precisely what comes of not taking witnesses seriously because they happen to be female. When justice isn't seen to be done, people take matters into their own hands."

The inspector stopped.

Dorothy turned to look at him. "What is it?"

"Ettie. Miss Leblanc's first name is Annette."

"Miss LeBlanc from the embassy? Surely you can't think she's involved? She's been so nice and helpful."

"In my experience, Miss Peto, murderers can be rather good at pretending to be nice, and you have only met her briefly. It was Miss LeBlanc who informed me of the relationship between Victor and Elsa, and it was Miss LeBlanc who made sure to give you the picture and we only have her word it was drawn by Alice."

"If you think Victor's half-sister could be behind this, then surely Clara is a more likely suspect. Mr Pomroy said it was possible she'd changed her name. She was at the theatre that night with Muller and Edith. She could have overheard him telling her that he was bringing Elsa over. Could we ask him if he knows Clara?"

"You may not have read yesterday evening's edition of the newspapers, but Mr Miller as we must now call him, is being congratulated for his part in helping us destroy a

Zeppelin over in Belgium. I can't very well ask a national hero if he associates with a woman known to be involved in the supply of drugs."

Dorothy didn't reply, remembering what Raymond had said.

The inspector began to walk on. "By the way, speaking of people with friends in high places. No doubt you'll be pleased to know Lord Sledmere has been released."

"Oh I'm so relieved you don't think it's him, Inspector," replied Dorothy smiling with delight.

"That isn't what I said, Miss Peto, but his solicitor turned up with a barrister and they both started quoting the Magna Carta to me and dropped the names of various high court judges. Now if you don't mind, I need to find out everything I can about Miss LeBlanc and thanks to Jones and Taylor following Clara Fleurot, I'm short-handed."

Dorothy opened her mouth to offer to help, but he had already disappeared across the road, waving his cane at a hooting delivery van. Dorothy watched him go and, with a sigh, realised she was alone on completely the wrong side of the city.

Chapter Nineteen

She took the underground back to Westminster, thinking of everything she'd learnt. It didn't matter how hard she tried, she simply couldn't imagine Miss LeBlanc being behind the murders, but the inspector was right—she barely knew the woman. With her dark hair, she matched the description of the maid who had visited Elsa at the hotel at Ramsgate. It was also true that they only had Miss LeBlanc's word for it that Alice had drawn any pictures, bright or otherwise.

With the inspection being short-handed, perhaps she could arrange for the WPV to set up a surveillance operation of their own. Some could go to the Belgian Embassy and others could attend the picnic the nuns were taking Alice on. Nina was bound to agree, but what about Margaret and Mary? This sort of police work would definitely come under the heading of ruffling feathers. She left the tube station and made her way to the WPV offices. With any luck, Mary and Margaret might still be away in Kent.

"Hello, I was hoping to find you here."

Dorothy stopped and looked up, startled. She had been so deep in thought, she hadn't noticed George standing outside the WPV offices, beaming from ear to ear.

"Good Lord, George! You startled me. What are you doing here?"

"I've come to say goodbye. I was released without charge first thing this morning." He thrust a huge bouquet of white roses towards her. "These are for you. I managed to get a message to Raymond to apologise for dragging him into all this. He wired back and told me how hard you'd been working on my behalf. Thanks awfully, Dorothy."

"It was nothing really. Hold on. What do you mean goodbye?"

"I sail for France tomorrow. Having been in the shadow of the noose, I'm rather looking forward to getting back to the front."

"Won't you be in trouble with your superior officers for contacting Elsa?"

"No. They got wind of what was going on, but it turns out Major Kingston, that's who gave me the orders regarding Elsa, served with Inspector Derwent out in Africa. The inspector explained everything to him, so it looks like I've escaped a court-martial too. Must be my lucky day!"

Dorothy smiled. It was so good to see him happy again. Then she remembered something that had been bothering her. "George, do you happen to remember a story about a gardener being poisoned in Yorkshire last year?"

He frowned for a second before nodding his head. "I do as a matter of fact. It was the only story that knocked my father's death off the front page of the *York Mercury*. I distinctly remember Gwen reading it out to me. I think she was trying to distract me. Bless her! She really was a smashing girl."

"Did Gwen bring her maid with her to the funeral?"

"Yes she did. Timid little thing, suffered with her skin, used to come out in a rash, always wore gloves, but Gwen was very fond of her. Petite Nanette. Edith used to call her."

"Nanette? I thought Nan was short for Nancy."

"No. I think she was half French. Gwen seemed to think it was rather glamorous to have a foreign maid. Suited the image of Edith Devine she'd created."

"Are you sure Nan wasn't half Belgian?" she pressed.

"Perhaps, I didn't really pay much attention."

A cold shiver of realisation ran through Dorothy. "Her name isn't Nan Lambert, but Nanette or Ettie Lambert with a silent T. Oh, George!"

"What's wrong, old girl?" he asked looking utterly bewildered.

"You might have mentioned this earlier. Never mind, thank you for the flowers. I need to go and make a telephone call." She reached up and kissed his cheek. "Good luck in France. Come home safe."

WITH THAT SHE dashed up the steps and into the WPV offices. She tossed the bouquet of flowers to a startled-looking Lucy and reached for the telephone. The Scotland Yard switchboard put her through to Inspector Derwent's office, but it seemed to take an eternity for someone to answer. Finally, she heard the voice of Sergeant Clark.

"I'm sorry, Miss Peto, the inspector isn't here. He and the other lads have gone to Southampton."

"I thought Victor Peeters's ship wasn't due to dock until early tomorrow morning."

"That's right but Clara Fleurot was seen boarding a train to Southampton. The inspector thinks she is on her way to meet Peeters. It looks like the two of them are working together after all. He's gone up with Jones, Brook and Taylor, leaving me to look into this young woman from the Belgian Embassy."

"Oh but it isn't Miss LeBlanc, it's the maid," Dorothy began to explain breathlessly. "Can't you get a message to the inspector somehow?"

"I can try contacting the Hampshire Constabulary, miss, but I can't promise anything."

"Sergeant, did the inspector write to Edith's mother about the compact?"

"He did. Her reply arrived this morning. She said she never received any compact."

"That's it! Proof!" exclaimed Dorothy. "Please, Sergeant, tell the inspector it is Nan Lambert. She's the one we are looking for. It's Clara Fleurot and Nan who have been working together."

"Edith Devine's maid? The shy little thing?"

"Yes."

There was a heavy sigh at the other end of the line. "Very well, Miss Peto, I'll try my best to pass that message on."

As the receiver clicked down, Dorothy prayed he meant it.

"Gosh, Dorothy! That all sounded very fraught. Is something wrong?" asked Lucy who had managed to locate a vase and was now happily arranging the roses.

"I'll explain later," Dorothy called over her shoulder as she quickly headed down the corridor to Margaret and Nina's office. She pushed the door open without knocking, then stopped abruptly when she saw the commandant and her three dogs had returned.

"Oh hello, Margaret, you're back. Is Mary with you?"

"No the poor thing is at home in bed resting her ankle. One of the horses at Danehill kicked her, although I'm sure it didn't mean to."

Dorothy cast an anxious look at Nina, who immediately stubbed out her cigarette.

"What's wrong, Dorothy?"

"I need you both to help me. I know who is responsible for the deaths of Edith and Elsa, and I'm afraid they might hurt Alice too."

"Who?" demanded Nina.

"Nan Lambert, Edith Devine's maid. She's Victor Peeters's half-sister and next of kin after Alice."

"Good heavens! Have you told Inspector Derwent?" asked Margaret.

"I've tried to get a message to him but he's gone chasing after Clara and he's got it into his head that the lady from the Belgian Embassy is Victor's half-sister."

"Are you sure she isn't?" asked Nina.

"Yes," insisted Dorothy. "George has just confirmed that Edith's maid's name is Nanette and that she's either half French or Belgian. She would have heard about how the gardener in Yorkshire was poisoned too. I think she's been working with Clara. They must have met at the theatre, when Edith started performing there and Clara began supplying her with drugs. Nan would have discovered Clara worked for Victor, and learnt that her estranged half-brother was very ill. Then when she heard Miller telling Edith he was bringing Elsa and Alice over to England, a plan began to form in her mind. A plan that would lead to Nan becoming Victor's only heir. Clara agreed to help her and they very nearly got away with it. The plan only failed when Alice ran away."

"Where are they both now?" asked Nina.

"I think Clara is in Southampton, that's where Inspector Derwent has gone, but Nan is here in London. I'm worried she might try to kidnap Alice today. The nuns are taking all the children on a picnic, and Nan has signed up to help. I won't be able to stop her on my own. Margaret, I need your permission for a group of us to go."

Margaret gave a nervous cough and began to chew her lip. "Oh dear. I'm not sure. Perhaps we should wait to hear from Inspector Derwent."

"There isn't time. The picnic will have already started," insisted Dorothy.

"I wish Mary was here to ask."

Nina clicked her tongue impatiently. "Well she isn't, Margaret, but as she always says you are the commandant. Think how proud she would be if the WPV were to thwart a possible kidnapping or worse. I'm sure you don't want that poor little girl to fall into the clutches of her mother's murderer."

Margaret nodded then rose to her feet, looking unusually determined. "Yes, you are quite right, Nina. We must focus on the little girl."

Dorothy, Nina and the three dogs followed her as she strode purposefully out of the office and waved to Joan who had joined Lucy in the sitting room.

"Ladies, follow me to Earl's Court!" she announced decisively.

The quickest way to travel the two miles from Westminster to Earl's Court was via the underground. The five of them caused quite a stir, running to jump on the next train with Margaret's three dogs woofing their heads off alongside them.

"Why on earth would anyone think a cemetery is the sort of place to take children for a picnic?" asked Lucy breathlessly, after Dorothy had briefly explained what was happening to her and Joan.

"Actually, it's a rather beautiful place," replied Margaret. "There's lots of wildlife and interesting architectural features."

"Perhaps, but I agree with Lucy. It sounds very Latin," said Nina.

Dorothy didn't join in the discussion. All she could think about was getting there before it was too late.

When they arrived at the cemetery, it was still warm, but the sky was beginning to darken and there was an ominous rumble of thunder in the distance. It seemed the picnic was almost over. Dozens of children were still running around playing hide-and-seek amongst the colonnades, but the nuns and their helpers were packing the plates and cups back into wicker baskets. Dorothy scanned the crowd, but she couldn't see Alice anywhere.

Nina tugged on Dorothy's arm and pointed. "Look over

there. It's the woman from the Belgian Embassy. Are you sure it isn't her?"

Dorothy looked over to where Miss LeBlanc was kneeling down, tying a little boy's shoelace.

"Perhaps you and Lucy should follow her, in case I'm wrong," said Dorothy beginning to doubt herself. Nina and Lucy made their way towards Miss LeBlanc while Margaret and Joan headed towards the colonnades. Dorothy began walking along a path that ran through the graves towards the Fulham Road. Suddenly she saw them. Alice clutching her pink rabbit as Nan led her away, holding her firmly by the hand.

Dorothy blew her whistle as loudly as she could, then yelled, "Stop!"

They both looked around in surprise, then Nan started to run, dragging Alice along with her. Dorothy chased after them, blowing her whistle for all she was worth. She soon caught up with them and grabbed the woman's arm. Despite her size, Nan was surprisingly strong and managed to escape her grasp. Then to Dorothy's horror, she pulled out a penknife and held it to the little girl's throat.

"Not another step or I'll kill her," she snarled. Her shy, timid demeanour had disappeared.

Dorothy immediately stopped and let her hands drop to her sides. "It's all right. I'll stay here. Please don't hurt her," she pleaded as Alice began to cry. From the corner of her eye, Dorothy could see Joan and Margaret heading towards them.

"Stay back! She has a knife!" she shouted.

Nan glanced nervously over her shoulder, but Dorothy's two colleagues had stopped running. However, nobody had stopped Margaret's dogs. Herbert, Topsy and Skip came flying down the path at full pelt. The hefty basset hound crashed straight into Nan's legs, knocking her clean off her feet. The knife flew from her hand and through the air and her grasp on Alice loosened enough for the little girl to escape. She ran straight into Dorothy's outstretched arms who held her tightly while watching Nan Lambert squirming on the ground trying to fend off the three excited dogs. Joan and Margaret leapt forward to grab her and were quickly joined by Lucy and Nina. The four of them managed to haul Nan to her feet and calm the dogs, then Margaret began to blow furiously on her whistle. Much to her relief, Dorothy saw two constables hurrying through the entrance gate.

Then everything seemed to happen very quickly. Two sisters from the convent came to find Alice. Dorothy tried to explain everything to them as she handed the little girl back into their care. Then she had to help convince the two sceptical constables that the petite young woman volunteering at the nun's picnic was a killer. Finally, at the very moment the Black Mariah arrived and Nan was bundled inside, the heavens opened and the cemetery emptied in minutes.

Over an hour later, back at the WPV offices, Dorothy and Nina collapsed on to one of the sofas, drenched and exhausted. Margaret was continuing to make a huge fuss of her dogs as she attempted to dry them with a small hand towel. Joan and Lucy had sensibly gone straight home.

"Thank heavens, you worked out it was that dreadful maid," said Margaret. "If we'd been a second later, I dread to think what might have happened to little Alice."

"I still don't understand why she killed Edith Devine, her employer," said Nina as she unlaced her boots.

"I think she did that on impulse," explained Dorothy. "When she overheard Miller telling Edith he couldn't see her anymore and that he was bringing Elsa over. Thanks to Clara, she knew Victor was out of the country and very ill. The two of them must have talked about who would inherit when he died. Now, thanks to Miller, Nan knew where the two people who stood between her and Victor's money would be. She knew she wouldn't be free to get close to Elsa and Alice and win their trust if she was still working for Edith, plus Edith knew her background, so she decided to remove her. Also, by killing Edith she saw a way of pointing the finger of blame at Miller. Don't forget it was her evidence the coroner based his verdict on. She made it seem like Edith's death was an accident or suicide but made sure the police knew Miller was one of the last people to see Edith and they had parted on bad terms. As her maid, Nan knew Edith hid the cocaine Clara brought her in her compact. She could easily have added some cyanide crystals that were kept in the caretaker's storeroom without her mistress noticing. As soon as Edith inhaled them, that was it." She paused to yank off her own boots before continuing.

"Then she and Clara needed to come up with a way of getting close to Elsa and Alice. Nan went to visit them in Ramsgate wearing her maid's outfit and one of Clara's dark wigs. She took Elsa gifts including the perfume bottle with dissolved soap flakes in it and the compact that originally belonged to Edith, containing face powder mixed with cyanide, and convinced Elsa that she was bringing them on behalf of Victor."

"And the two women shared the same initials!" exclaimed Nina. Dorothy nodded.

"Elsa trusted Nan and gave her the thank you letters she'd written to Victor and Pomroy to deliver by hand. However, Nan didn't deliver them, she read the letters herself instead. When she discovered Elsa was running out of money and needed to leave Ramsgate, Clara must have suggested Elsa and Alice move to one of Victor's properties in London. Nan would have made it seem like the offer came from Victor himself."

"And the poor mother and daughter ended up in Seven Dials," said Nina, who was now peeling off her sopping-wet stockings.

Dorothy nodded. "Yes. Nan had already begun slowly poisoning Elsa and they needed her to be somewhere they could keep an eye on her. I think they also realised that in a less educated and wealthy district, people would be more suspicious of a foreigner and be less likely to speak Elsa's language. Elsa of course wouldn't have known how poor the area was but was tempted to go there by the idea of being close to the opera house. She had the advertisement from when Caruso performed there. Perhaps the poor woman even thought she might get the chance to return to the stage herself."

"How very sad," Margaret said with a sigh. "She must have been devastated when she arrived in Seven Dials. Why didn't she try to find somewhere else?"

"She was probably too weak from the cyanide. You see, Nan must have realised Elsa was very different to Edith.

Herman Muller told us she barely drank and never in front of Alice. She certainly wouldn't have taken drugs voluntarily. Nan had to think of another way of poisoning her; then she remembered the story about the Yorkshire gardener. She would have read about it in the local papers when she went there with Edith for the funeral of the late Lord Derwent. Combining that with seeing how red and sore the hands of the women working for Clara in the laundries were, and her own case of nervous eczema, she came up with the idea of putting something in the perfume to irritate Elsa's skin then adding cyanide to the powder in the compact. Elsa grew weaker at the same time as she was running out of money and wanting to leave Ramsgate. The timing worked perfectly until the night she actually died. Clara had been keeping a close eye on Elsa and reporting back to Nan. As Clara was known to work for Victor, collecting rent for him, nobody would think anything of seeing her around Seven Dials."

"How awful! Imagine the two of them just waiting for the poor woman to die," said Margaret with a shudder.

"When Clara looked through the window and saw Elsa lying on the floor, she let herself in, but didn't see Alice hiding under the sofa. She set about adding the cocaine to her face, hoping an overstretched police force might simply assume that was how she died. Then for good measure she smashed a bottle of gin on the floor. This is what scared Alice and made her run away. Clara went to try to find her, perhaps checking with neighbours like Olive Clayton, not knowing that Alice had run back to the station that had brought her into London. It was a route she often walked with her mother. Perhaps she thought she could get back to Ramsgate where she had been happy. People saw her and just assumed she was begging when Mary and I found her."

"Was it when Clara was looking for Alice that Olive Clayton went in and stole the compact and perfume bottle?" asked Nina.

"Yes, Clara had planned to remove them herself, but when she returned to the house, she saw George leaving and didn't dare go in case he had called the police. Then the Zeppelin came over and she had to get to safety and no doubt report back to Nan."

"But afterwards she kept watching over the place?"

"Yes, she needed to find out if anyone had found the compact and perfume bottle. Perhaps someone had seen Olive Clayton visit the pawnbroker's or perhaps it was because she saw her speaking to me, but while I was in Elsa's house with Inspector Derwent, she killed Olive."

At that moment, the telephone in Margaret's office began to ring. She bustled through with the dogs at her heels and Nina, who had pulled her boots back on, stood up and shivered.

"It's no good. I'm exhausted and if I stay in these wet clothes much longer, I'll catch pneumonia." She bent down and gave Dorothy a hug. "We'll celebrate your excellent detective work properly another day when we are all less soggy and sleepy."

Dorothy watched her go then rested her head against the back of the sofa and listened to Margaret, who had a tendency to shout when she was on the telephone. It seemed it was Sir Edward Henry calling to congratulate them. Dorothy closed her eyes and smiled to herself as Margaret tried to convince him to begin recruiting basset hounds as police dogs.

Chapter Twenty

WHEN SHE OPENED her eyes again, it was morning and Mary was glaring down at her.

"What on earth do you think you are doing, Dorothy?" she demanded.

Dorothy yawned and stretched. "I'm terribly sorry, Mary. I must have fallen asleep."

"Margaret said she'd left you dozing here. She didn't have the heart to wake you although I doubt she expected you to be here all night."

"Did Margaret also tell you what happened yesterday?"

"She did. I have to say it all sounds very irregular, and you were very lucky that child wasn't injured because of your reckless actions." Mary was clearly put out not to have been involved in the arrest of a double murderer. "And, you can't go out on patrol like that. Your uniform is terribly creased. Go home and change, immediately."

Dorothy didn't argue. She was still awfully tired and aching from spending the night on the sofa. Stepping outside into the morning sunshine, she was thankful the heavy rain from the previous evening had stopped. She was so preoccupied with dodging the puddles littering the pavement, that at first she didn't notice the large black automobile pull up alongside her.

"Miss Peto! Miss Peto!"

She stopped and turned to see Inspector Derwent's head sticking out of the rear window.

"Oh hello there, Inspector. Is something wrong?"

The inspector shook his head. "Not at all. Congratulations are in order. Nan Lambert isn't as hardened as her accomplice, Clara Fleurot. After a night in the cells, she confessed to everything. I have to say that it never occurred to me that she might be our killer."

"It didn't to me either, until I talked to George," admitted Dorothy. "What happened with Clara and Victor Peeters?"

"After we received your message, we arrested Clara on Southampton dock."

"Was she trying to get to Victor?"

"No. Quite the opposite. She had a ticket to sail to America, on the next crossing. With Clara safely on the other side of the Atlantic, Nan would wait for Victor to die, claim her inheritance and then join her. You see Nan had signed the form for the picnic using Clara's name. This meant there was nothing to connect Nan to our investigation, but they knew we would be looking for Clara after Alice disappeared."

"I saw her signing the form at the convent. If only I had thought to check it," groaned Dorothy.

"Don't be too hard on yourself. The important thing is Alice is safe and we caught up with Clara before she sailed. Then we had to wait and explain everything to Victor. He was understandably shocked and desperate to see Alice. Actually, I'm on my way to see them reunited at the Belgian

Embassy. I thought you might like to join me."

"I would love to," replied Dorothy happily.

The inspector climbed out and held the door open for her. As they drove towards Kensington, Dorothy couldn't help recalling her very different journey there with the little girl asleep on her back.

When she and Inspector Derwent arrived in the garden of the embassy, Victor Peeters was already there standing beneath the shade of a horse chestnut tree. He was thinner and greyer than his photos but still a handsome man. He and the inspector exchanged the briefest of nods, then the inspector introduced him to Dorothy. Victor gave her a charming smile, then bowed and kissed her hand.

"Miss Peto, I am forever in your debt. It is thanks to you that Elsa's killers have been brought to justice and I am able to spend whatever time I have left with my daughter."

Dorothy felt herself blush. "It was nothing really," she murmured.

Then they all turned to watch as Miss LeBlanc and Mr Pomroy arrived with Alice.

"Please excuse me," said Victor as he hurried towards them with his arms outstretched. They watched as he dropped to his knees and with a little encouragement from Miss LeBlanc, Alice stepped forward and he embraced his little girl.

"Alice and Miss LeBlanc seem to have formed quite an attachment," whispered Dorothy.

"Indeed. Apparently, as of this morning, she no longer works at the embassy. Victor has employed her to act as Alice's nanny. Although the American doctor's treatment has been effective, Victor probably only has a few months left and he wanted to make sure Alice is surrounded by people with her best interests at heart. He's also made Pomroy her guardian when the inevitable happens."

The man from the embassy appeared carrying a ledger, inkstand and pen. After a brief conversation with Pomroy, Victor signed several documents and returned them to the embassy official.

"What are they doing?" asked Dorothy.

"Completing the paperwork to change Alice's name from Dubois to Peeters. That's why the reunion had to take place here at the embassy," explained the inspector.

"More name changes," she sighed. "I can't help thinking life would be much simpler if everyone stuck with the name they'd been born with."

He turned to look at her. "I expect you'll feel differently when you marry. I'm sure Lady Sledmere will be a very nice name to have."

Dorothy looked at him incredulously. "I could never marry George."

"Forgive me, I thought because you were so keen to clear his name…"

"Because he's like a brother to me. A sometimes infuriating, but much-loved younger brother."

The two of them stood silently for several moments. Then watched as father and daughter walked towards the side gate that led to Kensington Gardens. They both turned and smiled at Dorothy. Victor blew her a kiss and Alice gave her a shy wave. After a few seconds, Alice reached up for her father's hand and began skipping along the path. Despite her best efforts, Dorothy could feel tears begin to well up in her eyes. She quickly brushed them away with the back of her hand. The inspector glanced across at her and cleared his throat.

"I don't believe I have thanked you for your assistance in this matter, Miss Peto. I admit, like many of my colleagues, I was extremely dubious about the idea of females being involved in policing, but I must say you were very useful. Picking up on the missing compact and scent bottle and so forth."

Dorothy raised her eyebrows. "Well, we women think of little else except perfume and face powder, Inspector."

To Dorothy's surprise, the inspector's face reddened slightly.

"Perhaps I expressed myself badly. What I meant to say was you noticed things I didn't. I should have paid more attention to Edith's compact, then I may have recognised it when I saw it again. You saw things from a different perspective, and you have good instincts too."

"I was wrong about Miller. I even thought he might be a spy at one point. Then it turned out he was but for us, not Germany."

The inspector shrugged. "That was understandable, but right from the start, you knew something was strange about Edith Devine's death. It was you who suggested that the two women sharing the same initials was important and you were certainly tenacious when it came to Clara Fleurot." He paused. "I doubt we would have solved the case without you, so thank you."

Dorothy could feel her cheeks beginning to burn at his

unexpected gratitude.

"I still don't understand why Clara was involved. Was Nan Lambert blackmailing her? Or was it simply for money?" she asked.

The inspector shook his head. "Neither, but an even more popular motive. Love. Nan confessed that she and Clara are in love and believed that with Victor's money they could create a new life together in America. That's what all that 'never again' business at the court was about. I believe Clara wanted to leave her life of crime and Nan her life in service behind." He paused. "I apologise if I have shocked you, Miss Peto."

"Not at all, Inspector. Since coming to London and joining the WPV, I'm not sure anything shocks me anymore. What will happen to them now?" she asked.

"They are due to appear before the magistrate tomorrow morning to be remanded in custody."

"Well, I only hope he doesn't believe their lies like last time."

Inspector Derwent's lips slowly turned upwards. It was the first time Dorothy had seen him smile.

"I think that's extremely unlikely. They are due to appear before Frederick Mead."

Dorothy smiled back at him. "Do you know, Inspector, I think that might be the first time I've been happy to hear that man's name."

The End

Author's Note

I first stumbled across Dorothy, Nina, Mary and Margaret when carrying out research for another book. I became fascinated by the story of these pioneering women who paved the way for women to join the police force, but who history largely seems to have forgotten. I wanted to write a mystery that featured them, so although this is a work of fiction, it is inspired by real events, people and places.

Margaret really was a slightly eccentric philanthropist who generously supported charities dedicated to helping animals and children. Mary was a committed suffragette who was imprisoned for breaking windows including those at the Home Office. She twice went on hunger strike and on the last occasion she was force-fed. Nina was a talented speaker and writer, with a quick wit and an excellent eye for publicity. I chose Dorothy Peto to be my main character because of her age and the role she went on to play in the Metropolitan Police. However, my Dorothy's background is based on the work of several suffragettes including Edith Watson and Annie Jones. The real Dorothy spent much of the First World War on patrol in Bristol and Bath.

When I first began writing this story, the UK's Prime Minster, Home Secretary and the Commissioner of the Metropolitan Police were all female, yet just over a hundred years before, women were told they could not be charged with upholding the law as they were not proper people. The change in our country is due in no small part to the work of Dorothy and countless other campaigners.

Acknowledgements

I hope you enjoy this first Lady in Blue Mystery and that you will want to discover more about these trailblazing women. I am very grateful to the following authors whose writing helped me research the story of Dorothy and her companions and provided background for this period in our history.

> Allen, Mary Sophia, *Lady in Blue: Reminiscences and Study of the Status of Women Police,* S. Paul, 1936
>
> Frances, Hilary, *The Sexual Politics of Four Edwardian Feminists from c.1910 to c.1935,* etheses.whiterose.ac.uk, 1996
>
> Lock, Joan, *The British Policewoman: Her Story,* Robert Hale Ltd, 1979
>
> Peto, Miss Dorothy Olivia Georgiana OBE, *The Memoirs of,* Organising Committee for the European Conference on Equal Opportunities in the Police, 1992
>
> White, Jerry, *Zeppelin Nights: London in the First World War,* Vintage, 2015
>
> Worsley, Paul QC, *The Postcard Murder: A Judges Tale,* Pilot Productions, 2019

There are also several organisations I should like to thank for their assistance.

    Black Country Living Museum
    Greater Manchester Police Museum and Archives
    National Archives
    Sevendials.com
    The Royal Parks
    West Midlands Police Museum
    University of York, Centre for Women's Studies

Exclusive Excerpt:
A Death in Chelsea
The Second Lady in Blue Mystery

"Dorothy! You must come quickly. I've found a dead body." Dorothy Peto rubbed her eyes and wondered if it was possible she was still dreaming. The ringing of the telephone had woken her and she'd stumbled out of bed and down the hallway to answer it. The longcase clock standing next to her told her it was just after six.

"Margaret is that you?" she asked, stifling a yawn and jamming a finger in her ear so she could hear the voice at the end of the crackling line more clearly.

"Yes, please come quickly. It's poor Mr Gaskill. He's dead."

"Who?" asked Dorothy but Margaret had already hung up.

Dorothy waited for the omnibus to come to a juddering halt, then stepped off on to Glebe Place with some relief. Although it was still early and a Sunday, the journey from Bloomsbury to Chelsea had been awfully hot and crowded. A taxi would have been quicker and more pleasant, but they were almost impossible to find these days. So many motor cabs had been turned into ambulances and almost all the horses had been taken for the army.

She hurried down the road and turned the corner on to Cheyne Row. She checked her watch. Margaret had telephoned her almost an hour ago. She'd sounded terribly agitated. After her call, Dorothy had dressed immediately and dashed across the city.

Margaret Damer Dawson was Commandant of the Women's Police Volunteers, the group that she had set up with Dorothy, Mary Allen and Nina Boyle to help the regular police when war broke out. Normally, Margaret would have had Mary with her, but both she and Nina were away helping train new recruits. Over the last twelve months, the number of WPV members had grown rapidly and the women, patrolling in their dark blue uniform soon became a familiar sight on the country's streets. This morning, nobody gave Dorothy a second glance as she walked briskly towards Margaret's house.

As she approached the row of smart terraced town houses, she saw Margaret hurrying towards her, accompanied as always by her three dogs: Topsy, Skip and Herbert.

"Oh, Dorothy, thank heavens you are here," she gasped breathlessly.

"Margaret, are you all right? It sounded like you were saying someone had died."

"They have! Poor Mr Gaskill. I woke early. It was so hot last night and I never sleep well when Mary is away. So I went to open my bedroom curtains and there he was!"

"In your bedroom?"

"No, Dorothy! Of course not. In his garden. He lives next door." She gestured to 12 Cheyne Row. It was identical to her own house, number 10. Four elegant storeys high with a basement and built of brick with black wrought-iron railings. The front door of number 12 was wide open.

"Come and take a look for yourself," said Margaret as she made her way inside. Dorothy followed her through the door. The layout of the house's interior was also the same as Margaret's, but the décor was far more old-fashioned and a little shabby. The phrase 'faded grandeur' came to Dorothy's mind.

"Did Mr Gaskill live alone?" she asked.

"Yes," replied Margaret, "well, except for the servants. There's a butler, a cook and a maid."

They stepped out into the garden and Dorothy saw at once poor Mr Gaskill. Wearing a faded tartan dressing gown, he was sprawled out across a neatly trimmed lawn next to a beautifully carved stone bird table. He was a thin, frail-looking man, who Dorothy guessed must be in his seventies. She knelt down to check his pulse, but as soon as she touched his papery skin, she knew he was dead. Despite the heat of the early morning sun, he was stone cold and running across his forehead was a dried trickle of bloody. His still-clenched fist was full of birdseed.

"He must have come out to feed the birds," she said.

"Yes, he does every morning," explained Margaret. "At seven o'clock exactly. Mary and I always joke that we could set our watches by him, but when I opened the curtains, it was barely six. I was quite stunned to see him outside already. At first, I thought he was sitting down. Well, you know how poor my eyesight is, Dorothy. I put my spectacles on and that's when I saw him properly. I opened the window and called his name, but there was no response so I dashed over here."

"Where were the servants?"

"They were just getting up. They thought he was still in bed. Mrs Platt the cook and Connie the maid were awfully upset. I told Duckworth the butler to take them down into the kitchen."

"Have you telephoned the police?" asked Dorothy.

"Yes. I only spoke to a desk sergeant. The silly man asked me if I was sure I hadn't been dreaming. Such a cheek! Anyway I left my details and he promised to pass them on and I told Annie to try telephoning again."

Dorothy nodded although she wasn't convinced Margaret's maid was the best person to enlist for such an important task. The young woman always leapt out of her skin whenever the telephone rang.

She stood up and looked around the garden. Like the house, it was almost identical to Margaret's. It was walled on all sides with a small wooden door leading out on to Cheyne Walk. There were two flower beds planted with roses on either side of the lawn and as well as the bird table, there was an equally ornate sundial.

"Do you think he might have fallen and hit his head on the bird table?" asked Margaret. "The leather on the sole of his slipper is coming away. He could have tripped."

Dorothy bent down. It was true. Like his dressing gown, the dead man's slippers were old and worn, but she shook her head.

"I don't think so. There isn't any blood on the stone base of the bird table," she said.

Margaret's hand flew to her mouth. "Oh my goodness," she gasped. "Then you think someone may have attacked him. How dreadful! This is such a nice, quiet neighbourhood. Who could have done such a thing?"

"A burglar perhaps? They could have come through that door at the bottom of the garden. I wonder if it's locked."

Dorothy was about to go and check, when in the distance, she could hear the unmistakable ringing bell of an approaching police car.

"It sounds like Scotland Yard got your message. I'll go and tell the servants to prepare themselves to be interviewed. You stay here with the body and, Margaret, do try and keep the dogs away," she said, pointing to Herbert, the basset hound, who was trying to eat the birdseed out of the dead man's hand.

Find out what happens next…
Available now at your favorite online retailer!

The Lady in Blue Mystery series

Book 1: *The Body in Seven Dials*

Book 2: *A Death in Chelsea*

Book 3: *Coming soon!*

Available now at your favorite online retailer!

More Books by H L Marsay

The Secrets of Hartwell series

Book 1: *Four Hidden Treasures*

Book 2: *Four Secrets Kept*

Book 3: *Four Silences Broken*

The Chief Inspector Shadow series

Book 1: *A Long Shadow*

Book 2: *A Viking's Shadow*

Book 3: *A Ghostly Shadow*

Book 4: *A Roman Shadow*

Book 5: *A Forgotten Shadow*

Book 6: *A Christmas Shadow*

Available now at your favorite online retailer!

About the Author

H L Marsay always loved detective stories and promised herself that one day, she would write one too. She is lucky enough to live in York, a city full of history and mystery. When not writing, the five men in her life keep her busy – two sons, two dogs and one husband.

Thank you for reading
The Body in Seven Dials

If you enjoyed this book, you can find more from all our great authors at TulePublishing.com, or from your favorite online retailer.